In Flight

By R.K. Lilley

This book is dedicated to my mother, Linda, for getting me hopelessly addicted to fiction, from my very earliest memories.

CHAPTER ONE

Mr. Cavendish

My hands trembled slightly as I prepared my galley for the first class, pre-board service. My whole body hummed nervously as I pulled a chilled bottle of champagne from the large drawer of ice at the bottom of my liquor cart. I felt more than heard my best friend, Stephan, sweep into the curtained galley behind me.

"Showtime, Bee," he said briskly.

I felt him tucking errant blond hairs back into my sleek chignon. In spite of his fussing, I knew it was smooth. Since we were departing from our hometown of Las Vegas, we had taken a shuttle from our airline's headquarters directly to the plane. This meant that we got to bypass security completely. No metal detectors meant bobby pins. And bobby pins meant that my smooth, pale blond hair would behave itself perfectly.

But Stephan liked to fuss over me. He was by far the most affectionate person I knew. And certainly the only one I would permit to touch me, even in a casual manner.

He had earned those rights with me over many years of being my best friend. Best friend and so much more. Constant companion, confidante, partner, former roommate, and currently, my neighbor. He was also my inflight buddy-bid partner. We were completely inseparable.

There were times when it felt like he was more of an extension of me than an actual separate person. We were that close. Yes, we were codependent, there was no question, but we'd been partners for too many years to operate any other way.

There was no question that he was the most important person in my life. When I heard the word family, I thought of only one person, and that person was Stephan.

"We already have five seated in first class. Where's my manifest?" he asked

I handed it to him without a word. I'd had the passenger list tucked into my leather menu sleeve. I had already glanced at it. *It* was the reason that my hands weren't quite steady. There was no other reason for me to be so nervous. I was preparing for a nearly empty redeye flight, with only a minimal service. The only challenge on this flight was normally to stay awake.

"You've got to get a look at 2D," Stephan was saying with an exaggerated, dreamy sigh. His statement, and that dreamy sigh, were both very un-Stephan like, but I knew well the reason for the change in him. That reason had elicited some very uncharacteristic responses from me, as well.

"Yes, that's Mr. Cavendish," I said in a steady voice.

Big, elegant hands smoothed over the shoulders of my fitted, charcoal-gray suit vest. "You sound like you know him." There was a question in his voice.

"Mmm hmm." I tried my best for casual. "He was on that charter flight I had to work without you last week. He was meeting with the CEO. Mr. Cavendish is that bigwig hotel owner."

Stephan snapped his fingers behind me. I finally turned to look at him, raising a brow.

The clear blue eyes that met my own could have belonged to

my brother, if I'd had one. In fact, you could say that about the two of us in general. Our golden blond hair was nearly the same shade, though his had a wavy texture. His was brushed back artfully and hung just past his ears. We were both tall and lean, though he had me beat by several inches. Even my heels didn't make up the difference. Also, our features had a similar, nordic cast. Yes, we could have easily passed for siblings. And I certainly thought of him as a brother. I had for close to a decade now.

"I've heard of him! That dude is a billionaire! Melissa will go into heat when she finds out. We're gonna see her backing, ass first, into first class, as soon as she realizes who we've got up here!"

I tried to smother a laugh at the visual he'd painted. And, sadly, he probably wasn't all that far off the mark.

Melissa was one of the three flight attendants working in the main cabin of the 757. We had just started our new schedule with a new main cabin crew. Stephan and I always worked together in first class, we bid it that way, but our main cabin crew changed every few months. Our current bid was scheduled to last three months, and we were just getting to know our other flying mates. We were all getting along fine, so far.

Melissa was the loudest personality of the bunch, and so, for better or worse, we were learning all about her first. She was one of those girls who had become a flight attendant to meet men. Or more specifically, to meet rich men. She was new to the airline, so she was stuck working in coach. Or, as she said, slumming it. She coveted my position of first class flight attendant, or even Stephan's position of Lead flight attendant.

Stephan and I had started at our small company four years ago, in the very first flight attendant class, and so had years of seniority over her. Melissa had started as an inflight maybe six months ago, which meant she wouldn't even be able to apply for a first class position for another six months. And after that she wouldn't be able to hold a line in first class for another six months.

Instead, she would be on call, with a totally chaotic schedule that wouldn't allow for any planned destinations. And when she did get a steady line, it would be the worst line available, with short overnight trips in hotels right by the airport. From what I'd gathered from the fortune-hunters I'd worked with over the years, none of those things were conducive to planning assignations with rich men.

Melissa had been beyond lucky to get on our line for the next three months. It was a coveted line, with regular weekly overnights in New York. We would stay in our best crew hotel, which was less than two blocks from Central Park. It was a senior line, and we'd all been surprised to get such a junior member on our crew. But she still complained, often pointing out that she was just *made* for first class. Her constant complaints were already starting to wear on the crew.

Stephan gave my shoulder a reassuring squeeze before heading into the flight deck to have a briefing with the pilots. This was the main reason that Stephan took the position of lead while I took the first class galley position. I hated dealing with pilots. Stephan handled them beautifully, often playing my boyfriend when they acted even slightly interested in me on a personal level. Half of the people we worked with thought we were an item. Stephan wasn't out openly. It was a personal choice he'd made a long time ago, and one I understood completely. He'd had a rough time of it when he came out to his parents about being gay, and just felt safer keeping his preferences to himself.

I popped the cork off of the champagne bottle quickly and quietly, filling five glasses with practiced ease. I took slow, deep breaths to manage my nerves. I was used to managing a certain amount of anxiety. I tended to be an anxious person, though I hid it well. I just wasn't used to this type of nervous tension, or this much of it. And the cause of it today was, well, out of character for me, to say the least.

I swept from the galley with a burst of forced confidence. If I could keep a full drink tray steady at thirty-five thousand feet, in three and a half inch heels and turbulence on a regular basis, I could certainly serve a few drinks on steady ground.

I was doing just fine, my tray-laden arm steady, my feet sure, right up until I looked up from the ground and into the vibrant turquoise eyes of Mr. Cavendish.

As seemed to be his habit in our very brief acquaintance, he was watching me intently. His lean, elegant figure was lounging in the cream leather seat with a casual boredom that his eyes lacked. *Was it his intent stare that unnerved me so badly?* Probably. That intent gaze seemed to hold me strangely captivated. It could also have something to do with the fact that he was hands-down the most attractive person I'd ever seen. And I saw a lot. I'd served all types. From soaps stars, to movie stars, to all types of models. Hell, even Stephan was undoubtedly model material. But this man was quite simply the most stunning person I'd laid eyes on in my twenty-three years.

It was not one feature in particular that made him stand out so starkly, though all of his seemed flawless. Perhaps it was his deep golden complexion, combined with his sandy brown hair, which hung straight, just hitting the collar of his crisp white dress shirt. It was that light brown color that sat somewhere between blonde and brown, choosing neither, but somehow hit a shade that was lovelier than both. And his deep tan belonged on a surfer, or at least someone with dark hair and eyes. But his eyes weren't dark. They were a bright turquoise and stood out starkly with his unusual coloring. And they were so damn piercing…I felt as though he knew things about me with just a look, things he couldn't possibly know.

As I stared at him, frozen in place, he smiled at me, his

4

expression almost affectionate. His mouth looked so soft, pretty even, framing his straight white teeth. Even his nose was perfect, straight and appealing. He was just so stunningly good-looking.

The thought struck me, not for the first time, how unfair it was for one man to be that devastatingly handsome and also a billionaire still in his twenties. Anyone born so privileged was surely an awful person. He'd probably never suffered a day in his life. He'd probably had everything handed to him so easily that he was already arrogant and dissolute, bored with things that the rest of us strived for. There was no outward sign of that, but how could I see past his stunning outward appearance when I was so easily distracted by the beauty of it?

I quickly snapped myself out of that line of thought. I was being unfair, I knew. I knew nothing about this man and I certainly couldn't judge his character poorly based on what I'd observed so far. I hadn't realized how bitter my attitude had become towards those born to privilege. My own upbringing had been stark and brutal, and I had personally experienced a profound level of poverty, but I couldn't let that be an excuse to pass harsh judgement on someone who had been nothing but polite to me. I had to keep telling myself that, but being hopelessly attracted to him wasn't helping. That unwilling attraction made me instinctively want to lash out.

I swallowed, trying to wet my suddenly dry throat. "Hello again, Mr. Cavendish." I tried to nod at him politely, but as I did so, my drink tray wobbled precariously.

Mr. Cavendish moved unbelievably fast, half-standing to steady my tray over the seat between us. I watched in abject horror as a splash of champagne made it onto the sleeve of his dark gray suit jacket. That suit undoubtedly cost more than I made in a month.

"I'm so sorry, Mr. Cavendish." My voice was breathless and soft, which further flustered me.

5

He ran his free hand restlessly through his straight, sandy hair. The silky strands seemed to stay artfully out of his face. It was supermodel hair. Damn him.

"Don't be sorry, Bianca," he admonished me in a velvety deep voice. Even his voice was unfair. I reeled at the knowledge that he'd remembered my name.

He steadied my arm gallantly, and eventually released my tray when I told him I had it under control.

He turned down my offer of a glass of champagne. I belatedly recalled that he didn't touch any kind of alcohol.

"Just some water, when you get a chance," he told me with a warm smile.

I finished my champagne pre-board service. I still had only five passengers, so it took me no time at all.

I set my tray on the counter in the galley and went back through to collect jackets and take orders for the inflight service.

As I approached Mr. Cavendish again, he looked up intently from his phone, and my heartbeat went into overdrive as our gazes met again. "Can I take your jacket, Mr. Cavendish?" I asked him, my voice still strangely breathless. "I could try to get that champagne out, or just hang it up, if you like."

He stood, having to step into the aisle to do so completely. He was suddenly so close to me that I gasped. I was mortified at my reaction to him. I prided myself on my professionalism. And my reaction to his close proximity was most definitely *not* professional.

I was tall, nearly five foot ten barefoot, and easily six one now in my work shoes. But the top of my head still only came up to his nose. He was at least Stephan's height, maybe an inch taller. I always felt a little awkward around shorter men, but this height, this extremely tall man, had the opposite effect. He made me feel feminine and small. I enjoyed the feeling, but was extremely unnerved by it.

He shrugged out of his finely tailored suit jacket, handing it to me. He remained in a fine white dress shirt with a pale blue tie. I saw that, although he was lean and elegant, he was also surprisingly muscular. The sight of that hard play of muscles under his shirt made my mouth go dry.

"Just hang it, please, Bianca," he told me softly.

"Yes, Sir," I murmured in a voice I scarcely recognized.

I finished my usual pre-board service in a bit of a daze, barely locking down all of the carts in my galley before it was time to step again in front of Mr. Cavendish for the safety demonstration.

He watched me intently, his gaze never leaving my face. I didn't understand his interest. Never once had his gaze left my face. I sensed that he was interested in me. *But in what way?* I had no idea. Usually when men hit on me, their eyes were all over my body, not unswervingly glued to my eyes.

My demonstration was unusually graceless. I even fumbled with the seat buckle in my nervousness. I took my seat for takeoff with a sense of relief. I needed a moment of peace to gather my composure. But it wasn't meant to be. My jump seat faced Mr. Cavendish almost perfectly. I had to make a conscious effort not to meet his eyes during the long taxi and then takeoff.

CHAPTER TWO

Mr. Generous

Stephan clutched my hand warmly as we took off. We both loved the feeling of takeoff. It represented good things for both of us. New places. New adventures. Leaving bad things behind us. I sent him a quick, affectionate smile before I looked out the window in the door to my right, avoiding looking at Mr. Cavendish for as long as I could.

Finally, I stole a furtive glance at him, and was baffled by the change I saw in him. He was still as a statue now, his eyes positively glacial. I followed his gaze to where my hand lay linked with Stephan's on the small space between our jump seats. It occurred to me that it must look as though we were a couple. Stephan and I often appeared that way, even encouraged it at times. All but our close friends and Stephan's lovers thought we were an item. But it made me uncomfortable that Mr. Cavendish might make that assumption. Even so, it couldn't account for his suddenly hostile demeanor. I barely knew the man.

We quickly reached ten thousand feet. At the double ding that indicated our altitude, I got up and quickly started preparing a hot towel service while Stephan made his usual announcements. He leaned in close against my back, nearly embracing me as he spoke in my ear. "Mind if I go help the main cabin?" he asked me. "They have a full house."

I sent him a puzzled glance. "I'll do it after the hot towels. It's my turn, remember?"

It was our usual routine to help out in back when the first class cabin was light and the main cabin was at capacity. We certainly didn't need two people to serve five passengers that were all probably about to pass out. But he had helped in coach last time, so we both knew it was my turn to help in back.

He just kissed the top of my head, shaking his. "I need to talk to Jake about that incident report from last week, and he's got the front cart, so we can chat while we work. Good luck up here." And with that, he disappeared. I sighed, exasperated. For once, I actually wanted to work back there. It would give me a little break from Mr. Beautiful up front. But I certainly wasn't going to put up a fuss about it, so I would just have to deal.

Mr. Cavendish barely glanced at me now as I handed out hot towels, then collected them. Why did that bother me so much? I didn't want to delve too deeply into the thought.

I took drink orders, and served the first round of drinks quickly. The couple on the last row of first class seemed to be heavy drinkers, but the others just had water and looked close to falling asleep. I'd be surprised if most of them weren't asleep before I'd even finished my short service.

I took a cart out, offering cheese, crackers, and an olive basil dip. It took me less than five minutes to serve the entire cabin. Mr. Cavendish took a small plate of cheese with water, and the couple in back took some, but the other two declined and were sleeping before I was even back in the galley.

As I collected the plates, I was surprised to find that even the couple who'd been drinking cocktails had fallen asleep. I had read them all wrong. They were the 'drink a few and fall asleep couple'. I had thought for sure they were just getting started.

Mr. Cavendish was suddenly the only passenger awake in my cabin. It felt strangely as though we were alone. The curtain was closed securely on main cabin, and the lights were dimmed to near darkness throughout the entire plane.

He was working quietly on his laptop, looking alert and nowhere close to sleep. *Would he work straight through the night?* I wondered. I couldn't imagine him getting to New York and taking a nap. He likely worked around the clock. Our flight time was four hours and forty-three minutes, and it was now the middle of the night. Something urgent must be keeping him up if he couldn't even take a small nap on the flight.

I approached him, leaning down to speak to him quietly, conscious of the other sleeping passengers, though they were all at the back of first class, and he was nearly at the front. "Can I get you anything else, Sir?"

For the first time since we'd taken off, he gave me his full attention. "May I ask you something, Bianca?" he asked me in a carefully bland tone.

I raised my brows in question. "Yes, Sir. What can I help you with?"

He sighed, indicating the empty seat next to his. "Can you sit for a minute to talk?"

I glanced around nervously, not knowing what to make of his request. It seemed unprofessional to sit down next to him, but he had asked, and he was the only one likely to see me do it.

"Sit, Bianca. Everyone else is beyond caring." I loved the way he said my name. Loved it and was disconcerted by it. It was nothing I could put my finger on, but something about his tone made it sound almost intimate.

I took a deep breath and finally just sat down beside him. I angled toward him slightly, my hands in my lap, tugging my skirt down and smoothing the dark gray material nervously.

"Are you and Stephan together?" he asked frankly, when I

finally looked up at him. I just blinked for a moment, stunned. I hadn't expected his interest, let alone this kind of bluntness. I guessed that men so busy they couldn't even take a nap on a plane weren't the type to beat around the bush.

"No, Sir," I answered, before I could really think it through. "We're best friends, but it's platonic." *Why am I telling him this?* I asked myself, even as the words left my mouth.

I watched with an avid fascination as one of his elegant hands reached towards mine, long fingers circling my left wrist lightly. I looked back at his face, and he was smiling now. My chest was rising and falling so heavily that I caught the motion at the edge of my vision. My chest was ample, too much so, making me look disproportionate to my own critical eye. And suddenly, I was all too conscious of my heavy breasts, rising and falling conspicuously. My nipples were tightening up in a pleasurable way as my breath caught.

As though he read my mind, his gaze traveled down to my chest for the first time that I'd noticed. Some men only looked at or spoke to my chest, and up until now he'd done the opposite of that, which I had found refreshing.

He reached a hand to the thin, mock men's tie that lay between my breasts, running a light finger along it. He made a deep humming noise in his throat, then pulled his hand quickly back.

He cleared his throat softly. "Are you seeing anyone?" he asked, finally looking back into my eyes.

I bit my lip and shook my head. His gaze went to my mouth at the motion. He watched me with a singleminded focus that I couldn't seem to look away from.

"Good," he said. *Is this really happening?* I thought, dazed. "I assume you're taking a nap when you get to your hotel. What time will you be waking up?"

Lord, he was direct. Unusually so. It seemed to be swaying me from my normal ways. I was used to gently turning men down before they could directly ask me out. The tactic had always served me well. It saved me awkwardness, and saved their pride. I couldn't seem to use it on Mr. Cavendish, though. When he asked me a question, I felt almost compelled to answer it truthfully.

"I usually sleep for about four hours, so I can still get to sleep at night. We have an early flight to Las Vegas on Saturday morning. If I slept any longer than that, I'd be up all night."

He did quick calculations in his head, then asked. "So noon?"

I nodded, wondering why I wasn't yet explaining that I wouldn't go out with him. Or do any of the things that he obviously had on his mind...

"I'll send a car to pick you up for lunch," he told me. So he wasn't going to ask me out. He was apparently going to order me out. Why was I having such a hard time getting the words out to tell him no? "You and I need to talk," he continued. "I have a proposition for you."

The word proposition, which to my ear had a seedy ring to it, finally brought me back to myself. I shook my head finally, galvanized back into my normal behavior. "No, Mr. Cavendish. I'm flattered that you're...interested in me in some way. But I'll have to politely decline. I don't date."

He blinked at me, clearly taken aback. He was silent for a moment before he tried another tact. "I don't date, either, actually. That was not exactly what I had in mind."

This is good, I told myself around my bruised ego. *Of course he wouldn't want to date you.* He probably only dated useless socialites who had never had to work a day in their lives. I wanted him to continue with his explanation now, sure it would kill every ounce of the unwilling interest I felt for him.

"Then what did you have in mind?" I asked him, my voice colder now.

His gaze was hot suddenly, his finger running again along my thin tie. I had to check the impulse to look down and make sure my hardening nipples weren't outlined through my shirt and vest. "I think you and I are very compatible. In fact, I'm sure of it. Come to lunch with me today and I'll show you. If you still aren't interested, I will, of course, leave you alone. But I promise I can make you interested. I'll treat you very well, Bianca. I'm a very generous man-"

I held up my free hand. I was so done with the conversation. I felt slightly ill, but more aroused, and the combination was troubling to me. "Please, no more," I told him stiffly. "I'm not interested in any of that, believe me. I don't know what impression you think I've given you, but I'm not some kind of fortune-hunter. I don't want your generosity. I don't want anything at all from you. We have a girl that works in back who seems more your style. I'll send her your way if your'e so hard up that you're offering random women money. Or whatever the the hell it is you were suggesting. But I can tell you for sure that I am not the kind of girl that you're looking for."

I tried to stand, but he didn't release my wrist. I sat back in the seat, glaring at the hand that held me captive. "That's not what I meant at all, Bianca. I didn't mean to sound so… indelicate. But I am very, very attracted to you, and I would very much like to do something about it." He smiled at me with a mixture of charm and heat that was very nearly irresistible. "Have lunch with me, where we can discuss this at length, and with some privacy." He released my wrist as he finished speaking.

"No, thank you, Mr. Cavendish." I got up quietly and walked back into the galley, closing the curtain behind me calmly.

I was taking deep breaths, counting, and just trying to get my anxiety under control, when he swept in after me.

I opened my mouth to tell him no again when he kissed me. It was a hungry, desperate kiss, and I'd never experienced anything like it before. That was perhaps why I didn't know how to respond. I just stood there, every part of my body stiff except

13

for my lips, which had softened automatically at the touch of his pretty mouth. It was so unfair, that he had this too, this impossibly intoxicating kiss. *He's probably good at absolutely everything*, I thought with a twinge of dismay. His tongue swept into my mouth and I moaned quietly in spite of myself. "Suck on my tongue," he ordered me roughly, when he pulled back for a breath, and I was shocked. I'd never done that. But I was obeying him even as I questioned myself, sucking carefully and then harder. He groaned and pressed against me slowly. I felt him keenly, my body more sensitive than I could ever remember. His erection pressed into my stomach very obviously and I pulled back at the realization. "Touch me," he ordered, and I finally looked up at him.

I swallowed hard. "Where?" I asked, my voice needy and rough.

"My chest and stomach. Touch all the places there that you want to be touched on your own body."

I obeyed, cupping the supple flesh around his nipples as though they were breasts, kneading him. I was watching his mouth, and he licked his lips, nodding at me to go on. I ran a hand down the muscles of his abdomen. He was all corded muscles, everywhere I felt. I stroked his arms, and they were far bigger and more muscular than I would have guessed. He just looked so elegant at first glance, it was hard to believe anyone so elegant could also be so built. He had to work out for hours everyday to achieve this kind of a build. It was so intimidating. And so unbelievably hot.

He unbuttoned several of the buttons along his chest and stomach. "Touch my skin," he ordered roughly. I obeyed, some part of me going, *Oh shit, I can't believe I'm doing this*. But it was so natural to just do as he asked. It felt good. I tried to fit both hands into his shirt, and he pulled one out gently. I stroked his hard, hot skin. I felt no hair, and wondered if he waxed it. It was so smooth.

He kissed the hand that he had grabbed, placing it firmly back onto his shoulder. I watched my own hand wander down his body, going straight to his groin. I gripped him through his slacks suddenly, and he groaned, wrenching my hand away quickly. He grinned at me, but it was a pained grin, all white teeth. "Not here. Not yet. The first time I want you in my bed."

He stepped back, putting a safe distance between us. He buttoned his shirt quickly and straightened his clothing, watching me. He pulled his phone out. "Give me your number," he told me.

I shook myself mentally. *What was I doing?* I did not want to get mixed up with him. I knew it absolutely. I just wasn't *feeling* my own certainty at that particular moment.

I shook my head at him. "No," I said firmly.

He looked genuinely surprised at my answer, and then amused. That made me mad.

I backed up until my butt bumped against the aircraft door. "Not interested." My tone was sure.

He put his hands in his pockets, leaning casually against the counter. He ran a tongue over his teeth. *He's enjoying this*, I thought, with no small amount of outrage. *The thought of someone saying no to him is so foreign that it just amuses him.* His voice was rich with mirth when he spoke again. "How about coffee? Is that neutral enough? Give me your number and we'll go for some coffee."

I shook my head. "No, thank you." I waved at the space between us. "I don't do this sort of thing. I'm just not interested."

A corner of his mouth quirked sardonically. His eyes were on my chest as it rose and fell in agitation. I finally looked down, mortified to see that my hardened nipples were showing clearly even through the three layers covering them. "I *will* put you over my knee every time you lie to me, Bianca." His voice was quiet now, but with a dangerous edge.

My brain short-circuited for a moment, my face going a little slack. *He's joking. Isn't he?* My whole body tensed at his comment, and I knew it was more desire than dismay that shocked a tremor through my body. "See. I'm not into any of that stuff, so we are clearly not compatible."

He ran a long finger down his own tie the way he had done to mine. "I'm not sure if that one was a lie or if you just don't know how pleasurable 'that stuff' can be. Or how well suited you are to it. I can show you. I would love to show you. When I'm done with you, I'll know your body better than you do, and you will be begging me for it. Every inch of your body is submitting to me, even as you're turning me down. Can you honestly tell me that the thought of submitting to me in bed doesn't make you wet?"

The question made me press my legs together, but my traitorous body would not shake my resolve. He obviously knew what he was doing, knew which buttons to push, knew how to control me sexually. But that was exactly what I didn't want. *Wasn't it?*

He seemed to read my mind, or more likely, my expression. He grinned. "I meant it about the spanking, Bianca. And the submission. You're going to learn very quickly that I always mean what I say."

"Please leave my galley, Mr. Cavendish. I won't change my mind."

He pulled out his wallet, never looking away from me as he pulled out a business card. He touched it to my cheek, running it lightly down to my chin, then to my neck. I shivered as he reached my collar bone. There was a tiny pocket on my vest, right over my right breast, and he slid the card into that pocket. "The number on the back is my cel. I would love to hear from you. Anytime, night or day."

I just waited stiffly until he finally left the galley to return to his seat.

16

I was still standing there, taking deep, calming breaths, when Stephan joined me a good thirty minutes later.

He was eyeing me curiously as he shut the curtain. "You ok, Buttercup?" he asked me carefully. I smiled a little at the ridiculous nickname he'd given me back when we were fourteen year old runaways. It always made me smile, which was why he used it.

I nodded. I'd tell him about the whole Mr. Beautiful fiasco, but just not right then. Or even that week.

"What do you think of Mr. Cavendish?" he asked carefully, even innocently. Too innocently.

My eyes narrowed as I looked at him. "Have you been talking to him?"

He did a little non-committal head bob. But he only did that bob when the answer was a yes. "I think he has a crush on you. Did he like ask you out or anything?"

I just glared at him. "What did he say to you?"

"Are you gonna go out with him?" he shot back.

"Of course not. You know I don't date. What's gotten into you?"

He shrugged, still looking too innocent. "You've gotta start sometime, Buttercup. A young, beautiful woman can't just 'not date' indefinitely. And it's not gonna get any better than *that* guy. I have a good feeling about him." He waved a hand in Mr. Cavendish's general direction.

I pointed a finger at him. "We're not doing this again. Everyone in the world does *not* need to date. I don't interfere in your life choices. You don't get to interfere with mine."

He raised both hands in surrender. "Just a little friendly advice, Bee. But I'll drop it now. You know I can't stand it when you're mad at me."

I was more than happy to drop it. He gave me a tight hug. "Love you, Bee," he murmured against my hair. It was just his way of being affectionate. It was how he showed love and sought comfort. It was not my way. Not with anyone but him.

I hugged him back. "Love you too, Steph," I murmured back.

The rest of the flight passed as slowly as I had expected it to. The red-eyes weren't my favorite. I liked to stay constantly busy. These flights were all about killing time. Even Mr. Cavendish was dozing when I checked on my cabin. I watched him sleep for a long time. Watching such a restless person at rest was fascinating. He was almost too pretty in his sleep, with no tension in his face. His long, thick, dark lashes making dark shadows on his face even in the near darkness. I could have watched him sleep all night. I admitted that fact to myself, though I didn't like it. And I wanted to touch him, badly. A stray lock of hair had fallen across one of his cheeks. I wanted to brush it away, and rub it in my fingers. I thought, with no small amount of regret, of all of the parts of him I'd wanted to touch, but that I would never allow myself to. The moment had passed, and I was determined to move on. I shook myself out of my ridiculous reverie as I realized it was time to prep the cabin for landing.

I found myself watching him again as we took our seats to land. He was still dozing, and I couldn't seem to look away, even when his eyes opened, and he blinked awake, disoriented. His gaze found me quickly, the sleep leaving his eyes as he met my stare and blinked. I schooled my face into neutral lines as he stared back at me. Eventually, I broke the stare, looking at Stephan instead. He was studying me as well, his look strange.

"You like him," he whispered to me, a fair amount of shock in his voice.

"Don't," was all I said in response.

CHAPTER THREE

Mr. Unnerving

The jet bridge at JFK-New York was different than the one in McCarran-Las Vegas, so the passengers departed out of the first door, having to make their way through the first class cabin. This meant that I had to hustle to get the passengers their jackets quickly so that the first class passengers wouldn't be delayed getting off of the plane.

I nodded politely at Mr. Cavendish as I handed him his suit jacket. "Have a nice day, Mr. Cavendish."

He gave me a slightly annoyed look. "Please, call me James," he chided me. He leaned in closer, speaking directly into my ear. "In private, though, you may call me Mr. Cavendish." With that unnerving exchange, he walked away.

Stephan raised his brows at me as I came back to stand beside him to see off the other passengers. "What did he say to you?" he asked, obviously curious. "The look on his face, and then on yours..."

I just shook my head. "You don't wanna know."

I went through the motions of our usual deplaning routine, not feeling at all like myself. Being around that man made me feel...strange. It felt a little like I'd been plucked away from my

19

own orderly life and placed in the middle of some kind of a game. A game with rules that I hadn't been told. And I had no frame of reference with which to learn those rules. I told myself firmly that I was only relieved that I had told James Cavendish no. He was just too much for me. He was too experienced, too jaded, too rich. And all of that would have been enough to dissuade me even if I was interested in dating, which I certainly was not. I never had been. And he was obviously into some kind of S&M besides. I had my own demons to deal with, and that sort of thing was the last thing I should be interested in. But still... in spite of myself, I did find it fascinating. And frightening. And exciting. I knew that it was probably because of my violent childhood that an excited shiver ran through me at the thought of some of the things he'd said. Like putting me over his knee... I knew from countless visits to a shrink that the things that horrified people in childhood could also excite us as adults. The thought was sobering. I worked really hard not to be a victim of my childhood. That made it all the more important that I stay away from someone like James Cavendish.

It took some convincing, but I felt I had adequately convinced myself of this as we got our luggage down, and then waited for the rest of the crew to join us.

Stephan and I walked in the front of our little inflight parade as we made our way briskly through JFK. "Mmmm, I'd kill for a coffee right now. Shall we grab one on our way out?" Stephan murmured to me as we approached a small coffee stand to our right.

I shot him a puzzled frown. "You know I'd never sleep a wink if I had coffee, but I'll wait in line with you while you get one."

He gave an odd little shrug, his eyes intently on the coffee stand. "Nah, I guess I'll wait til' after a nap."

I followed his gaze to see Mr. Cavendish waiting at the coffee counter. He gave us an enigmatic smile, nodding cordially to Stephan. My head whipped around to eye Stephan suspiciously. He was nodding back at James Cavendish, smiling.

"What are you up to, Stephan?" I growled at him, my voice pitched low so that the rest of the crew wouldn't hear.

He pursed his lips. I nodded stiffly as we made our way past Mr. Cavendish. I was going for polite, but cold. I thought I pulled it off well.

"What? I can't be polite?" he asked, his tone all innocence. I didn't trust that tone at all. When I'd met Stephan he'd been a fourteen year old street hustler who could lie the wallet off of anyone breathing. He had long ago mastered the art of playing dumb. But I knew him better than anyone, and I wasn't fooled for a second.

"That smile you shared with him was downright conspiratorial. Tell me what you did. Did you give him my number?"

He sent me a wounded glance. "I wouldn't do that."

I was relieved. Stephan could skate around the truth like a pro, but he would never outright lie to me. If he said he wouldn't give James my number, I knew it was the truth, so I left it alone after that.

The crew van to the hotel was full of excited chatter about the plans for the evening. Apparently, everyone was planning to go out for drinks together at the bar on the corner near our hotel. Karaoke night. I cringed a little at the thought. It sounded a little too loud and embarrassing for my taste, or my mood. But I would be a good sport. It was a new crew, and I'd hate to be the only anti-social one in the bunch, when they were all so obviously excited.

Also, I knew Stephan liked one of the bartenders at that bar. They'd been feeling each other out slowly for the last couple of months. We went there for either lunch or dinner almost every week, when we came to town. Stephan was ninety percent sure that the bartender was flirting with him, and not just a friendly guy. But it took him a long time to work up to actually asking a guy out.

Stephan wasn't out of the closet. I didn't know if he would ever be ready for that. Gay guys who were out of the closet usually just weren't okay with dating in secret as though they were doing something wrong.

I knew that Stephan also preferred dating other men who weren't out, because it made it easier to keep it low-key. But this made it much harder for him to date. I'd suggested to him that he could probably find people easier online, considering his restrictions, but he wouldn't even consider it. He said online dating just felt wrong for him. He was a little old-fashioned about the strangest things.

"You're quiet, Buttercup," he whispered in my ear. Melissa was describing to the van at large what she was planning to wear that night, and what she was planning to sing for her karaoke numbers. Her selection of 'Sexy Back' did not surprise me in the least. "You'll come with us to the bar, right?" he asked me, a plea already in his voice. He thought I was going to try to duck out. I wasn't. The bartender was the first guy he'd been interested in since a particularly hard breakup a year ago, and if he needed me there for moral support, I'd be there.

I looked at him. His eyes were wide and doing their best 'Puss in Boots' impression for me already. *Wow, he's ready to bring out the big guns to get me to go tonight.* I decided to let him off the hook. "I'll go. But you have to swear not to make me sing or dance."

He nodded earnestly, smiling his happiest, boyish smile. "I know better. You'd have to be pretty drunk to get up on that stage. And I can't remember the last time you had a drink."

It'd been years, I knew. The month I'd turned twenty-one had been fun, and I'd indulged at a few parties then, but me and alcohol just didn't mix well. It was a family trait. Still, I considered having a few drinks with the crew. I was just so damned tense. Maybe I would indulge. Just let myself relax for a few hours. I couldn't find a good reason not to. "Maybe I'll have a few drinks tonight," I told him.

His eyes widened. "Yeah?" He was a moderate drinker himself, but he indulged more than I did.

I shrugged. "Maybe."

"Okay, Chickee," he said, drawing the end of the word into a long eeee sound. He put his arm along the back of my seat, giving my shoulder a squeeze.

"You two are so darn cute," Melissa gushed, when she saw his affectionate gesture.

We both gave her neutral smiles. We didn't know her well enough to explain ourselves to her, and frankly, I doubted we'd ever be close enough friends with her to do so. I tried to always give people a chance, but so far Melissa had not impressed me. I just found her untrustworthy, though I had nothing concrete so far to prove that. Although, she did openly admit that her goal in life was to find a rich man to take care of her. That seemed pretty damned shady to me.

"And I just love all those pet names he has for you."

Stephan gave her his most charming smile. "I'll call you Chickee, too, if you like."

She giggled. She was always like this when pilots were around, just way sweeter than she acted if they weren't present. "I think that's adorable. But my favorite is Buttercup. I heard you call her that the other day."

He gave me a soft smile that was all for me. "That one is only for Bee."

She clapped her hands together. "Oh, oh, oh, is there a story behind that pet name? I love stories!"

My nose crinkled. She was laying it on a little thick today. I shot a glance at the two pilots who were watching our interaction from the front row of seats in the huge van. I was guessing that she liked one of them, from the affected way she was acting.

The First Officer was younger and better looking than the Captain. Jeff, I recalled his name. He had dark brown hair, and attractive brown eyes. He was tall, with a rangy build. But my bet was she liked the Captain, since he made twice Jeff's salary.

The Captain, whose name I was ninety percent sure was Peter, was older, with balding gray hair, a beer gut, and eyes that never strayed north of a woman's chest.

She reaffirmed my guess almost as I thought it, sending the captain a positively beaming smile. "Don't you just love stories, too, Peter?" she asked him.

He gave her what I thought was a slightly greasy smile. "You betcha."

Stephan shook his head. "That story is between me and Bee. But, Peter, I'm dying to know what song you'll choose to serenade us with tonight." Stephan changed the subject easily, and with much charm. He had Peter laughingly refusing to sing and steering the conversation in the direction he chose with no effort whatsoever.

CHAPTER FOUR

Mr. Beautiful

I awoke to the sound of my alarm with even less enthusiasm than usual. I had tossed and turned for four hours. I'd been trying to catch enough sleep to make it through until at least eight p.m. I had failed. I would be dead on my feet by late afternoon, I guessed. I was in a positively sour mood as I stalked into my hotel room's bathroom.

"We working out?" Stephan called out to me from his room as I came back out.

Our rooms adjoined, as they usually did when we were in this hotel. We came here often, and knew the front desk staff well enough to arrange our rooms how we preferred. We just kept the door between our rooms open. We'd been roommates for years, and only recently become neighbors instead, so it was a relaxed, effortless arrangement. We both found comfort in the other's presence.

My only response was a mannerless grunt. He laughed. "The times when you don't want to the most, are the times that you definitely should," he told me.

I made a raspberry noise at him, and he laughed harder.

A moment later he came into my room, already in his gym

clothes and carrying a cup of coffee from my favorite cafe on the corner. The sight cheered me instantly.

He smiled at me, wiggling his brows. "Will this change your mind? Large mocha with soy, no whip, and an extra shot of espresso." He named off my order, though he hadn't needed to. I'd known as soon as I saw the cup that he'd know just what I'd want.

I grinned. "You're the best."

"It's a fact," he agreed.

We worked out for an hour. The hotel's gym was tiny and unimpressive, with one treadmill, one elliptical, one stationary bike, and some free weights. I stuck to the elliptical for the full hour, but Stephan flitted around from the bike, to the treadmill, and spent a half an hour lifting weights. It was his usual routine, and I watched him, feeling good as I listened to music on my phone and worked out.

Stephan had been right. I had been so tempted to skip a workout today, but it had ended up being just what I needed. I felt worlds better when we finished up.

We grabbed a quick sandwich for lunch. It was a beautiful late spring day in New York City, and I enjoyed our walk along the bustling street. "Wanna eat in the park?" I asked Stephan as we waited in line at a crowded local deli.

He nodded. "For sure. Picnic style."

We didn't precisely eat picnic style. Instead, we settled for finding an empty bench to sit on and people watch while we ate. "Whatcha gonna wear to the bar?" Stephan asked me between big bites.

We ate fast, as though afraid the food would disappear if we didn't finish it quickly. We both ate like hungry street kids if we didn't make a conscious effort not to. We didn't bother eating any differently when it was just the two of us. We had nothing to hide from each other. It was one of the reasons we were damn near inseparable.

"Iyonno," I said with too much food in my mouth. I swallowed, washing the mouthful down with a big swig of water from the refillable bottle I'd taken to carrying around almost constantly, to save money on bottled water.

"I don't know," I said more clearly. "It's nice and warm, so some shorts and a blouse, I guess. I don't feel like dressing up, but I don't wanna look like a slob when I know everyone else will be dressing up." I gestured at the comfortable gray workout T-shirt, black cheer shorts, and neon green running shoes I was wearing. "What I'd like to wear is this. But I know you'd harass me, so I'll try to look halfway decent, I suppose."

"You'll have to help me pick out my outfit. I wanna look really hot tonight. I think I just might be ready to ask Melvin out this time," Stephan said. I smiled. He had said the same thing for the last three weeks, but I just agreed.

We went back to our rooms to shower and get ready for the night ahead. We chatted amiably as we got ready.

I chose some cuffed, pleated black shorts and a sleeveless black and white blouse with flowery ruffles at the neck. It was the kind of outfit I liked best. It was comfortable but feminine. Some earrings and the right shoes, and it was dressy enough for just about anything. Add practical shoes, and poof, not overdressed.

I chose sandals with a short heel tonight. I picked silver hoops from the small bag of jewelry that I always packed. I wore my hair down. It was pin-straight and the pale length hung to my mid-back.

I put my makeup on quickly, just opting for mascara and some soft pink lip gloss. I finished getting ready first, since I didn't particularly care how I looked for the outing. I sat on Stephan's bed and patiently watched him try on everything he'd packed.

We finally settled on a fitted pale gray polo with some blue and gray plaid cargo shorts that hung from his slim hips in a very attractive way. He adopted the preppy look often, and I thought it suited him. He looked like a live Abercrombie and Fitch ad. I told him so. He laughed it off, but I could tell that he was pleased by the comparison, though it was only the truth.

We got to the bar a little before four p.m., but it was already a bit of a crush. It was not a fancy bar, just an old fashioned Irish pub with a few karaoke nights a week, but it was in the heart of Manhattan and it was Friday night, so I was not at all surprised by the crowd.

Stephan worked his magic and within minutes we had snagged seats at the bar where Melvin was working. I'd had no doubt that he would. He had a rare combination of charm and charisma and he just seemed to make things work out that way. Most of the people in this place would never find a seat on a night this crowded.

We greeted Melvin warmly, and he seemed genuinely pleased to see us. Especially Stephan, though he was very nice to me. I always went out of my way to try and befriend anyone Stephan was interested in. He was my only family, and it was important to me that I be friends with anyone he found significant.

I guessed Melvin was about our age, somewhere in his early twenties. He was just shy of six feet tall, and very slender, nearly delicate. I couldn't begin to guess his race, a mix of some kind. His skin was a naturally pale coffee color, his black hair cropped very close to his head. His eyes were a pale green. He was very handsome, and had a very engaging smile. *Stephan has great taste,* I thought.

"What can I get you?" Melvin had to raise his voice a little to be heard above the growing crowd. I bit my lip, looking at Stephan. I hadn't had any kind of alcohol in so long that my mind went blank. Stephan just shrugged and winked at Melvin. Whoa, that was bold for him. Melvin blushed a little and smiled back shyly.

"Surprise us.   Something with liquor," Stephan told him playfully.

Melvin grinned. "Shots or cocktails?"

"One of each. Make us your favorite of each," I declared. He left with a happy whistle to accommodate us.

I was distracted by the sound of some out-of-tune singing. We were far enough from the stage not to be deafened, but close enough to have a perfect view. That was always how it seemed to go around Stephan. He led a charmed life. "They start the Karaoke this early?" I asked Stephan, surprised.

He shrugged. "I guess so. It does seem awfully early for that, though. They need to let us get a little more buzzed before we have to listen to that."

I agreed, laughing.

Melvin was back in short order. He'd made us each a Pom-tini, which was delicious enough that I didn't think it could possibly get me drunk. He'd also brought us a shot he called 'surfer on acid'. I'd never heard of it. I smelled it, and my nose wrinkled. It was strong. "What is it?" I asked him.

"Jagermeister, pineapple juice, and coconut rum. Trust me, it's good."

Stephan grinned at him.   "I trust you," he declared, and downed it. He gasped as it went down. "Damn, it is good."

I downed mine. There was only one way to do a shot, as far as I was concerned, and that way was fast. They were right, it was very good, and I felt a nearly instant, fuzzy buzz. *Okaaay*, I thought. I needed to slow it down. Even one shot was a shock to my system after so much time without. Though it *was* a shot that packed a hell of a punch.

Melvin brought us each a glass of ice water without us having to ask, then went to tend to the growing crowd. Stephan would have to stay late into the night if he hoped for much of Melvin's attention. The bar was getting more crowded by the second.

Melvin was extremely busy, but still managed to stop near us to have short conversations with Stephan every few minutes, and I took this as an encouraging sign. He was definitely giving Stephan special attention, beyond being simply friendly. I finished my first Pom-tini way too fast. "Damn tiny martini glasses," I muttered to Stephan, my voice way louder than I'd intended. Yep, I definitely needed to slow it down on the drinking. Stephan laughed at me, finishing his as well.

Melvin immediately had martini and shot refills in front of us. Okay, we were definitely getting special treatment. He wagged a finger at us. "Your next round will be a new surprise." He winked at Stephan as he walked away. I smiled broadly at Stephan. He smiled back at me. He was the happiest I'd seen him in a while, and it brightened my mood a lot just to see him like that. He'd been majorly hung up on his Ex from a year ago, and it was a relief to see that he was finally moving on. "We better drink these fast. I want to see our next surprise," Stephan teased me.

I laughed and took the shot. Screw slowing down. I wanted our next surprise. Stephan and I unwisely raced to finish the Pom-tini. I pointed at him, laughing, as I finished mine just a second ahead of him. "I win," I said.

With perfect timing, Melvin slid a new shot and martini in front of us just as Stephan set down his glass. "A Kamikaze, and a Razzle-tini," he told us, having to almost shout now with the horrible rendition of 'Moves Like Jagger' a group of three were belting out from the stage. I thanked him. Stephan did the same, squeezing Melvin's hand just as he was pulling back. It was a surprisingly bold move for Stephan. Melvin blushed and smiled at Stephan as he went back to tend to customers.

I practically beamed at Stephan. "He's soooo interested. You know that, right?" I asked him.

He nodded, looking suddenly shy, but very pleased. "Yeah, I'm finally sure of it."

It wasn't long before the crew started showing up. Brenda

showed up first. She was a middle-aged woman, in her mid-forties, I guessed. I saw her less than anyone else on the crew, since she worked in the back galley of the plane, and I worked in the front, but she seemed very nice. I thought we could easily be friends, if we spent a little time together. She walked up to us, smiling.

She had dark brown hair cut in a bob that flattered her bone structure nicely. She had a medium build and was very pretty. I knew she was married with some teenage children, but I didn't know all the details yet. I made a note to ask her more about her family. She seemed like she would be a good mom, with her kind eyes and calm manner.

We greeted her a little more loudly and boisterously than was our habit, and she laughed at us with good humor. "You guys have been at it for awhile, huh?"

Stephan insisted she take his chair, and she did so, thanking him with a dimpled smile. "He's one of the last throwbacks to a true gentleman," she said to me. I could tell she was assuming that he and I were an item, and I didn't correct her.

Within five minutes, Stephan had secured the seat on the other side of me. I giggled at him. "How do you always do that?" I asked, turning in the direction of his new seat.

He arched a brow at me. "You should know better than anyone, Bee. I've been hustling since I was a kid. Talking someone out of a seat at the bar is child's play."

Melissa was the next to show up, already looking around with boredom as she approached us. Probably looking for Captain Peter, I thought.

She was in rare form, wearing a white micro-mini skirt and a clingy pink top that sort of clashed with her dark red hair. The top was so thin that I could tell two things; her boobs were fake, and she wasn't wearing a bra.

She couldn't be more than five foot two barefoot, but she was making up for it tonight. Her white, rhinestone-studded stilettos were easily over five inches tall. She handled them well, too, gliding in them as though she wore heels like that every day. For all I knew, she did. She had a heavy layer of makeup on, her lips bright red and her lashes so thick and black they looked like something you'd see on an old-fashioned pin-up model. She was very pretty. What she lacked in taste she more than made up for in sheer good looks.

"Hey guys," she said without smiling. It was as though she didn't want to waste a good smile on us.

"Hey," I said. Brenda and Stephan greeted her. I noticed that Stephan didn't offer her his chair. I knew that she got on his nerves just a bit without him having to say it. She wasn't exactly a hard worker, and she seemed to think she was entitled to more than other people. Those were two qualities that he and I just had trouble relating to.

The pilots were the next to show. They came in together. I'm not sure I would have recognized either of them out of uniform. I only knew they had arrived when Melissa's personality suddenly got real bubbly. Stephan and I shared a short, pointed look.

We all said our greetings, and by then Melissa had managed to snag the seat next to Brenda. Captain Peter was practically glued to the back of her chair. I tried not to stare. They weren't being subtle. Those two were likely going to end the night together.

My eyes snagged on the ring on the Captain's left hand as he rubbed it all over Melissa's nearly bare back. *Ewww*, I thought. I hated that. I didn't understand why people got married, and then acted like that. But it certainly knocked my opinion of Melissa down even further. There was no way she had missed the wedding ring on his finger if I had seen it from several feet away. Hell, she probably felt it on her back, he was rubbing her so hard with it.

I made an easy decision to just try to ignore them for the

duration of the evening. They were a major buzz-kill.

I noticed with a little dismay that the first officer, Jeff, had ended up standing by my chair, his body angled towards me. He smiled at me as I noticed him. He waved at the glasses in front of me. "What're you drinking? It looks like a good time."

I told him, and he stepped closer as I spoke. I moved back a bit. I hated when people tried to casually touch me, and he just seemed like the type to try it.

Sure enough, a few minutes later, after he had downed his own shot, he reached out a hand, touching a strand of my hair. I shrank back just a little. "I love your hair." He was nearly shouting over the rowdy crowd. "It looks so hot when you wear it down."

I turned away from him at that, finishing my current round of drinks. Yes, it was official. I was drunk. I caught Stephan and Melvin sharing a look, and I knew exactly what it meant. Stephan was trying to tell Melvin to cut off my alcohol.

I glared, leaning closer to him. I pointed a finger at his chest threateningly. "Don't you dare. I barely ever drink, and I really need to relax tonight. This is the first time in days that I've been able to unwind and just forget about Mr. Beautiful."

Stephan had looked ready to argue until that last embarrassing sentence left my mouth. But as I finished, he sputtered out a laugh. "Mr. Beautiful?"

I nodded, and he laughed harder. "Well, he is. James Cavendish is too damned beautiful to be real. He scares the shit outta me," I confided.

Stephan stopped laughing at that. "Why?" he asked seriously.

I shook my head. "Not like that. A different kind of scary. I haven't figured it out. All I know for sure is, I need to stay the hell away from Mr. Beautiful." I over-enunciated the last sentence so much that, even drunk, I noticed it.

Stephan's eyes widened as he looked at a spot above and

behind me.

"What?" I asked him in a loud, belligerent tone. Yes, I was definitely drunk. "What? Is Mr. Beautiful standing behind me or something?"

Stephan pursed his lips and I suddenly had an awful feeling that I'd hit that one right on the head. I turned my spinning head around and looked up, and up, into bright blue eyes. "Hello, Mr. Beautiful," I said in a quieter, but still obviously drunk, voice.

CHAPTER FIVE

Mr. Persistent

       I spun almost immediately to glare at Stephan. "Traitor," I said to him, my words slurred.

He threw his hands up, giving me his innocent look. "I didn't give out your number or anything. He asked if we were going out tonight. I just told him where. No harm done."

I mouthed a few choice words at him. I felt a hard cheek press to the hair near my ear and knew it was Mr. Beautiful himself. "Mr. Beautiful, huh?" he whispered in my ear. I knew my whole body was bright red with embarrassment. "I'm going to take that as a compliment, though I have to say, it's a new one."

"Hello, Mr. Cavendish," I said stiffly, without turning.

"I told you, call me James. Or Mr. Beautiful, if you prefer. You can save the Mr. Cavendish for when we're in private." It was the second time he'd said that, and I just couldn't tell if he was teasing. *Did I even want to know?* I wondered. *No,* I told myself firmly.

I tried to just ignore everyone for awhile after that. Except for Melvin. Him, I tried to flag down to get another drink, but *he* was ignoring *me.* Vaguely, I could hear Stephan and James chatting amiably at my back.

James hadn't moved, and he was standing close enough to my back to indicate that he and I were together. He was so close that it made the skin of my back tingle. If I shifted even an inch backward, we'd be touching.

I turned my head slightly and saw that the co-pilot had been forced to move away from me. He was looking between Stephan and James, an odd look on his face. He didn't know what to make of the situation. I didn't really care what he made of it. I was just relieved that he seemed to get the picture that I was clearly not available.

I lurched suddenly to my feet. I had expected to be a little unsteady on my feet, but it was much worse than I'd thought. I had to clutch the bar for several moments to gain my balance.

"Whoa, careful there, Buttercup," Stephan was saying to me.

I felt a hard arm going around my waist for support, and I knew it wasn't Stephan. "Buttercup?" James asked him, his voice amused.

I looked at Stephan, who was looking a little sheepish. "It's an old nickname, from when we were kids. Bee will have to tell you the story sometime."

"I look forward to it. Does she drink like this often?" James asked casually, but I thought there was a slight edge to his voice. He was still just talking to Stephan. About me, and in front of me. It was infuriating.

"All the time," I said loudly.

"This is the first time she's had a drink since the month she turned twenty-one," Stephen said quietly. "At least two years ago."

James's mouth was at my ear again. "You remember what I told you about lying to me," he warned softly. "That's two."

He'd said he'd put me over his knee. "He's a kinky bastard," I thought drunkenly.

Oops, I'd said that out loud. Luckily, only James had heard.

He laughed, showing even white teeth. He hadn't taken it as an insult. He nodded at me, making very solid eye contact. He agreed.

"I need to go to the bathroom," I declared loudly.

"I'll help you get there, Buttercup," James told me. Stephan rose as we moved, as though to help. James waved him down. "I've got her."

And he did. He wrapped my arm around him and took the brunt of my weight as he led me effortlessly through the crowd toward the restrooms.

"Why are you here?" I asked him bluntly.

"Well, I came here because I very much want to fuck you until neither of us can walk. I want you so bad I can't see straight. But since that won't be happening now, I'm staying to make sure you make it back to your room in one piece."

"Why won't that be happening now?" I asked him. I knew it was a bad question, one that implied that I was disappointed that it wouldn't be happening, but I was just too drunk and curious to care.

He looked at me, brow raised. "I won't touch you while you're impaired. Never. I just don't do that."

"So you give up?" I challenged, but it came out as more of a whine.

He surprised me by kissing the top of my head. "Far from it. I still intend to fuck you senseless. Just not tonight, Buttercup. And I'd appreciate it if you could refrain from ever getting yourself into this condition again." His arms and the kiss had been soft and sweet, but his words and his tone were icy.

What a strange man, I thought. How could someone sound so cold while calling me Buttercup?

I stopped suddenly. We were against the wall now, close to the hallway that led to the restrooms. I turned in his arms, pressing up against him. He sucked in a breath at the sudden contact. I looked into his eyes. He looked back, his eyes hard.

"Yes?" he asked me sharply.

"My condition isn't your business, James." I emphasized his name. It was the first time I'd used it.

His gaze was steady. "I intend for it to be my business."

"You don't want to date me, you said," I told him.

He sighed. "It's true. But I want other things. I at least want the chance to talk to you about what I do want."

"So talk," I told him.

"We will talk. When you're sober. And when we have some actual privacy."

I wagged a finger at him, then stood on my tiptoes to be sure he heard me as I spoke directly into his face. "That doesn't sound like talking." My words were slurred, and he visibly flinched.

He hated how drunk I was, I could tell. He had a real serious problem with it. My extremely drunk mind started to hatch up a drunk scheme to use that to my advantage. If he didn't like drunk, I would show him some drunk behavior that would scare him off for good. I nodded at him, turning away. Just as soon as I went to the bathroom, I was gonna make him run the other way in a hurry.

I used the restroom. It was a sign of how drunk I was that I was proud when I used the bathroom successfully and without a mess.

I was washing up when Melissa came bursting through the door, looking excited. "Who is that gorgeous man?" she asked me breathlessly. She was the most animated I'd ever seen her without a man she liked in the room. Of course, that's just because she happened to be talking about one right at that moment.

I didn't have to ask who she was talking about. "That is Mr. Beautiful," I said. I was going for a breezy tone, but I heard my voice, and knew it just sounded drunk and slurred.

I walked out before she could ask me anything else. James

took my arm before I could even locate him. "Have you ever been so drunk that you can't look yourself in the eyes when you see a mirror?" I asked him. It was a serious question. I was really that drunk. He just looked at me.

"Answer me, James," I tried to order him.

"No," he said immediately.

"Dance with me," I told him. Time for operation 'Hot Mess'. He hated drunk. I'd show him drunk.

"No," he said firmly.

"Fine. Somebody'll dance with me. Just you watch." His hand tightened on my arm when I tried to walk away.

"No, they won't. If you have to dance, it'll be by yourself tonight."

I gasped at him in outrage. I was momentarily distracted when we walked back out into the huge bar and found it had considerably less people than it had when we went in.

"Whats'appened to all the people?" I asked. My slur was getting more pronounced, but I couldn't seem to help it. I looked at him. He just shrugged. "Is it that late?" I pondered, reaching into my small handbag for my phone. "Where's ma'phone?" I mumbled.

"You left it at the bar," he told me. I started to lurch in that direction. He stayed me, holding my phone in front of my face. "I grabbed it for you."

I snatched it from him, glaring. I glanced at the face of it, pushing the front button to show the time. "S'only eight clock. Why d'ya spose everyone is leaving? Is something happening? Are they closing?"

His only answers were shrugs. His hands were in his pockets. I studied him, suddenly realizing how bored and detached he looked. I recalled what he'd said about only sticking around to make sure I got back in one piece. "You don't have to stay here. I'm just fine."

He pulled me against him suddenly. I stiffened, but he just

pushed my cheek into his chest. "You're an infuriating woman," he said into my hair. I tried to shove away from him for that comment, but I couldn't seem to budge him. "I would be happy to walk you back to your room, but I'm not leaving you here when you're acting like this."

"You don't know anything about me. I may act this way all the time," I said, but the words were muffled into his shirt.

He was wearing the softest T-shirt I'd ever felt. I was suddenly nuzzling against it. I realized that I hadn't even seen what he was wearing. It wasn't a suit, and I hadn't even gotten a chance to check him out.

I pulled back, looking with fascination at his casual attire. His shirt was a navy V-neck T-shirt with a small pocket over the left side of his chest. Right over his nipple, I thought. It was fitted, showing off his sleek muscles. And it was sooo soft.

I started running my hands over it, and he didn't stop me. He wore casual gray slacks with navy running shoes. He looked positively edible.

"Someday soon I'm going to tie you up and tease you just the way you're teasing me right now, with no hope for release for at least a night." His voice was soft and earnest. His words stilled my hands immediately. Apparently I wasn't doing a great job of scaring him off. Yet.

I snapped my fingers at him as I got an idea. I was steadier on my feet as I pulled completely out of his arms. Just a few minutes without imbibing was improving my balance.

"I have a surprise for you," I told him ominously, and stalked toward the Karaoke DJ.

I whispered my request in the strange man's ear, and he nodded, shooting a look at James.

I put a finger over my lips. "Shhh. It's a surprise for Mr. Beautiful."

James watched me stoically as I climbed onto the tiny stage. Surprisingly, there was no one in line, so I got to go immediately. Before I'd gone to the bathroom there had been a line nearly out the door of people waiting to perform. Now the place was just getting emptier by the second.

That was fine with me. This hot mess of a show was all for James Cavendish.

I couldn't help it. I started to giggle as the first notes of S&M came on and I saw his eyes widen. I got myself under control enough to start singing to it when the words came on the screen, shooting him sassy looks and even throwing in a little bit of wiggling to the beat. I even bent down to flip my hair at a small pause in the song. *Oh, lord*, that almost knocked me off the stage.

He moved closer at my reckless action, as though to catch me if I really did fall off.

I got a little off track when Melissa strutted over and started talking to him. *Did she really have to stand so close to him?* Apparently, she did. She even pressed against him as she spoke into his ear.

He didn't seem to mind either, talking to her now more than he was watching me. It seemed to be a very serious conversation for two people who had just met. *Or did they know each other?*

That's it, I decided. I was going to find out.

The music hadn't even stopped when I stomped off the stage.

James gave me a small smile as I approached. Melissa wasn't touching him anymore, but she was still standing way too close to him.

"Thank you for the surprise, Bianca. I won't forget that for as long as I live." His voice was warm and full of good humor. *Dammit.* That had not been what I was going for.

"Do you two know each other?" I asked abruptly.

James looked a little surprised. "We just met. She works with you, right?"

"So what were you talking about?" I asked pointedly.

"She said she was a good friend of yours. I was asking her about you."

I looked at Melissa. She looked a little miffed, but hardly deterred. If she had any clue how much James was worth, she'd *really* be all over him.

I toyed with the idea of telling her. That might solve the whole situation right there. For reasons I didn't want to analyze, I decided against it almost immediately.

She studied me briefly, and her expression brightened. She grabbed my hand suddenly, all bubbly girl again. "Come on, chicky," she said to me fondly, leading me back to the Dj.

CHAPTER SIX

Mr. Perverse

I didn't have to wonder what she was up to for long. She had us duet-ing a version of 'Back that thing Up' in no time.

I mostly tried to rap to the vaguely obscene lyrics while watching her in fascination. She quickly had her ass to the audience, doing some pretty impressive booty dancing.

I was more stacked than her in the chest department, and mine were very much natural, but she had waaay more junk in the trunk. And I had to admit it was very nice junk. And she very much knew it.

She threw smiles over her shoulder at the crowd as she crouched nearly to the floor. Yep, she was backing that thing up.

I was rapping, "Call me big daddy when you back that thang up," when Stephan caught my gaze from the crowd. He'd left his spot at the bar, where he'd been in close conversation with Melvin since we'd come out of the bathroom.

Ah, damn. I had interrupted them with my antics. He had finally gotten a chance to make his move, and I had distracted him. I felt instantly guilty.

43

He was giving me wide eyes. I could tell he was about ready to carry me home. He would not approve of operation 'hot mess', I knew for sure. He'd been acting as my protective older brother for too long to just idly stand by while I drunkenly embarrassed myself.

I was relieved when he didn't immediately come and carry me from the stage. But my relief was short-lived as I saw him speaking earnestly to James. James was listening intently, nodding in agreement.

I got distracted by the lyrics screen as the the beat got faster for a moment. I substituted any words I couldn't say that started with N with the word chicky. I thought it fit rather well into the song, and was mentally patting myself on the back when the song ended.

Melissa laughingly hugged me when we finished. She was breathless from all that shaking. Did she suddenly like me? Or was this some kind of a show for James's benefit? With what I knew of Melissa, I suspected the latter, but I didn't really care just then.

I approached the two tall men who looked to be having a serious conversation that I was positive was all about me.

James sent me a wide-eyed look. He looked shocked about something.

I stalked up to Stephan and bumped his shoulder with my own. "What are you telling him?" I asked him, my voice angry. "Go sit back down at the bar, Stephan. I am just fine."

Stephan leaned down to me. He seemed visibly upset, and I was on alert at once. What the hell was going on with these two?

He hugged me, speaking into my ear. "Please don't be mad at me. I know it's not my place to butt in, but I just had to see what kind of a guy he is. I think he'll treat you well. And if he doesn't, I told him I'd kick his billionaire ass."

I scrunched my nose up at him. "That's why you thought I'd

44

be mad at you?"

He didn't look any less upset, so I knew that wasn't it. He couldn't look me in the eye, and he was trembling a little. He hated it when I was mad at him. He had serious issues with people being upset with him, and especially with me being mad. Issues that stemmed from some truly horrible things that had happened to him when he was a kid. I'd been his only family for years, so he feared my anger. He had this irrational fear that if he ever made me really angry with him, I would desert him, like his family had. I'd told him many times that it would never happen, but he still didn't know how to cope with any kind of conflict.

He was shaking his head, and I could see a certain panic in his eyes that I dreaded. It did a great deal towards sobering me up. "What is it?" I asked him.

"I told him that you were a virgin," he whispered in my ear. I stiffened. "I just didn't want him to hurt you. Or to…have the wrong impression of you with the way you were acting. Please don't be mad."

I couldn't seem to help it. I was instantly mad. I pushed him back, pointing at him. "Go. Back. To. Your. Seat."

He obeyed, doing a pretty good impression of a 'Charley Brown walk' back over to Melvin. I had probably just ruined his whole night, but he had no right to share personal information about me. Especially not with Mr. Beautiful.

I turned back to James, glaring. "So, are you done yet? You can see now that this is not going to happen. My V-card should be more than enough of a reason to make someone like you run screaming in the other direction." *Maybe Stephan had found me a better final solution to this strange problem*, I realized, even as I spoke.

The shock was long gone from his face. Now his face was carefully blank. The blankness didn't quite reach his eyes, though. They were as intense as ever. "Come here," he told me.

A few feet separated us. I closed the distance before I thought to defy him. He fisted a hand very, very carefully into my hair, pulling my head back slightly. He leaned down to my ear. "I'm going to ruin you," he breathed. "I'll be your first, and I'll fuck you so thoroughly that I'll be your last, too. You won't want any other man after I've gotten my hands on you. Every last inch of you." A shudder ran through my entire body at his roughly whispered words.

My brow furrowed. Had he somehow sensed I was a virgin even before Stephan told him? Is that why he was pursuing me? Did he have some weird fetish? "So you prefer virgins?" I whispered the question back at him.

His brows shot up in surprise. "I've never been with one, so no. But I can't say I'm displeased with the notion. In fact, I love it that I'll be your first."

I didn't even bother to tell him that he was assuming a whole lot right there. I was suddenly very tired. Tired enough to pass out. And we had to be up at five a.m to get ready for the morning flight. "I'm ready to go," I told him. His face brightened instantly.

"Good. Let's go tell Stephan."

Stephan wouldn't even look at me as we approached.

"Bianca is calling it a night," James told Stephan. "I'll see her to her room. What time should I set her alarm for?" I rolled my eyes. There he went, talking about me in front of me again.

"Five," Stephan and I answered at the same time. The men nodded at each other cordially, Stephan never looking at me.

I knew it would bother him all night if I didn't tell him he was forgiven. I stepped forward, kissing him softly on the forehead.

"I'm not mad at you," I told him, and was surprised that it was true. He'd had no right to do it, but I knew he was only trying to protect me. It had been his job for years now, and it was a job he took very seriously.

He sniffed a little, and I was shocked when I saw one tear slip down his cheek as he looked at his lap.

"Thank you," he said, and I heard the relief in his voice. He was so relieved that he was crying, when he never cried. That was how strongly my anger affected him.

"Please don't," I told him. It broke my heart to see him like that.

He lifted his head, and he looked better. "I'm good. Really. Go get some sleep. I'll see you in the morning." He smiled and waved me off. I smiled back, and we left.

James held my arm on our short walk back to the hotel. He had a firm grip on the back of my arm, just above my elbow. He seemed to like that spot. "Stephan and I spoke at length. He knows I would never take advantage of you when you're impaired." James seemed to feel the need to explain this to me. "If I didn't know otherwise, I would think he was your older brother," he continued. "How long have you two been close?" he asked.

I sent him a sideways glance. He was fishing for information about me, I could tell. I didn't play that game. Especially when I knew next to nothing about him.

"A long time," I answered vaguely. That's the best he would get. I had already sobered up considerably, so he'd missed the boat on any carelessly thrown information. Especially since I was planning to never drink again. I was already mortified by some of my antics that night, and I wasn't even completely sober yet.

"You need to get on the pill." He abruptly changed the subject, his voice authoritative.

I sent him another sideways glance. This glance was on its way to a glare. "My body, my business," I told him stiffly.

"When we're having sex, it will be my business as well. And you need to get started. It can take weeks to months before it becomes effective."

My glance became a glare. "For your information, I'm already on the pill. I have bad periods, and it helps make them milder. I've actually been on them since I was a teenager... for personal reasons." Reasons I would never tell him. Like the fact that Stephan and I had lived in an abandoned building with a bunch of other homeless people and I'd been terrified of being raped and getting pregnant. I hadn't been able to sleep for the fear. A trip to the free clinic had given me a great deal of peace of mind. About the pregnancy aspect, at least. "But you are outrageous, you know that? I've never agreed to have sex with you."

"What personal reasons?" he asked. Of course he would zero in on the thing I was the least willing to talk about.

"I prefer to keep those reasons personal." I stuck my tongue out at him.

His hand squeezed my arm in a warning. "You are exasperating."

"Let me bombard you with a bunch of personal questions and see how you like it," I shot back.

"Give it a try. I think the tradeoff might just be worthwhile for me."

I fell silent at that.

We made our way into the hotel without a word. I nodded at the girl working the front desk as we walked by. Her name was Sarah, and she knew Stephan and I. We'd even gone out with her a few times. She gave me wide eyes. She probably thought Stephan and I were a couple, as so many people did.

"Hey, Sarah," I called out, without stopping.

"Hey, Bianca," she called back.

"The security here is deplorable," James said as the elevator doors closed on us. He was shaking his head in dismay.

I giggled. "What did you expect? It's a crew hotel in downtown manhattan. The security isn't deplorable. It's non-existant." I giggled harder. Rich people could be funny.

He gave me a disgruntled look. "It's terrifying. Anyone could come in here."

I just kept giggling. "That's what locks and police are for. If you think this is bad, you should see some of the places Stephan and I have stayed." *Oh shit.* I hadn't meant to say that out loud.

His intent eyes searched my face. "Where? What do you mean? Do you still stay in those places?"

I shrugged, trying to blow past the whole thing. "Um, not really. I guess this is our least secure crew hotel at the moment." The thought made me start giggling again.

He held a hand out for my key card, and I gave it to him without a word.

"I would prefer if you stay at a more secure place when you visit the city. I'll arrange it," he said, shocking me.

I shook my head. "No. No. No," I told him clearly. "I don't know what you think is going on here, but you are not going to take control of my life. You can just rule out that scenario right now."

His mouth set in a hard line. "We'll talk about it when you're sober."

He was crazy, I decided. "You can talk all you want. That is not happening."

He noticed the open connecting door as we entered my room. He gave me a questioning look, going through the door, as though he had the right to search the place.

"Stephan's room?" he asked from Stephan's room.

"Yes," I answered.

He came back in, closing and locking the door without asking. I just went to the bed and lay down, closing my eyes.

"I need to set my alarm," I told myself out loud, reaching for my little bag. I had dropped it on the floor somewhere between the door and my bed.

"I've got it," James told me, and I heard him moving around.

I heard the little sound that meant my phone had been plugged into a charger.

"Thank you," I murmured, eyes still closed. "You can go now. I'll wake up on time. I've never been late to work. I'm not gonna start the habit tomorrow. As soon as my head stops this spinning, I'll be falling asleep."

He didn't respond, and I heard him moving around my room. He went into the bathroom, coming out just a moment later. The bed dipped as he sat beside me on the bed. I felt and smelled a cool, makeup removing wipe on my face.

I tensed up in surprise. *What's he doing?* He gently wiped my entire face, even wiping my eyelashes carefully to remove my mascara.

"You hardly wear any makeup," he said absently. "You have a lovely complexion." That was such a sweet thing to say that I had to snort.

"Look who's talking, Mr. Beautiful," I said.

"Perhaps I'll just call you Mrs. Beautiful," he said to me, leaning down to kiss just the tip of my nose.

I felt him get up again, returning after just a moment. When I felt his fingers on the button of the waistband of my shorts, my eyes shot open, my hands moving to block him. The only light in the room came from the bathroom, but I could still make him out.

"What are you doing?" I asked slowly.

He brushed my hands away, unbuttoning my shorts and sweeping them down my legs in a quick, smooth motion.

"Taking care of you," he said mildly. "I told you and Stephan that I would. I'm getting you ready for bed right now. And if you start throwing up all of that poison you drank tonight, I'll take you to the bathroom and hold your hair out of your face for you. Hold still. I'll have you changed faster if you don't fidget so much."

Strangely, I obeyed him, and he had me out of my clothes

and into the thin cotton shift I had packed as a nightgown.

He removed my bra like a pro, never touching a thing beyond my back and shoulders. He barely jostled me as he did it. It was rather impressive. He even folded my shorts carefully, and hung my blouse up, as though he did this everyday. He tucked me in carefully.

What a strange billionaire, I thought to myself.

When he finished, he came to stand over me. He looked down at me, hands in his pockets, looking like he wasn't sure what to do next. It was a strange look for him.

"You can sleep here," I told him. "If you can handle the lack of security." I couldn't help but tease him about that.

He sucked in a breath. "Do you mind if I just sleep in my boxers? It's much more comfortable, and I swear I won't try a thing. Tonight."

Did I mind? I was dying to see his body. I just had to know if he was that tan everywhere.

"Okay," I said in a breathless voice.

He didn't hesitate after that, stripping off his shoes, socks, shirt and slacks in short order. I wished fervently that the lights were on, never taking my eyes off of him. He slid onto the other side of the bed from me, lying on his back on top of the covers.

"Go to sleep," he told me.

"Are you tan like that everywhere?" I asked him, just on the edge of sleep. If he answered me, I never heard him as I drifted off.

CHAPTER SEVEN

Mr. Moody

The sound of my alarm woke me from a deep sleep. I never slept that hard, and coming out of it was something I was unaccustomed to. I knew instantly that it was gonna be a rough morning by the pounding in my temples.

The clock showed five a.m, but my body still thought it was two a.m. A twenty-four hour layover was never enough time to adjust to the time difference.

I wasn't surprised to find that James had left, though I was strangely disappointed.

Since there were no longer any lingering effects of alcohol buzzing through my system, I knew I had a problem. I was starting to like that kinky rich bastard.

I went directly into the shower, pinning my hair up and keeping it carefully dry. There was no way I'd have time to dry it if I washed it.

I threw my shift back on my slightly damp skin, planning to wear it until it was time to change into work clothes. I was so used to sharing adjoining rooms with Stephan that it was just second nature for me to stay at least partially decent while I got ready.

My bathroom door was slightly ajar, so when my hotel room door clicked open and then closed, I froze in alarm. I peaked out of the door, both surprised and relieved to see that it was James.

He joined me in the bathroom without asking. Even Stephan wasn't so familiar with me, so it caught me off guard that he would join me so casually in the bathroom right after I'd showered.

He handed me a cup of coffee and two white tablets. He set two bottles of water on the counter.

"The pills are for the hangover," he told me. "And the water will help. You're dehydrated."

I took the pills, downing most of the first bottle in the process. A long drink of the coffee and I felt nearly human again.

I saw that he had changed his clothes. He was back in a suit, looking fresh and well rested.

"You went back to your place?" I knew little about him, but I did know that he lived primarily in New York. My eyes were on his impeccable suit. It was a soft gray, his shirt and tie blue today. I'd never gotten a chance to get a good look at him without his clothes on. *Dammit.*

As I looked at him, my eyes moved up to his in the mirror. We were both facing it, and his lovely turquoise eyes were glued to my body with an intensity that made my eyes follow his.

My thin shift, combined with my slightly damp skin, had, not surprisingly, made my nightgown transparent. *I might as well be naked*, I thought, a little stunned.

And he was drinking in the sight of me hungrily, as though he'd never seen anything so appetizing in his life. It was an intoxicating feeling, to put that look in his eyes.

He stepped in directly behind me, his eyes steadily on my chest. My breasts felt heavy and I wanted him to touch them so badly.

I unconsciously arched my back a little, my shoulders going back, my chest forward, my nipples clearly visible as they rubbed against the thin fabric of my shift. They were pebbled to hardness, and tightened even more as I watched them.

"I don't want to make you late for work," he murmured. "But I need to do something."

He pressed up against my back, his arousal hard and heavy against my tailbone. His hands covered my breasts, finally, and I moaned, arching back. He kneaded them firmly and my eyes fell closed.

"Look at me," he snapped, and I obeyed automatically, meeting his intense eyes in the mirror.

"I like this nightgown," he said almost absently, as he continued to touch me. "Spread your legs more," he told me, and they just shifted apart, as though my body and his mouth had some sort of agreement that I wasn't yet privy to.

One hand stayed kneading my breast, and plucking at my nipple just perfectly while the other ran along my ribs, down my abdomen, and straight between my legs.

They started to shut instinctively against the invasion.

"Open wider," he ordered, and they just did. "I want to pleasure every inch of you, but for the moment, I'm just going to make you come. I just need to touch you. Lay your head back against my shoulder."

He quickly found and rubbed my clitoris with his thumb while his index and middle finger played at my entrance almost teasingly.

He sucked in a breath as he felt me. "God, a fucking wet virgin. You are too much, Bianca."

He pushed one finger into me slowly, and groaned. The fit was excruciatingly tight. I masturbated sometimes with my own fingers, but his were just so much bigger and rougher, and more talented. He knew how to touch me with far more skill than I knew how to touch myself. The thought was a little daunting, but my mind quickly wandered back to the sensations at hand.

He worked his finger all the way in and began to stroke, his finger seeking out just the right spot inside of me. His thumb never stopped circling my clit, and his other hand still kneaded my tender breast with consummate skill. He was a hell of a multi-tasker.

As he stroked, his arousal brushed against my back with increasing pressure. He slipped a second finger in and I felt impossibly full. I cried out, grinding against him.

He stopped suddenly. "Ask me for it," he ordered, and I didn't mistake his meaning.

"Please." I didn't hesitate.

"Say, please, Mr. Cavendish, make me come."

"Please, Mr. Cavendish, make me come."

He pinched my nipple hard as he stroked that perfect spot harder. I came in seconds, before I even really knew it was happening.

I hadn't realized that an orgasm could be like that, erupting so swiftly. Or so powerfully. I felt like I may have lost myself for a moment.

We were both panting heavily as I came back to myself. He caught my gaze in the mirror as he shifted his fingers out of me. I watched, absolutely mesmerized, as he raised them to his mouth and licked them clean.

When he finished, he grabbed my chin and turned my head to his for a deep kiss. "You are the most perfect fucking thing I've ever seen in my life," he murmured against my mouth.

I tried to reach for his still heavy arousal. He caught my hand, knowing where it was headed. "There's no time. Get dressed." He sounded almost angry now.

He was apparently frustrated and moody about it.

I got dressed in record time, in my little dress suit that was designed to look like a mock man's suit, little tie and all.

James watched me the entire time, not giving me a second of

privacy. I was in too much of a hurry to worry about it.

"That is the hottest fucking flight attendant uniform I've ever seen. That thing should be illegal. I'm going to do some illegal things to you with that little tease of a tie," he said, his tone serious. I just laughed.

"I can do my hair and makeup in the van. Stephan will help me." I licked my lower lip and waved a hand at his still obviously heavy arousal. "I still have ten minutes to spare. There has to be something I can do for you. I don't like feeling like I've left you unsatisfied."

He smiled at me, and it was pained. "You are too perfect. But it's not happening this morning. I'm not coming again until I can be buried inside of you. Preferably for days."

I took a step closer to him, licking my lips again. Impulsively, I knelt in front of him.

"You could bury yourself somewhere else," I said, my voice turning breathy.

My face hovered just inches from his groin, but I checked the urge to touch him, just looking up at him instead.

He gripped my hair a little roughly. "Have you done that before?" he asked, his voice unsteady.

I shook my head, licking my lips again. "Like I've told you, I don't date. I don't do any of this stuff. I don't know what's gotten into me, but you should take me up on the offer before I change my mind."

He had his slacks unbuttoned and his arousal out so fast that I blinked at the sight of him. He was..spectacular. And right in my face.

It was no hardship at all to take him into my mouth and start sucking on him hungrily. Just the opposite. I'd never wanted something so much in my life. Though I couldn't fit much more than the tip past my teeth.

"Use your hands at the base," he told me. He used his hands to show me. He used the moisture that my mouth had spread on the tip and the shaft to lubricate my hands. He coached them into a twisting motion at the base.

"Harder," he ordered. "Pull your lips over your teeth and suck harder," he gasped. "Yes, that's perfect, Bianca."

"I'm coming," he warned me several intoxicating moments later. Both of his hands were gripped in my hair tightly. "If you don't want me to come in your mouth, you should pull back now." His voice was absolutely raw with his need, and I loved it. I could get addicted to this feeling. To this act.

Instead of pulling back, I sucked harder, swallowing instinctively when the warm essence of him shot against the back of my throat.

He pulled me up and kissed me. His hands were rough in my hair, almost to the point of pain, but, caught up in the moment, I loved it.

He finally set me down, glancing at the clock. "You're late. We'll talk later. I don't want you to get into trouble. I've seen how important your work ethic is to you."

I just nodded, in full rush mode.

I grabbed my bags and my half-empty cup of coffee on the way out, not saying goodbye. Frankly, I just didn't know what to say. I'd never done such intimate things in my entire life, and I'd never even agreed to give Mr. Beautiful my phone number.

It was like I wasn't myself anymore, once I got into his orbit. He just took over. And so far, I was batting zero at resisting him. When he touched me, I lost all control, and he took all of it, and it just felt so good to let go. In fact, it felt more than good. It felt so perfect to me that I didn't even know how to resist.

CHAPTER EIGHT

Mr. Stalker

I felt a huge wave of relief as I noted, coming down into the lobby five minutes late, that Stephan and I were the only crew members that had shown up so far.

I'd never been late before, not even five minutes late, but it wouldn't count against me this time. If we got a crew delay today, it would be whoever showed up last that caused it, and not me, since I had shown up second.

Stephan gave me a tentative smile when he saw me. "Good morning, Buttercup."

"Morning. How was the rest of your night?" I asked, hoping it had ended well for him.

He grinned. "It was great. We went back to Melvin's place and talked for hours. We're taking it slow, but we understand each other now."

I grinned back. "That's awesome. Guess we'll be sticking to New York for awhile, huh?"

He sighed. "I hope so. So how did it go with Mr. Beautiful?" he asked me with a smile. "You are looking much more chipper this morning than I had thought possible, considering the condition you were in when you left the bar. I assume he kept his promise to be a perfect gentleman last night?" He made the last into a question.

I nodded carefully. "Yes, he was a perfect gentleman last night. He was very sweet, actually. He even washed off my makeup. And he brought me coffee and aspirin this morning."

Something caught his eye behind me, and I turned, expecting one of the tardy crew members. I shouldn't have been surprised that it was James. I *had* left him behind in my room. He had to pass through the lobby in order to leave. But it was still a little shock to see him so soon after what we'd just done.

My eyes traveled unbidden down to the area of his body that I'd just given special attention to. I licked my lower lip. His blue eyes were positively vivid as he stared back at me, striding straight up to me.

He nodded politely to Stephan. They both murmured a good morning. James's warm hand landed possessively on the nape of my neck. My eyes wandered back down south. His fingers bit harder into my nape, and my eyes shot back up to his.

"Our Buttercup is a handful, Stephan," he said idly to the other man.

Stephan laughed. "She is that."

"A fucking perfect handful," James murmured to me.

Stephan heard him, and laughed harder. "Well, I wouldn't exactly know about that, but I'll take your word for it."

"Walk me to the door, please?" James asked me politely.

I did. He lowered his hand from my neck when we reached the door.

"I'm going to tie you to my bed and take your hymen. I can't seem to think about anything else," he told me quietly. "Tell me when I can see you again."

I swallowed hard. "I'm not sure. I have a twelve hour day tomorrow. We're doing a turn to DC."

"What about today?"

I just blinked at him. "I'm flying back to Las Vegas."

He just nodded as though that was helpful, and left.

The other flight attendants came down in short order, starting with Brenda. She was a solid ten minutes late from our showtime. Melissa and Jake came down a few minutes after that.

We waited another ten minutes before Stephan had to phone headquarters.

"Yes, I'm just making sure that we are sharing an airport shuttle with our pilots this morning," he murmured into his phone. "Okay, thank you."

The disheveled looking pilots showed just as he was hanging up his phone. We had already loaded up our bags, so we piled in while the pilots got theirs loaded up.

We rushed through the airport, the entire crew hustling to avoid a delay.

Stephan had braided my hair into one sleek braid in the van, while I applied a minimal amount of makeup at red lights. There was no way I could have done it while the maniac driver was swerving around. Even after years of New York layovers, I had yet to get used to the crazy thing New Yorkers called 'driving.'

We made it to the gate in record time, and an exasperated gate agent let us onto the jetway. She was plump, middle-aged, and harried looking.

"You guys are borderline late," she scolded us. "If this flight is delayed, I'm putting down the flight crew as the cause."

Stephan gave her his most charming smile. "Sweetheart, let's not be delayed then. Send them down anytime you like. We have the A team working today. We don't need any prep time at all."

She smiled back, instantly relieved by his attitude. "That's what I like to hear. Some flight crews need thirty minutes to prep."

Stephan gave the Captain a meaningful look. "Well, that ain't us, right Captain?" he prompted him. Some pilots took forever to prep, too.

Captain Peter nodded, smiling. "Like he said, we're on our A game today, so send 'em on down."

It was a slight gamble. If we were unlucky enough to have any mechanical problems, we would have a plane full of passengers for the delay. But we were hoping for lucky today. It was that or a write-up.

"I'll start the pre-board beverage service for you and have Jake man the door so you can take inventory in the galley. The caterers have come and gone by now. Hopefully they left us everything we need," Stephan delved into the liquor cart as he spoke, pulling out glasses.

"Wanna take out a tray of mimosas?" I asked him. "They're usually a hit in the morning, especially on this flight, and it saves time, since we have twenty-one up here."

He nodded absently, digging around. He could never find anything in the galley, and I didn't know why he even tried anymore.

I opened a drawer full of cold bottles of water, pointing. "Just put those out for them. I'll do the rest of the mimosa prep while you do that."

I was already popping the cork on the champagne as he strode back into the cabin.

It was going to be a hectic morning. It just had that feeling to it. I liked that, though. Staying busy was never a bad thing, as far as I was concerned.

I had a tray of mimosas waiting when he came back a few minutes later. He headed immediately back out.

I had accounted for all of the drinks we needed. I began to count the meals, and prepare the menus. I handed Stephan the menus to hand out and he handed me a list of drink orders. No glasses remained on the tray.

"I should be good after you hand out those menus," I told him. "Do I need to take out another tray of mimosas?"

"Nope, you made the perfect amount. And you have a surprise in 2D, Buttercup." He grinned at me as he swept back out into the cabin.

I was only half listening, making drinks as quickly as possible. Pre-board service could be tricky when we were this pressed for time.

I strode out with the first round of drink orders. I was delivering the orders back to front, because that was how Stephan had written it down. It must have been the order they'd boarded in. The gate agents sometimes liked to mix it up, though only god knew why.

I unloaded the drinks quickly. There were some loud, boisterous New Yorkers up front today. I just smiled at them. A few men almost shouted at each other as they argued about some sports team. I counted five of them together that may be a possible problem, or may just need a firm shushing if they kept it up.

They got suddenly quiet as they noticed me.

"Hey, sugar. You're a sight for sore eyes," the loudest one said to me finally, after they'd all stared at me rudely while I set down their drinks. I looked up and smiled at him pleasantly. Neutrally. He was maybe in his late forties, with dark hair and swarthy skin. He looked like a New Yorker down to his toes.

"Good morning," I murmured, heading back into the galley for the next round.

I only had a few more drinks to make after that. The waters and mimosas had been enough for most of them.

I handed out the next small round, collecting already empty glasses on my tray as I passed back in. I started from the front again, collecting jackets, and making sure no one needed anything.

I froze, my cool composure slipping for a heartbeat when I saw the man occupying 2D. I was surprised that I hadn't noticed him sooner. It seemed as though my body should have sensed his very presence by the way it instantly reacted.

I recovered more quickly to the sight of him this time than I had the last time he'd been in that seat. I hoped that meant I was getting used to him.

He can't continue to affect me this way every time I see him, I told myself. I knew it was just wishful thinking.

"May I get you anything else, Mr. Cavendish?" I inquired cooly. He already had one of the bottles of water that Stephan had handed out. Water seemed to be the only thing he drank. "May I hang your jacket?"

His face was tense, but he was silent as he stood and removed his suit jacket. The seat beside him was the only vacant one in first class, and I guessed that he had purchased it to gain some semblance of privacy.

I remembered from overhearing him speaking to our CEO on the charter flight where I had met him that he didn't often fly commercial. *Why on earth would he?* He had a private jet. *Why was he suddenly flying with us so often?* I guessed it was most likely because he was looking into backing us financially in some way.

As he straightened in the aisle, he was suddenly only inches from me.

I took a deep breath, inhaling the scent of him. He smelled so wonderful, with just a hint of spicy cologne over his own natural scent.

"Why didn't you tell me you were taking this flight?" I murmured the question to him as I took his jacket, my voice pitched low.

"It was a last minute decision. I didn't know until this morning that I had urgent business in Las Vegas that needed attention today," he murmured back, his voice soft, but his face still hard and tense.

I searched his face briefly, but had to quickly move on. There was just no time right then for figuring out what Mr. Beautiful was up to.

I barely got the glasses collected and the galley secured in time for the safety demonstration. I pointedly avoided looking at James and got through it with my usual composure.

The group of New Yorkers made a few raunchy comments about me loudly enough that I heard it as I passed them while I was doing a seat belt check. I ignored them easily. It was nothing unusual. In fact, it was par for the course on this particular flight.

It was Saturday morning, and there was usually a group of old school New York men on this flight. They were heading to Vegas, had just paid for an upgrade to first class, and were getting their party started. They were obnoxious and rude, but also a common feature on JFK flights.

I paused briefly by James. His fists were clenched, his hard face tilted toward the small window. He looked very out of sorts.

"Can I help you with anything, Mr. Cavendish?" I asked him quietly. I couldn't begin to imagine what had him so agitated.

He shook his head slightly. He quickly contradicted himself. "Tell Stephan I want to speak to him as soon as he's available," he said shortly.

"Okaaay," I said, confused, and moved on.

CHAPTER NINE

Mr. Angry

"What was that all about?" I asked Stephan, as we buckled into our jump seats. He and James had had a brief but intense looking exchange right before Stephan came to sit beside me.

He just shook his head, looking out the window.

I elbowed him in the ribs.

"Ow," he said, shooting me a surprised look. "What's gotten into you?"

My eyes widened with incredulity. "Me? What about you? How did Mr. Beautiful over there get you in his corner so fast? You're supposed to help me avoid guys like that. Instead, you've been helping him. And now you're close-mouthed about talks you're having with him."

He sighed. "It was about that rowdy crowd in rows five and six. They've been keeping up a non-stop dialogue about you, and it's not sitting well with James. I need to have a word with them once we reach ten thousand feet."

He smirked suddenly. "Or else I think Mr. Beautiful might start throwing punches."

I rolled my eyes, shooting an exasperated look at James,

who was directly in my view. He still had his gaze trained on the window, but his eyes were glassed over, his fists clenched hard. He looked even more agitated now.

"It's just the usual good ol' boy Vegas crowd," I told Stephan. "Same type of crowd we get almost every week. The've been easy to ignore so far. Don't get them unnecessarily riled up."

Now it was Stephan's turn to look exasperated. "I don't think you heard the worst of what they've been saying. James told me, and it wasn't pretty. They are being particularly raunchy and using a lot of profanity loudly enough for the rest of the cabin to be disturbed. I need to address it. Better to nip it in the bud. And look at James. He is seriously agitated. Better to piss off a few jerks than to have an all out brawl on our hands."

I did look at James. I studied him closely. His agitation seemed to be growing by the second.

His eyes snapped wide suddenly, his gaze shooting to us, his hands going to his seat belt as though he were preparing to get up.

"Ah, shit," Stephan muttered, trepidation in his voice.

James seemed to get himself under control, carefully letting go of his seat belt and unclenching his hands. He closed his eyes, his lips moving.

"He's counting to ten," I said stupidly. "Can you hear what they're saying that's getting him all riled up? I can't hear a thing."

"I can hear their voices, but I can't make out what they're saying at all," Stephan said, watching James carefully.

Stephan was painfully tense. I knew he hated fighting more than just about anything else in the world. I had also seen him fight several times, though it had been years since he'd had to. He was exceptionally good at it. Whatever happened, he would be able to handle himself, I knew. But he would hate it. He abhorred violence of any kind.

James opened his eyes suddenly, looking more furious than

I'd ever seen him. Apparently counting to ten hadn't worked. His hands shot again to his seat belt and I watched in horror as he shot from his seat, striding to the troublemakers with violence in every quick step.

"Fuck," Stephan cursed. "Stay here. Please," he pleaded, going after James in a flash.

There was a very tense exchange. James was leaning down close to speak to the man who had addressed me earlier, and I couldn't see his face or hear what he was saying.

Stephan was pointing at one of the other men and his voice was raised, though I couldn't make out the words over the plane engine and the distance. I was surprised that Stephan didn't even look at James, making no attempt whatsoever to make him return to his seat.

Shit, I thought. That probably meant his own temper was flaring up as well. It really would be a brawl if Stephan started throwing punches.

I saw the man who Stephan was clearly reaming out raise his hands, as though in surrender. That didn't seem to appease Stephan, though, who just turned to the man who James had taken special exception to. I assumed he was still talking to the man, though I couldn't hear him.

He was speaking quietly, while Stephan was just getting louder.

"I mean it. One more word out of any of you, and we are diverting this plane and there will be law enforcement waiting for you at the gate." With that, Stephan stormed back to the seat beside me. He still hadn't bothered to make James take his seat.

A few tense moments later, James straightened, walking stiffly back to his seat. He didn't look at me, just sat, buckled up, and closed his eyes.

I felt a relief so huge it almost shamed me. Seeing that, although he'd really wanted to pound someone, he had restrained himself, was something I'd almost needed to see. Whatever else I didn't know about him, at least I knew he could practice self-control.

Uncontrolled violence and aggression were the monsters of my childhood, and I felt almost limp with relief to see that I wouldn't find them in James. Not in the way I had feared. The way I always feared, despite a decent amount of time and therapy.

"What happened? What were they saying that would involve law enforcement?" I asked Stephan finally.

He just shook his head. "I'll tell you later. Please, just give me a minute to compose myself." His voice was pleading, so I dropped the issue. If he said he'd tell me later, I knew he would.

I was up the second I heard the double ding that indicated we were at ten thousand feet. I started my usual routine, preparing my galley for our breakfast service. I liked the routine, liked routines in general. I found them soothing, in a way.

The chaos of my adolescence made me crave stability in my adult life. So my life, even with all of the traveling, followed a schedule and routine that I enjoyed. Saturday morning breakfast service out of New York was a part of that.

Our airline prided itself on its first class service, so our breakfast service was extensive. We would be busy until we landed. With first class full, Stephan stayed up front to help me.

I worked the galley, and he served. That suited me, especially today, with a volatile James, and some apparently degenerate men in the cabin.

Stephan and I didn't even speak for the first hour as we worked. He was brooding, and we didn't really need to talk to communicate.

We worked together effortlessly, after all these years. He took the passengers' orders and I read them and made them. As he served, I worked on the next step. We were fast and effective even without speaking.

I loved this part of the job. I wasn't even sure why. Just the busy feel in the air, the familiar galley routine, making sure everyone felt like they had received exceptional service, and like we had done a good job. I supposed I had just spent a large part of my life feeling worthless and lost, and this job, on a good day, made me feel like I had some worth. When I thought of it that way, it sounded pathetic, but that didn't make it any less true.

I noticed everything we served to James, of course. He drank water exclusively, that I had seen. No ice, just the bottle and a glass. I started putting a slice of lemon in his glass, and he didn't complain, so I continued to do so.

For breakfast, he ordered the only healthy thing we served on the first flight of the day. It was greek yogurt with fresh blueberries and raw pecans. I wasn't surprised that he was the only one to order it. We usually didn't have any takers, so Stephan and I often had it for breakfast ourselves. I could've guessed from what I had seen of his body that he ate healthy, but that confirmed it.

Could I ever be comfortable getting naked with someone that good looking, who had a flawless body, so far as I could tell? I didn't know how. I tried to stay in shape but I had junk food sometimes, and I probably didn't work out as often as I could.

I thought my thighs were too big, and my ankles were too small, like toothpicks. And my arms were thin, but my hips were a little wide and my shoulders were too broad, to my critical eye. Like every woman, I had body issues. Would James notice them when I was naked? I tried not to dwell on it, but I did anyways. I was relieved when we got too busy for me to think about it anymore.

It was a solid two and a half hours into the flight before Stephan could make his way back to check on the main cabin.

"I'll be back in a few minutes. Brenda is baking the cookies back there right now. I'll bring some back to add to the cheese service," Stephan told me as he hung up the inflight phone.

I nodded absently. I was prepping our three-tiered cart for the cheese service. There was nothing he could help me with in first class for at least ten minutes, so it was good timing.

I heard the bathroom door opening on the other side of the curtain, and shifted the cart to make sure the passenger could get back to their seat before I moved it into position.

I was startled when James entered the enclosed galley. He looked much calmer than he had before.

I offered him a small smile. "Hey," I said, studying him carefully, trying to read his mood.

He gave me a small smile back. He moved my cart for me, seeing that I was bearing its weight. He used it to block the aisle completely, just outside of the curtained area, managing to stay behind the curtain completely as he did so.

"Oh," I said softly as I watched him rearrange the galley, getting an inkling of what he intended. He was arranging a moment of privacy for...something.

I just watched him, mesmerized.

He set the brake on the cart with the toe of his shoe easily, as though he did it every day. He took a deep breath, his back to me for one long moment.

Abruptly, he turned, pacing to me. He grabbed my braid, pulling my head back. He kissed me, and it was hot and angry and hungry.

In spite of myself, I melted in an instant, melding my body as close to his as I could get it.

He backed me up against the counter, lifting me onto the only small bit of empty counter space available. I barely fit. He didn't stop kissing me.

I murmured a protest as I felt his fingers inching my fitted skirt up my legs. He had my thighs bared in a flash, and I pulled back, panting.

"What are you doing?" I asked, a little panicked at his intent.

"Shh," he told me, and started kissing me again, his hands still pushing my skirt up impatiently. "I need to do this."

That didn't make me feel reassured, but he stopped abruptly when his hands had shoved my skirt up far enough to bare my garters and the tops of my stockings. He shoved the skirt higher roughly.

He cursed when he saw my lacy lime green thong. "This is the type of panty you were wearing last night, too, wasn't it? But that one was blue."

I just nodded, feeling a little disoriented. "They're the most comfortable underwear I've ever worn. I can't wear anything else, since I discovered them."

"I fucking love them," he told me, and it made me smile at him.

Then he surprised me again by kneeling in front of me in one fluid movement. He handed me a cloth. An old fashioned handkerchief, I observed "Put that in your mouth and bite down. Try not to make too much noise." I obeyed him without hesitating, my whole body vibrating in anticipation at what he was going to do.

"Grip my hair," he told me. My hands stroked through it hungrily. It was perfect, of course, soft as silk, and so smooth and thick. I saw all of the different shades of light brown and dark blond, highlighted by the sun shinning through the small window in the door of the plane just to our left. People paid a fortune for highlights not half as beautiful as that shifting, golden color.

My mind went blank, my head suddenly falling back. He had shoved my thong to the side and buried his face against me.

I was lost instantly in the shocking wash of sensation from his accomplished tongue lapping at the core of me with singleminded purpose.

His masterful fingers thrust into me, a finger stroking along just the perfect spot. I whimpered into the cloth I was biting, not quite muffling the high-pitched noise.

Almost hurriedly, his tongue moved up to my clit. He sucked at it, hard, and I came without warning. I'd had no idea it could happen so fast, even with our earlier episode in the hotel bathroom.

He continued to nuzzle me, even when I went still after the powerful aftershocks subsided. I felt his head pulling back, and looked down at him. He propped his chin on the material of my skirt, just above my pelvis.

"One more," he ordered, and went back to his exquisite ministrations.

I screamed into the cloth when I came that time, just as surprised by this orgasm as I was by the last one. He'd brought it on even faster, as though his tongue had just found and pushed my orgasm button. Or perhaps the last one had had me primed and ready. I wasn't experienced enough to know for sure. I hadn't known my body could be played like an instrument, until James had gotten his hands on me.

He lapped at me a few more times after my tremors had subsided.

"I could eat you all day," he told me as he stood. He pulled the handkerchief from my mouth, shoving it between my thighs to sop up the excess moisture.

"I love how wet you are," he murmured, delving down to kiss me. His tongue swept into my mouth, licking, and I was a little scandalized to realize that I was tasting myself in a way I'd never imagined.

I sucked on his tongue, and he groaned. I knew he definitely liked that, and I sucked harder.

He didn't kiss me long, pulling back to lift me down from the counter. It didn't seem to strain him at all to lift me. I loved that, loved feeling small and feminine compared to his strength.

He shoved the dirty handkerchief into his pocket and started to straighten my clothes with an almost impersonal efficiency.

He was still pulling my skirt back down to my knees when Stephan burst through the curtain, looking baffled, and then shocked at what he saw.

It must have been obvious from James lowering my skirt that we had obviously been doing something much too intimate for the galley of an aircraft.

Stephan's shocked eyes flew to my face. Then he blushed like I'd never seen him blush before.

"Was that noise you? That muffled scream?" he asked slowly.

I knew I turned just as pink as him, but I nodded. No point in denying it.

Stephan was still bright pink as he gave James a censuring look. "Really, James? On a morning flight? With a group of perverts just a few feet away?"

Apparently, Stephan was heaping the responsibility of this embarrassing episode squarely on Mr. Beautiful's shoulders.

James looked a little shame-faced at the assessment. It made him look almost boyish. It was hard to reconcile that look with the James I knew.

I just blinked at them both, at a loss. I had never been in anything even approaching a situation like this.

Stephan pointed in the general direction of James's seat. "I think you should go sit down now."

James did so without so much as a word or a look.

CHAPTER TEN

Mr. Kinky

The rest of the flight went by in a kind of a blur for me. We did the wine and cheese service, and I deliberately refrained from making any eye contact, knowing I would be mortified if they gave me strange looks.

I wanted to just pretend that no one had heard us in the galley, and that they certainly hadn't taken the noises for what they actually were. As long as I didn't look at anyone directly, I could just keep trying to convince myself that that was the case.

I especially avoided looking at James as we served him. I had pulled my cool composure around me like armor after our sordid scene, but I knew one look at him could undo all of that.

My side of the cart was lined up to serve him by a stroke of bad luck, so I quietly asked him what he'd like without ever looking directly at him.

He said he would take one slice of the brie and some grapes. I set the small plate on his tray table, the sight that met me there stilling me for a long moment.

I noticed several things at once.

He had rolled up the sleeves of his dress shirt, revealing tanned forearms, both presented wrist up as he affected a relaxed pose. With the sunlight streaming through his window I could see faint white lines tracing thin scars around his wrists. I was instantly curious about the marks, but *they* weren't what caught my rapt attention at a glance.

He'd removed his tie, leaving his tanned throat and just a hint of his chest visible. The sight of his smooth golden skin made me wild. I felt deprived of it, especially with how little I'd gotten to see of it, considering all that we'd done to each other.

The sight of him like that was incredibly sexy, seeming to me almost too intimate for airplane attire. That was ridiculous, of course. There weren't special rules against him showing any of his skin in public, just because it was so much finer than everyone else's.

Yes, the sight of him like that turned me on acutely in an instant. But that wasn't what had stopped me in my tracks. It was the object in his hand that did that.

His right hand lay on his knee, just beside his tray table, empty. But his left hand lay across his tray table, as though displaying the object clutched in his hand like a trophy.

It was the handkerchief he had used on me in the galley. His hand was fisting it reflexively, as though it relaxed him.

I made myself look away from him. I didn't look back again.

The thought occurred to me quite vividly that he was impossibly out of my league. He was way too experienced. And rich. And kinky. And I was just about as close to the polar opposite of all of that as a person could get. The thought was sobering.

Somewhere along the way I had decided that I would have sex with him. But I had to remember that it wasn't going any further than that. He obviously liked the pursuit. I would give in. He would fuck me for a few memorable days, if I was lucky, and then we would go our separate ways. I certainly didn't want anything more.

Relationships terrified me to my very core. So what better

candidate to rid me of my virginity? At twenty-three, it was nothing but a burden. I just hadn't bothered to do anything about it before because no one had interested me enough to try to get past some of my hangups.

Masturbation and some rather sordid online porn had cured the rare urges I'd had. And I'd certainly never felt this sort of all-consuming attraction before.

So I would do it. I would have sex with him. I would satisfy my curiosity, and then I would get back to my normal life.

I managed not to look at James again until we were taking our jump seats for landing.

He smiled at me when I did finally look at him. It was an intimate smile, unlike any I'd ever been on the receiving end of. I couldn't find the will to smile back, or do anything but stare at him dumbly, trying not to look at the thing still clutched in his hand.

I didn't come close to stifling the gasp that rushed out of me as he brought the handkerchief to his face, inhaling deeply, his eyes closing as though he were savoring the smell.

"What the hell?" Stephan muttered the question beside me.

I didn't answer, not even sure if it was directed at me, or James.

I looked out the window hastily, blushing from the top of my head to the tips of my toes. *Yes*, I thought to myself, a little stunned. *He is worlds out of my league, but I'm going to go through with this anyways.*

Somehow, over the course of the flight, I had managed to forget all about the near brawl that had almost happened over me. Stephan's announcement as we taxied to our gate was what reminded me of the tense event.

"Ladies and Gentlemen, I'm going to need everyone to remain seated when we arrive at the gate. Our plane is being met by law enforcement, so we're going to need everyone to remain patient for just a few minutes.   I will make an announcement when it is okay to deplane. Again, please stay in your seats when we pull up to the gate."

Oh shit, I thought, stunned.

I gave Stephan wide eyes. "What did they do to get the royal treatment?" I asked him. It seemed a little excessive to get the police involved over the little I had actually heard.

He shook his head. "I'll explain it all later. James and I will have to talk to the police for their report, and perhaps anyone else in first class that'll admit to hearing anything. The flight paperwork is going to be a bitch, too. But the stuff they were talking about was illegal, and I just think they need a report filed on them, in case they were really considering doing some of the stuff they were talking about. It might have all just been some particularly huge jerks talking shit, but I wouldn't feel right if I didn't do all that I could to make sure they were discouraged from acting like that. And worse-case scenario, if they really end up doing something horrible to some poor girl, this incident could help prosecute them later on."

I just stared at him. I really had been out of the loop. "You are sooo gonna tell me what all happened back there."

He nodded. "Yeah, I will. Later."

It was a curiously drama-free deplaning after that. Stephan consulted with the police while I answered the call buttons that started lighting up a few seconds before we arrived at the gate.

After a brief exchange, the men were escorted off, seeming to cooperate sedately with the two police officers who led them off. James followed immediately behind them. To give his side of the story, I assumed. The couple seated directly behind him followed as well, and the two men who had been across the aisle from the first couple that departed. For the same reason, I assumed.

I got caught in the back galley when passengers were

allowed to deplane scant seconds later.

Brenda and Melissa, who used the jump seats in the back galley, bombarded me with questions while I waited a little impatiently for the plane to empty.

"What happened up there?" Brenda asked me, her eyes wide.

"Was that James Cavendish I saw following the police off with those men?" Melissa asked, her expression nearly predatory. She had that laser sharp look she got in her eye when she was into a guy. I had seen it in her eyes way too often, considering how short a time I'd known her.

So she found out his name, I thought, a little uneasily. She probably knew more about him than I did now. I actively avoided all social networking, and I didn't even own a television. I only knew he came from a wealthy family with a massive hotel chain around the world. I had never even searched his name online to find out anything. I was guessing that by now Melissa couldn't say the same.

"Yes, that was him," I answered her question first, curious to see her reaction.

She gave me a considering look. "I didn't even know he was on this flight. You've gotta tell me when you see the hot, rich ones, Bianca. I thought we were friends." Her voice was all offended sweetness, a strange new affectation for her.

I just stared at her, not knowing what to say for a long moment.

"I know you two ladies aren't on the market, but I'm gonna say it anyways. I call dibs on that one." She giggled as she said it, so I honestly couldn't tell if she was joking. Either way, though, it was at that moment that I knew she was crazy.

I shook my head, startled to feel a hostility towards her that I didn't want to investigate.

"That's not how it works," I told her.

She giggled again. "Whatever. I wasn't really worried about

it. Men want who they want, and I can tell I'm just his type. I'll have his number before we get to headquarters."

Brenda and I shared a look. Brenda went straight back to her own line of questioning. "Why were the cops called? I saw a commotion when we took off, but I couldn't tell what happened, and there didn't seem to be a problem after that."

Brenda seemed to have adopted the skill of just ignoring Melissa when she got crazy. I made a note to emulate her methods.

I told them what I knew, leaving out James's specific involvement. Melissa zeroed in on the oversight immediately. "Why did James follow them off?"

Was she really on a first name basis after one short conversation with him? Was I missing something here?

"He and some of the other people in first class heard a lot of what they were saying, I suppose."

I was saved from having to answer anything else when Stephan strode into the galley.

He looked at the other two women. "Last passenger is off, ladies. Bianca and I need to speak to the police and write incident reports, but you guys are good to go, since you weren't involved. We'll see you first thing in the morning."

Brenda smiled, grabbing her bags and saying goodbye before hurrying off. Our employee bus was on a twenty minute timer. She'd have to get down to the bus stop in three minutes or wait another twenty, I observed as I checked my watch.

It was a plain metal watch with a dark blue face. It was looking a little the worse for wear, I noticed for the first time. It had lasted two years, and it looked like I needed a replacement, by all the nicks and dents in it. Watches in good condition were actually a job requirement for us, so I'd have to buckle down and go shopping for once.

I'd been on a super tight budget for the last six months. This would be the first time I'd gone shopping for anything besides food in that time. *Shit.* That gave me an uncomfortable thought.

I looked up at Stephan, who was staring at Melissa. I could tell he was wondering why she hadn't left yet.

She just beamed at him. "I'm gonna stick around for a bit, make sure you guys get everything squared away okay." She put an awkward arm around my shoulders. Especially awkward considering she was six inches shorter than I was, even in her ultra-tall heels.

Stephan and I shared a look.

"She's been through an ordeal, poor thing, with those men saying those awful things about her," Melissa said, her voice dripping with false sympathy.

I ignored her, talking to Stephan. "I forgot to pay for my drinks last night. I'm sorry. What do I owe you?"

He'd been on a budget similar to mine lately, and for the same reason, so I knew he couldn't afford to be buying me drinks at the bar.

We had both saved money from working steady amounts of overtime over the last four years. We had taken that savings and found two nearly new houses that had recently been foreclosed on, right next door to each other. We'd both been able to successfully buy the small houses, and were now proud homeowners. And neighbors.

It had been something we'd fantasized about as homeless teenagers. We'd talked about it endlessly, how someday we wouldn't be homeless. Instead, we had promised, we'd always live right next to each other. And we'd been serious about it.

We'd worked and saved, and it had been one of the happiest days of my life, the day we moved from our small shared apartment and into our small, side-by-side houses.

He grinned at me. It was a shit-eating grin. "You don't. James bought out the bar for the night. That's why it emptied out so fast. He covered all of our drinks for the night, and

Melvin said his tip for last night was a month's worth of his normal pay. And all thanks to you, Buttercup."

I stared at him, stunned speechless, my mind racing.

"Why thanks to her?" Melissa asked him, her voice sharp. "What is going on with you two? It almost sounds like you're pimping your girlfriend out."

Stephan looked at her, and his eyes were as cold as I'd ever seen them. I'd never been on the receiving end of that icy stare. Melissa took it better than I would have.

"Bianca is the most important person in the world to me," Stephan told her coldly. "She's my best friend and my only family. She is not, however, my girlfriend. And it's thanks to her because James Cavendish is crazy about her. So crazy, in fact, that he rented that entire bar out for the night. All just so that he could get her number, and spend some time with her."

Now it was Melissa's turn to look stunned, but she recovered almost immediately. It turned into a catty glance at me.

She gave me an insulting once over. "I bet you misunderstood. Stephan just thinks you're special because you've been BFF's forever." And with that heartwarming assessment, she stalked out of the galley.

Stephan and I shared a look that communicated what we were starting to think about the little red-headed gold-digger.

The mess that awaited us outside of the plane was dealt with more quickly than I would have thought possible.

They were holding the loud-mouthed men somewhere in the airport, questioning them extensively. Probably scaring the hell out of them, I thought. One police officer was waiting for us when we deplaned, and interviewed me briefly about what I'd seen and heard personally.

My part was short. And I got to hear Stephan's account first hand, so I got a pretty clear picture of what had gone down.

It had started out as raunchy chatter by the men, though Stephan had heard about that second-hand from James.

Comments about my body, things they'd like to do to me, graphic and disgusting, but nothing we'd call the police about, usually.

And then on takeoff, one of them had apparently gotten especially loud and graphic, talking about some drugs he had with him just for women like me, and that they should follow me through the airport and buy me a drink. And drug it. And then try to get me alone in their hotel room.

That encouraged the others to add in what they would do to me when I was drugged and unconscious, and there I got a clearer picture of why the police had been called.

I doubted the men would get arrested, unless the drugs they had mentioned really were in one of their suitcases. I thought it more likely they would lose a few hours of their precious vacation time and get the hell scared out of them by the police.

Stephan finished telling his version of the events shortly, and without any unnecessary embellishment.

The police officer nodded and wrote as he went on. Just as he finished up, I saw James approaching with another police officer. Neither of these officers had been there to meet the plane.

Just how many police were involved in this fiasco? I wondered, a little baffled.

I stiffened a little when I saw that Melissa was walking beside him, touching the back of his arm in an overly friendly way as she chattered away about God only knew what. I tried to ignore her.

James looked stoic and unreadable as the trio got closer to us. I noticed that he wore only his dress shirt, still with no tie or jacket.

"Did we leave his suit jacket on the plane?" I asked Stephan.

Stephan blinked. "Must have," he said.

"I'll go get it," I told him, and turned briskly to do so.

The plane was deserted as I came back on, and I was

relieved that another crew hadn't yet taken it over.

I dug a pen and a piece of hotel stationary from my carryon, jotting down my name and number, and slipped the small piece of paper into James's jacket.

I'd done a whole hell of a lot more already, so it seemed silly not to give the man my number.

CHAPTER ELEVEN

Mr. Spellcaster

Both officers were absent, but James, Stephan, and Melissa were still waiting when I reemerged from the jetway. James and Melissa were speaking, but James looked up when he saw me, giving me his full, intense regard.

Stephan was writing furiously. He was filling out an incident report, I was sure.

I handed James his jacket without a word.

"Do I need to fill out my own, or can I just add to yours and sign?" I asked Stephan, referring to his paperwork.

"We can share," he told me without looking up. "I'm almost done. I got most of it down during the flight. I just left the end blank because I wasn't sure those boneheads wouldn't do something else that I'd need to add."

"K," I said, waiting in a sort of awkward silence. Even Melissa wasn't chattering, and James just continued to stare at me without a word, as though he expected me to do something.

Finally, after watching me in silence for long, pregnant minutes, he spoke. "Can I talk to you for a minute? I need to go soon."

I nodded, walking away from the others in silence. I half-expected Melissa to follow us, but she didn't, just watching us with a strange look on her face.

"I have to work until this evening, but I want to see you. I'll send a driver to pick you up at six. Give me your number and address."

He had his phone out, waiting. I just looked at him for a moment. This wouldn't do at all.

"I put my number in your suit pocket," I began. "And I'll drive to your place. What's your address."

He definitely looked like he wanted to argue, but I didn't think he wanted to push his luck, so he gave me his address stiffly.

"I'll try to get done with my work earlier, if you want," he told me, as I GPS'd his address into my phone.

Not bad, I thought. Only twenty minutes from my house. That was downright convenient.

"Don't do so on my account. I'm going home to take a two hour nap, and then I have some errands to run." I ran a hand over my watch absently. "I need to replace this old thing before I get written up for wearing an eyesore. I just realized how bad it's looking."

I had forgotten who I was talking to, and flushed. I felt shabby enough in his presence. I certainly didn't need to go broadcasting how poor I was to him.

His hand snaked out, grabbing my wrist to look at my watch. His fingers circled my wrist as he studied it. "You're so delicate," he murmured.

I barely heard him. My eyes were on his tan collarbone, still peaking out from his crisp shirt.

"I don't know why it is, but the sight of even the smallest amount of your skin doesn't seem appropriate to me in public. Your throat looks so naked." I hadn't meant to speak the thought out loud, and immediately blushed.

He looked up at me with just his eyes, not lifting his head, a wicked grin on his face. "You only think that because the things you want me to do to you aren't appropriate in public."

"I want to see your body," I told him. I couldn't seem to stop myself. I had been thinking about it almost constantly since I'd met him.

His smile dropped, and he straightened, taking a step closer to me. "You're going to. Tonight. And I'm going to see and touch every inch of you."

I took a step back, trying to shake away the strange spell he seemed to cast on me. *Not here. Not now.*

"I'll see you tonight," I told him, walking back to Stephan. Anything else we needed to say, we could discuss later, when we weren't in public and I wasn't still in uniform.

James took my dismissal in stride, nodding at the other flight attendants and then striding away toward the terminal.

I added a small paragraph of what I'd heard to Stephan's report and signed. We headed to the bus stop.

Melissa was still trailing us, I noticed, but none of us spoke. She seemed sullen and strange, but I frankly didn't want to know why and didn't care.

We dropped our paperwork off at headquarters and Stephan drove us home.

We took turns driving to work. We were almost always able to carpool, and it saved us both money we could use for other things. Like watches, I thought, sighing. I really wasn't in the mood for a trip to the mall.

"I need to run some errands after I take a nap," I told Stephan as he backed out.

"K. I'll come with. I could use a few things. Where are we going?"

"I need a watch." I held my old watch out. The face was even cracked. *How had I not noticed that sooner? Had it just happened?* "And some groceries. And some paint, paper, and canvas."

Painting was my favorite hobby, and I had a room full of

paintings to prove it. I was dabbling with oils lately, but watercolors and acrylics had always been my strength, and were more affordable in general. I needed to stock up on almost all of my supplies.

"Perfect. I've been needing a frame for that mountain landscape you made me. It's going in my living room. It's my all time favorite."

I smiled at him fondly. "You don't have to do that. I won't feel bad if you don't hang it up. I paint things for you because I like to. You don't have to decorate your entire house with my junk just to humor me."

He sent me a bewildered look. "You think that's why I've covered my entire home with your paintings? To humor you?"

I shrugged, feeling self-conscious. I hadn't gone to art school, had no training whatsoever, so I always questioned if people were sincere when they complimented my work. Stephan deserved better than my doubting him, though.

"I love your paintings, Bianca. Every time I look at any of the ones I have displayed, I feel joy. They help make my house a happy, healthy place for me. I think of where we've come from, all that we've been through, and the astoundingly beautiful things you can create, and it never fails to amaze me. It makes me hopeful about the future."

I flushed a bit, but smiled. "I painted that mountain landscape because it made me think of you. It was so strong, and stark, and beautiful. And every color I used in that painting, I got from studying you. I used the color of your hair and skin for the desert mountains, and your eyes were the sky. It's very nearly an abstract portrait of you."

He laughed, a carefree, joyous sound.

We're in a good place, I thought. We'd overcome so much, and left so much of the bad stuff behind. Over the years, the lingering dark shadows of our pasts seemed to be fading from us, more and more.

"Well, now I love it even more," he said. "You know how much I love pictures of myself."

I laughed, because it was pretty much true. Both of our houses sported portraits of Stephan, some his idea. He liked to pose for me, and he was a great subject, waiting patiently for hours if I needed him to.

Our houses were only fifteen minutes from the airport, just off of the 215 west. It was an ideal airport location, with a new track of houses and a short commute.

Seeing my small house still made me smile. I'd opted to keep the all-desert landscape that my yard had sported when I purchased the house, figuring it was for the best to forgo the grass, since we lived in the desert and we were often out of town.

Stephan had stubbornly refused to stay content with rocks and cacti, planting a small row of flowers along his front steps and a compact square of grass in the front yard. So far he was winning the battle against the desert, his grass still green and his flowers blooming as we pulled up.

"I'll text you when I wake up," I told him, walking the scant distance to my house.

I punched in my alarm code. I had splurged and purchased the best security system I could afford. It was important that my house feel like a safe place for me, so the peace of mind the system brought me was well worth the cost of it.

I unlocked the gated door, and the two locks on the actual door. I did the same routine on the other side, padding to the inside security panel and punching in my code.

I had thirty seconds to get the code in before an automatic alarm went off and the security dispatch station would give me a call, and put out a call to law enforcement. I had made the timer particularly short because it made me feel more secure.

I headed back into my bedroom, satisfied that the house was secure for my nap.

The last few days had been overwhelming. I barely got undressed before I was laying on my bed, and asleep in an instant.

I awoke in a near stupor, bleary eyes taking long moments to read my bedside clock. That couldn't be right, I thought. It was showing 3:44 p.m. I had crashed just before 10 a.m, with the intention to sleep for two hours. *Dammit.* I'd forgotten to set an alarm.

I was digging my phone out almost immediately, texting Stephan.

Bianca: I'm so sorry. I overslept. Errands on Monday?

He had responded by the time I was done in the bathroom.

Stephan: No worries. Monday sounds great. Got a hot date tonight?

Bianca: Seeing James. Not a date.

Stephan: Well, good luck, B. Let me know if you need anything. I'll see you in the morning.

Bianca: Kk. We r leaving at 5:45am in my car, right?

Stephan: Yep

I set to work packing, and then re-packing my small flight bag for the DC turn in the morning.

A turn was when we flew somewhere, usually on the east coast for us, then turned around and came immediately back. It was the best way to work a lot of hours on our job, but it could easily be a fourteen hour or longer day if we had even a slight delay. This turn was a part of our set weekly schedule, but we often picked up extra turns on our days off to get overtime.

My mortgage was reasonable, and fit into my budget, but I was trying to replenish the savings I had depleted almost completely in order to put a down payment on my house, and then the extra costs of a few upgrades and repairs to the house.

It made me very nervous to live paycheck to paycheck, so I was quickly trying to rectify the situation. I would have three days total off for the week, and planned to pick up extra hours on at least one of them.

I hung the work clothes that I had uncharacteristically strewn all over the floor into a dry cleaning bag. I had many uniforms, but at least half of them needed a trip to the dry cleaner.

I gathered them up and put them in my car, planning to stop by on the way to James's house. We got a small dry cleaning allowance from the company. They wanted us to look polished on the job, but it didn't cover even half of the cost that I spent at the cleaners. Perhaps it was all of those extra hours I worked that wracked my dry cleaning bill up so high...

I showered and washed my hair. I shaved just about every part of my body, the actions giving me a feeling of anticipation that they never had before. I always shaved my legs. But I'd never done it for a man before. I felt odd, so unlike myself.

I rubbed oil and then lotion into my skin, and left my hair to air dry. I could do some painting outside while it was wet. Las Vegas in the late spring was like nature's hair dryer.

I wore a baggy old teal-colored cotton sundress outside to paint. It was comfortable and I didn't really care if it got some paint on it, so I often wore it and several other threadbare dresses when I painted.

My backyard was small, but it had high walls. This made it fairly private, so I could wear what I wanted. I hadn't worn underwear. I often didn't if I was just puttering around the house by myself, but today it felt different.

I moved my easel around, and felt the brush of my breasts against my threadbare dress in a completely new way. It was like James could do foreplay without even being present. I was priming myself for him with no effort on his part. It wasn't fair for anyone to be that wickedly attractive. I kept picturing the way he had looked at me while he put that handkerchief to his face, brazenly inhaling it. I shivered at just the thought. I kept thinking about his spanking threats, as well. In fact, I thought of that the most.

Would he do that tonight? Would he spank me and then take my virginity? And tie me up? In what order? I squeezed my legs together just at the thought. The not knowing was a pull to me, even if it did frighten me.

If I was honest with myself, being frightened was a pull for me as well. I knew James could take me to some dark places, but I would find pleasure there, and I wanted that.

I had a board mounted with some watercolor paper that I had prepped before I left. I began to paint with an uncharacteristically short amount of prep. Usually I did a lot of sketching and planning, taking pictures and pinning them up. But today, I just painted. I knew exactly where to start.

I mixed some blue, a bright azure with a watery aquamarine and then added a touch of green. It didn't take long to mix exactly what I wanted, a vivid turquoise blue that I shaped into a pair of eyes that I couldn't get out of my head.

CHAPTER TWELVE

Mr. Dominant

I got caught up painting, and so lost track of time. When I noticed the time, I cursed. I was actually running late, which I never did. Now it had happened twice in two days.

That can't become a habit, I thought. It was hell on my nerves.

I knew it wasn't a date, but I still had to take some time and care with my hair and makeup, lining my eyes with a soft brown, and putting a double layer of black mascara on my lashes. The effect was dramatic for a bit of makeup. I added a light gold shadow to my eyes, and stained my lips with a dusky red.

I smoothed my hair out, and left it down and straight.

I wore a short black dress with violet flowers splashed across it. It was a little transparent, not see-through enough to need a slip underneath, just enough to hint at the figure beneath. It was sleeveless, with a scoop neck that showed more cleavage than I usually preferred.

The thin black lace bra I chose clearly outlined my nipples. I wouldn't normally pair the two together, but it seemed appropriate for a night like this.

I found one of my lacy thongs that matched the flowers on my dress. Someone would probably be seeing my panties tonight, so why not have them match?

As I studied my reflection in the mirror, I reached a hand up, gripping my breast, massaging it and plucking at the nipple until it showed clearly through the thin dress.

What am I doing? I wondered, even as I inched my dress up to my hips, running a finger inside my panties. *I'm late, I* thought, but even so, began stroking myself.

My phone rang, and it startled me out of my strange little trance. I answered in a breathless voice. "Hello?"

"Where are you?" James's voice bit at me with no preamble. He sounded harsh, almost angry.

I looked at the clock. It was 5:49 p.m. I was supposed to be at his house in eleven minutes.

"I was just about to head out. I'll be there in about twenty minutes, if I don't make any wrong turns."

"What's going on? You sound strange. And you're going to be late. This is one of many reasons why I wanted to send a driver."

"I'll be right there." I had started stroking myself again, the sound of his voice turning me on, even angry, perhaps because of that.

"What are you doing? Why do you sound so breathless?" he asked, his own voice changing to a purr.

Oh God, I thought, *he knows what I'm doing.* "Nothing," I told him, but I hadn't stopped.

"Are you touching yourself?" The purr had an edge to it now.

"No," I said, because I just couldn't admit it, even though I couldn't stop. *What came over me when I got into this man's orbit?*

"Do you remember what I said I'd do to you if you lied to me? I believe that's three times now. Don't make yourself come. Your cunt is mine, and so is your pleasure. You're not allowed to come unless I say so."

I just moaned.

This time his voice barked at me. "If you don't get into your car this second, I'm coming there, and then I won't let you come for hours."

I was obeying, letting my dress drop and grabbing my purse, moving swiftly to my garage.

He didn't say another word, just hung up on me. I pulled up the GPS on my phone and started to drive.

There was almost no traffic, so I made it there in an even fifteen minutes.

As I pulled up to the massive gates surrounding the palatial compound he called a house, they swung open immediately, then closed behind me.

I loved my car. It was a 2008 civic, a very reliable little car, and I'd gotten a great deal on it. But it sat out in the Vegas sun when I went on trips for several days a week, and the black paint job had become faded. I suddenly became conscious that a car like mine would stick out like a sore thumb in a place like this.

I tried to shrug it off. This affair was going to be brief and memorable, and I didn't need to waste a second of it worrying about our drastic lifestyle differences.

I parked as close as I could get to the elaborately carved front door in the massive circular drive. There were no other cars in the driveway. I figured they were parked in the huge attached garage that seemed larger than my entire house.

The front door opened before I took even one of the steps that led up to it. I froze when I saw James.

He was shirtless, wearing just a pair of black athletic shorts with white stripes down the sides. His torso was a work of art, his golden skin ripped up by tight muscles along every inch of its long, lean length. I couldn't see a hint of hair on it, and I had a feeling it wasn't from waxing.

His shorts hung dangerously low on his lean hips. His hips

and his sexy pelvic muscles stuck out starkly, shaped into a defined V, and I wanted to lick every inch of him. His shorts were baggy, and the shadows weren't in my favor, so I couldn't make anything else out below that but knees, calves, and feet. Even those were spectacularly sexy, long, with starkly defined muscles running along his calves.

"Get in here," he said by way of greeting, his voice gravelly and rough. I'd been standing and just ogling him for a good five minutes.

I obeyed, just brushing past him. He sucked in a harsh breath at our almost contact.

"I had dinner ready, but that's going to have to wait. You're a little minx, you know that?"

I didn't know that, so I just shook my head, looking around at his intimidating entryway.

I sooo don't belong here, was my first thought, as I eyed up all the marble floors and clean columns, and the double stairway leading to the second floor. It was beautifully decorated in desert colors, with heavy, expensive looking vases and artwork.

"I gave my entire staff the night off, so we're quite alone," he told me, as though that was my concern. The thought of his staff hadn't even occurred to me.

I walked up to one of the stairways, running a finger along the heavy dark wood of the rail. The room had the feel of a modern twist on a southwestern decor theme. It was tasteful and lovely, but I just felt overwhelmed.

I didn't like the idea of being with someone this rich. Someone who I had nothing in common with. I forgot for a second what I was even doing there.

James stepped up behind me, not touching, but unbearably close, and I remembered then. Oh yeah, *that.*

"Where's your bedroom?" I asked bluntly. Perhaps it would be less intimidating than what I had seen so far. I highly doubted it.

A strong hand fell on my nape, squeezing, then massaging. I leaned into the contact. Even his simplest touch was pleasurable.

He grabbed my hair there, pulling the strands together into a ponytail. He used it like a handle. Or a leash. He pulled me, not ungently, up the stairs by it. My chin lifted up with his handling. It was firm and controlling, but with no pain. Yet.

We passed by eight doors in the long hallway to his bedroom. His room was on the very end, the door already opened.

He took me just inside of it, stopping to let me take it all in.

The room was softly lit and colossal. Double doors opened into a well lit bathroom on the opposite side of the room. The walls were a medium taupe, the colors themed to the desert, similar to the rest of what I'd seen of the house.

His bed was massive. I'd never seen a bed like that. It had to have been custom made. It had a massive four poster frame, made up of heavy dark wood that was intricately carved and nearly reached the high ceiling.

It was topped by a heavy, latticed top of the same wood. It was patterned and carved into a piece of art. It was beautiful and frightening. It was a bed made for beauty and pleasure. And bondage and pain.

I picked out the more alarming little details slowly, as I took in the entire massive bedroom. Restraints were hanging, attached to the latticed top. And more were fastened to the posters themselves, laid out neatly against the crisp white sheets.

"Are those ropes?" I asked in a breathless voice. There was some kind of cushioned ramp in the middle of the bed, in a sandy beige that matched the carpet. I wasn't sure what it was for.

"Yes," he answered, and didn't elaborate.

My eyes caught on the object they had perhaps been avoiding. A black riding crop lay on the ramp. "Is that a riding crop?" I asked, my voice catching, but I knew the answer.

"Yes," he answered, moving for the first time since we'd entered the room, nudging me forward by his grip on my hair until I was several steps closer to the bed. "I have more toys that I want to use on you, but I didn't want to intimidate you by laying them all out."

I laughed, and it was a desperate kind of noise. So this was how he tried *not* to intimidate me?

"You need to pick a safe word," he told me. It was an order.

I took a deep breath. "I assume you know I've never done any of this before?" It was a question.

"Yes," he breathed, his voice thick and intense.

My mind went blank. "Sotnos," I said finally. It was as though my mind had worked independently of my brain.

"Sotnos?" he asked archly. He imitated the accenting of the word perfectly on the first try.

"Yes." I wouldn't tell him why. I was shocked at myself for choosing it, though it made a sick kind of sense. But I certainly wouldn't explain it to him.

He tugged on my hair, hard, tilting my head back and to the side until I looked at him. His gaze was hard. "There are rules in here. I become your master in here, and I will punish you when you defy me. I will read your reactions, and try not to go too far, but if I do, or if there's something you just can't handle, that's the word you use."

"What about outside of here? Didn't you say you would punish me for lying to you? But we weren't in here when I lied to you."

He smiled at me, and it was wicked. "There are exceptions. I will never lie to you, and I expect you to learn to do the same. Tell me what your safe word means."

I shook my head stubbornly. "No."

"Would you rather take more lashes than just tell me what that means?"

I nodded. "Yes." I tried to sound sure, but I wasn't. I had no concept of how hard he would hit me, or how much it would hurt, but I had spent my formative years being conditioned for pain, and I couldn't imagine that I wouldn't have a higher tolerance for this than most.

He ran a tongue over his teeth. It was incredibly hot, watching that skilled tongue run across his straight white teeth. I hadn't seen it before, but the teeth on the outside of his canines were a little sharp, almost faint fangs, the four teeth between them straight and perfect. Even his teeth were impossibly sexy.

Figures, I thought, almost resentfully.

"How about an exchange? Is there something I could give you in exchange for that information? Something you want to know about me? Something you want in general?" His voice had turned to velvet as he spoke.

I wasn't even tempted. I was not talking about it. I shook my head. He gripped my hair, hard.

"You're driving me crazy," he said softly, then nudged me towards the bed. "We need to talk. We need to figure out this arrangement. But I can't wait any more for this. Nothing has ever made me feel this wild before. I need to mark you. I need to own you. I need to punish you. I need to open you up and strip every detail out of you. And I will get you to tell me what that word means to you."

The last two sentences made my heart beat the fastest. That was never going to happen, but I couldn't find the voice to tell him that just now. I couldn't find the breath. It was panting out of me in a harsh rhythm of mindless fear and anticipation.

CHAPTER THIRTEEN

Mr. BDSM

"Lift your arms," he told me, when we were a scant foot from his forbidding bed.

I did, and he lifted my dress off in one smooth move. He sucked in a breath and circled me slowly. I barely noticed how he perused my body. I was too busy drinking in the sight of him.

His exquisite torso was even closer now, and the lighting was much better. He was even more perfect than I had realized. There wasn't an ounce of fat on him. Just hard, rippling muscles roping his tall form.

His hair was the color of caramel in the soft light. It trailed into his stunning face temptingly. I wanted to touch it, I wanted to touch *him*, but he had said there were rules in here, and the thought gave me pause.

He bent down in a swift move when he reached my left breast, biting me hard through my lacy black bra.

I made a little yelp at the sharp bite, and he pulled back, continuing to circle me. He snapped my thong as he reached my hip.

"You are too much," he told me. He stopped at my back. "A

virgin with the sexiest body I've ever seen in my life. Too fucking perfect." As he spoke, I felt him kneel behind me. I puzzled over what he was doing only a moment before he bit my butt, hard.

I sobbed in a breath. It had hurt. I glanced back. He was kissing the wound now, his teeth marks clearly imprinted into my skin. I glanced at the nipple he had bitten. Teeth marks were clearly imprinted there as well, though he hadn't bitten me there anywhere near as hard.

"I want to cut all of your clothes off, but I love everything I see you wear, and I have no idea where you got any of it, so I don't know how to replace it." He fingered my panties as he spoke.

"The thongs are from Victoria's Secret. So is the bra," I told him. Just trying to be helpful.

He gave me an approving smile that was all teeth, followed by a sharp slap on the ass.

"Don't move," he told me, moving to the closest bedside table.

My eyes widened. I don't know what I had expected when he said cut, but the sight of a knife in this room of pain sent a streak of panic through me.

How far would he go? How far would I let him go?

He laughed wickedly at the look on my face. "It's just for cutting clothes. I would never cut your skin. The thought is abhorrent to me. I just want to blister it a little."

He came back to me, grabbing the front of my bra and tugging it out from my breasts, cutting it in one clean motion, directly between the cups. His gaze was glued to my small, rosy nipples, and I felt them getting impossibly tighter by the second. He pinched them one by one, softly, then harder, finally giving them a firm pinch.

"How sensitive are they? Did you like the first touch better, or the last?" He pinched them harder still, and I moaned. "Or the fourth time?" he asked.

I swallowed. It was an easy answer for me. I just couldn't seem to get the words out. I cleared my throat. "The fourth."

"Good. I have something for you." He walked back to the side table, reaching inside and taking out some sort of light silver chain.

He was back in front of me, fastening some kind of clamp onto both of my nipples before I even had a clue what they were.

"Nipple clamps. Are they too tight?"

I shook my head, looking down at them. Each nipple was pinched by a small, peach colored clamp, the silver chain connected between them. He wrapped the chain around the back of my neck, fastening it there. The sight of that thin chain, and those hungry little clamps, and the feel, god, the feel, was so erotic that I had to press my thighs together to try to stop the rush of liquid there.

He sliced each side of my thong, removing it and stuffing it in his pocket.

"Climb on the bed," he ordered me, his voice low and hoarse. I did so. "Climb over to that ramp until your knees are touching it. Yes, right there."

I felt him climbing up right behind me. Just as my knees touched the ramp, his hand applied a firm pressure to the nape of my neck, pushing until I was face down on the ramp. My cheek lay on the broad end of the riding crop he had left there. My face was low, my ass lifted. *Perfect spanking position*, I thought.

"This isn't your knee," I told him.

He laughed, and it was a very pleased noise. "It is not. My lap isn't a safe place for you at the moment. We'll get to that, though, I promise." As he spoke, I felt him slipping a rope over my ankle. He tightened it firmly, but it wasn't at all uncomfortable.

"The more you struggle, the more these will chafe. Keep that in mind." He secured my other ankle and my wrists with swift, economical movements.

He climbed back to a position behind me and the ramp. He leaned over me then, his torso pressing into my back, his groin against my butt. I wiggled, and a hard hand swatted me lightly.

"Hold still," he told me, slipping the crop out from under my cheek. He lifted his weight completely off of me. I moaned at the loss. He swatted me with his hand for that, too.

There was a long pause while I waited for him, breath held.

"Do you have anything to say before I begin?" he asked me.

"I'm sorry, Mr. Cavendish," I told him, my tone repentant. Instinctively, I arched my back.

He made a delicious little humming noise in his throat and began to work. The first slap of the leather was more startling than painful, but the slaps got harder as he warmed up. As I had expected, I felt the pain, but my reaction to it wasn't a negative one. I moaned and wriggled helplessly when the crop hit lower, closer to my sex. He began to slap the crop against me hard and fast.

Abruptly, he stopped. I had received only twenty slaps, distributed all over my butt and the backs of my thighs.

I arched and muttered a protest then and I could hear his breathing, harsh and uneven, behind me. I rubbed my clamped nipples against the soft material of the ramp, liking the harsh bite of sensation it caused.

James remained still behind me for long moments.

"I need to stop there. I don't want you too sore to lie on your back when I take you. Fuck. I can see the liquid running down your legs." I felt his fingers stroking my thighs, sliding through the moisture there.

"We need to do a few things before I fuck you. I have a health exam on the table over there. I've been tested. All the results are clean. Do you want to see it? It's available for you. I want to bury my cock in you bare, if you'll allow. You said you're on the pill, right?"

I nodded. "I am. I'll take your word for it. If I thought you would lie about something like that, I wouldn't be letting you tie me up and pound the V-card out of me, now would I?"

He laughed, a happy sound, and I felt him kiss my cheek from behind in a surprisingly sweet gesture.

He slid the ramp from underneath me with no warning, knocking it right off the bed. I fell to the bed with a soft little whoosh.

He had my ankles free in the next instant, gripping them with his hands. He pushed me up higher on the bed, and in a shocking movement flipped me onto my back with just that contact. My arms twisted above my head, confining me even more. He had my legs spread wide when he tied them this time, and if I'd thought they were tight before, I'd been mistaken. I couldn't move them at all now. No more wiggling for me.

He studied me in my new position, and I studied him. His gaze was so intense it was mesmerizing. His eyes drank in every inch of me, and then he bent to start on me with his mouth. He started with a soft chaste kiss on the mouth. And then he moved down and not an inch of the front of my body was left chaste. He kissed me from my jaw, down my neck, to my collar bone. Not a nerve in my body was safe. And all the while, I couldn't move an inch.

He buried his face between my breasts, and pulled up in a quick push-up motion, the chain between the clamps clenched in his teeth.

I cried out at the harsh sensation, but it was a cry of pleasure more than pain. He kept pushing up until my nipples were pulled up, the chain taut. It was exquisitely agonizing. He finally released the chain, opening his mouth, and that was just as devastating, the end of the torture making me sob out a plea.

He suckled each breast then, soft and conciliatory noises

coming from his throat as he tended to them.

He licked to the undersides of my heavy breasts, down to my ribs, into my naval, nuzzling my hips, and stopping at my shaved sex. The tiniest patch of trimmed blond hair remained there. He fingered it, looking up at me.

"Fucking perfect," he murmured, his face serious, and buried his face there to work it's magic.

I was so wet and ready that he had me coming in seconds. Two fingers inside my cleft and his tongue on my clitoris, his knowledge of those two perfect buttons mind-boggling, and I was so gone, screaming without holding back. His head lifted briefly, and I looked down the length of my body at him. He was framed perfectly between my heaving breasts. I felt absolutely drugged from his attentions.

His caramel-colored hair trailed into his eyes. "Again," he told me, and did it again.

He straightened after that, slipping his shorts off to finally reveal his full naked self to me. I swallowed hard at the sight of him. That was when I started begging.

His rock hard length looked too big to fit inside of me, but I didn't care. I wanted it inside of me. If he made me wait another second, I thought I would cry.

"I can't wait anymore," he told me in a rough voice. "This is going to hurt. From what I've heard, that's unavoidable."

I didn't care. "Please, James. Please, please, please."

He didn't hesitate after that, lowering himself on top of me, and lining his cock up against my slick cleft. Sleek muscles sharply defined his broad shoulders as he held himself over me.

An exquisite work of art is about to fuck me, I thought, dazed and out of my mind turned on.

He thrust into me with one hard, brutal motion, piercing my hymen without further ado. I cried out at the shock. I felt so impossibly full. He didn't stop, thrusting fast and hard, setting an inexhaustible pace that had his sweat dripping down onto me in delicious trails. That initial sharp, biting pain faded as he thrust, turning into the purest pleasure, and the empty space at my core was filled to bursting with a wash of sensations that I could never have imagined.

I couldn't keep back the sobs that escaped my throat, the tears that trailed down the sides of my face at the exquisite feeling of being both dominated and filled by this man.

He watched me the entire time with those intensely vivid turquoise eyes. My eyes started to close with the pleasure once, and he barked out a harsh order for me to open my eyes and look at him.

I obeyed, though the intimacy of that extra contact was almost too much for me. It was hard to remember that we weren't supposed to feel anything for each other when he looked at me like I was more important than his next breath.

He pulled out almost completely, had me pleading with him to stay, before he pounded back in with a growl. If I had thought he was letting go before, now he was pounding me into the mattress until I thought I might leave a permanent imprint.

He reached a hand down between us, rubbing circles around my clit without slowing his furious pace.

"Come, Bianca, now," he ordered, and his order worked as a trigger. I screamed as I came, and he shouted my name as he followed me, burying himself to the hilt as tremors wracked him, his neck arcing with his pleasure. As the waves started to subside a little, he gripped my chin, looking at me with an almost angry, and certainly possessive, gleam.

"You're mine," he told me. I had no idea what to say to that, but I didn't need to respond. In the next instant, he was kissing me passionately, desperately.

He released my wrists and ankles and undid my nipple clamps more quickly than I would have thought possible. He pulled me against him, lining us up flesh to flesh, and started kissing my mouth again, as though he would never stop.

"Thank you," he told me quietly, just once, when he came up for air, then began kissing me again.

CHAPTER FOURTEEN

Mr. Sensitive

Eventually he stopped kissing me and pulled my cheek against his chest. I was reeling with the realization that casual sex could feel so intimate. I felt so cherished as he stroked my back reverently and whispered sweet words to me.

He left me. "Don't move," he said, his voice almost a whisper, as though afraid to intrude on the moment with noise.

I heard him start the bath, and couldn't think of anything that sounded more perfect than a hot bath at that moment.

I lay on my back, exactly as he had left me, feeling more relaxed in every part of my body than I could ever remember. I felt...peaceful. It was a revelation.

When he'd been gone for several minutes, I opened my eyes to look around.

He stood at the foot of the bed, watching me, his eyes ablaze. I glanced down my body and realized there was blood spread around on the sheets rather messily.

"I didn't realize I would bleed so much," I said, starting to sit up.

"Don't," he told me, and I lay back down. We watched each other. I saw that his erection was as hard as though he'd never come.

I pointed at it. "Can you go again? Is that possible?"

He smiled, and stroked his cock idly with one hand. "Oh, yes. But you're too sore tonight. I was just enjoying the view. Embedding this image into my brain."

He came to my side, lifting me until I was cradled against his chest. He rose from the bed with my weight in his arms. He showed no visible strain. I loved that, his strength, and all of the amazing things he could do with his body, seemingly effortlessly.

"Let's take a bath and talk about what we're gonna do about this," he said, stroking my hair, as though the 'this' was me.

It made me smile for some odd reason, though the thought of talking about anything held no appeal for me at that moment.

He stepped into the biggest tub I'd ever seen, still holding me.

The bathroom was one giant slab of greenish-black granite, so far as I could see. The tub was square and he slid down against one side of it, holding me in front of him until we were sitting up together, him spooning me from behind.

He pumped some divine smelling soap out of a built-in granite dispenser and began to lather soap over my entire body leisurely. It smelled like him, and I breathed it in. I felt positively decadent, laying there bonelessly while he tended to my bath.

"I love that soap. It smells like you," I told him, eyes closed in pleasure.

He brought his lips to my ear, biting the lobe teasingly. "Now you smell like me. I love *that*."

He washed me in silence for a few minutes, stroking as much as cleaning. He kept coming back to my breasts, stroking and kneading the pliable flesh thoroughly.

"We need to talk," he told me.

I groaned, and not in pleasure this time. "I'd prefer that you spank me again. Can we do that instead?" I was only half-joking.

He made a delicious purring noise against my neck. "Not tonight. We need to set up the rules for this. If my self-control hadn't deserted me tonight, we would have settled it before I ever touched you."

I cringed at his terminology. The word 'settled' gave me a bad feeling. I didn't think it boded well for the conversation to come.

"What is there to talk about?" I finally asked.

He sighed, the motion shifting me where I lay with my back on his chest.

"Well, I suppose I'd like to know what you would like out of our arrangement. What's important to you?" As he spoke, he turned me so that he could see my face more clearly, my head supported by the crook of his elbow.

I wrinkled my nose at him. The term 'arrangement' was even worse than 'settled'.

"Really, the only thing I expect from you is an exclusive sexual relationship while we're...having sex, even if we're done with each other in a week. And by done, I mean some type of communication before you start seeing anybody else, sexually or otherwise. And if that's a struggle for you, just let me know so I can bail out on the whole mess now."

He blinked at me, looking stunned, and I thought for an awful moment that he considered that too much of a concession. I was about a second away from getting the hell out of there when he spoke. "Yes, of course." His tone implied that he hadn't even considered anything else.

"And you want to not date," I prompted him. I was avidly curious to know what that meant for him.

He nodded, studying my face. "I want to see you, though, as often as possible. I would just prefer for our relationship to remain private. So most of our meetings will be at one of my homes or yours. I won't be taking you out to a lot of public places, I regret."

Sure he did, I thought cynically.

I made my face go blank, suddenly feeling a little delicate for reasons I wasn't willing to examine at that moment.

"Sounds great. Isn't that enough to settle things for the moment? If we're done with each other in a week, this seems like an awful lot of unnecessary talk, doesn't it? And if it lasts for two or three weeks, we'll take that hurdle when we come to it."

His face hardened as I spoke. His own questions seemed harsh. "Is that what you think? That we'll be done with each other in a week? Or two or three?"

I shrugged, closing my eyes as though I might drift off at any moment.

"I don't want to *think* about it. However long it lasts, if you're just honest with me when you're done, and don't just start seeing other people without telling me, that's enough for me."

He went back to washing and stroking me, tenderly washing and conditioning my hair, silent for a time.

"I would give just about anything to know what's behind that cool composure of yours. And I would kill to know what you're thinking," he whispered against my hair. "I'm so afraid I'll offend you beyond all repair, and that you'll never let me know how. You'll just leave and never speak to me again. Would you do that?"

I never opened my eyes, just shrugging again. Though it was uncanny to me how he'd realized that about me with how little he knew me.

"It's possible. It's hard to say without specifics."

He cursed softly. "I need to feel more secure about this. You terrify me."

I smiled wryly, eyes still closed.

"Wrong word, Mr. Beautiful. The term you're looking for is more in-control, not more secure. But I like my life. I'm not making a lot of concessions there, so don't even try. I'm usually in New York one full day a week. You live there, right?"

"Primarily, yes."

"Okay, well, I'll let you know when I'm in New York, and maybe we can meet up somewhere private."

His arms tightened around me. "This is what I'm talking about. Are you saying this because I've somehow offended you? Or are you really so indifferent?"

I suddenly wanted, badly, to leave. He wasn't one to leave a subject alone until he was satisfied, and I was absolutely done talking about anything that involved my indifference or lack thereof. I felt an instant need to get away from him, away from this feeling of intimacy. It was suddenly unbearable to me.

"I need to get home. I work early." I stood. I was relieved when he let me step out of the bath.

"Have you eaten dinner?" he asked me, his voice stiff and cool.

I thought about it, my mind going blank. *When was the last time I'd eaten?* I recalled scarfing down a protein bar as I painted, but that had been all since my yogurt on the plane.

"Um, I guess not," I finally answered. "But I can grab something later."

His nostrils flared, his eyes getting a little wild.

"Please, at least stay to eat with me. I'll feel like a complete bastard if you come here, we do all of that," he waved a hand at the bedroom, "and you leave as though you can't even stand to share a meal with me. I have some salmon prepped that only needs fifteen minutes to bake."

I nodded. "Okay," I agreed readily enough. I didn't want to storm out like a drama queen. I *would* prefer to leave with some dignity after a civilized meal.

He wrapped a towel around me, drying himself quickly and wrapping a towel low around his hips in a mouth-watering display. I looked away. He took off for the kitchen like he was afraid I would leave if it took him too long to get the salmon ready. He was uncanny at reading my intentions…

I slipped my dress back on, having nothing else. The lack of a bra and panties made it into a somewhat obscene outfit, but I didn't think it mattered. I would be going from James's house directly to my garage. I could probably get away with being naked, in a pinch.

I towel dried my hair a bit, used the restroom, which I found in its own room within the bathroom, and padded barefoot from his room.

I searched for and found the kitchen, but I stopped in the daunting dining room and sat there.

The table was set in almost a romantic fashion, so I assumed this was where we were meant to eat. I'd rather wait in a room by myself than tempt James into trying to have another 'talk' with me.

He joined me just a moment later, carrying two delicious looking salads. He set them down on the settings, darting back into the kitchen. He came back with two glasses of water with lemon.

I thought he might have actually forgotten that he was wearing nothing but a damp towel. It was impossible for me to forget such a thing. *Looking that incredible should be illegal.* He really was tan everywhere. It was a heady sight.

I waited politely for him to sit to my left before eating. It was mixed greens with feta cheese and pecans. I couldn't put my finger on what the lightly flavored dressing was, but it was quite good.

"It's delicious," I told him after a few bites.

He smiled at me. It was a careful smile. He was still in his 'afraid to offend me' mood.

"I actually cooked the whole meal tonight. I don't get to do it often, but I wanted to for you. I can't pretend, though, that this is a common occurrence. I have a great housekeeper here who usually does most of the cooking at this house."

I nodded pleasantly, trying not to look uncomfortable with the casual reminder of his wealth.

"Do your parents live in Las Vegas, as well?" he asked me after he'd finished his salad.

I froze, but recovered quickly. "They're dead," I said, my face and voice blank.

He looked startled. "I'm sorry. I didn't know. What happened?"

"Where do your parents live?" I asked him pointedly, rather than answering.

He looked uncomfortable. "They're dead as well. They died when I was thirteen, in a car crash."

I gave him an apologetic grimace. "Sorry. I don't like to talk about my parents, but I didn't mean to be insensitive about yours."

He reached across the table, putting his hand over mine. "Don't be sorry. That wasn't insensitive. You didn't know, either."

I gave him a wry smile. "I should have looked you up online. I could have saved us at least one awkward moment."

He gave me a wry smile back. "That wouldn't help me learn about you, though."

We went back to eating for a minute, and the silence was awkward.

"When is your birthday?" he asked suddenly. I knew what he was doing. He was so afraid to offend me, to scare me off, that he was trying to find neutral things to talk about. He couldn't have known that my birthday was another touchy subject.

"October." I answered. "How about you?"

"June 5th. October what?"

I sighed. "24th." I stifled the urge to say, *Why do you care? You won't even remember my name by then. That would be rude*, I told myself. And he seemed to be oddly sensitive.

He nodded, as though making a note of it.

Yeah, right.

The oven timer went off, and he walked into the kitchen, seemingly oblivious to the fact that that clingy towel looked in danger of falling off with every step.

I made myself look away.

He brought in two impressive dishes a moment later. He had already dished the food onto the plates, arranging the meal with a chef's flourish.

It was an offering of asparagus, freshly baked salmon seasoned to perfection, and some type of grain I'd never seen before.

I tasted it, then pointed to it with my fork. "I don't even know what that is, but it's delicious. It's all divine. Is there anything you're bad at?"

He smiled, the first self-deprecating smile I'd seen on him. It was disarming and all too charming.

"Learning about you. Getting you to spend the night with me. And that grain is quinoa."

I just continued to eat, ignoring the first things he mentioned. I still felt that itching under my skin, that strong need to withdraw from the intimacy we'd shared.

"Oh, I got you a present," he told me, smiling at me as we were finishing our meal. "Do you want desert before or after the gift?"

I waved him off. "Oh, I couldn't. I'm so stuffed already."

He looked genuinely disappointed. "Just a bite? It's just a light custard with some fresh fruit. We could share."

I smiled, genuinely charmed by his boyish need to impress me with his cooking. "Okay, we can share."

CHAPTER FIFTEEN

Mr. Insatiable

He was back quickly with the desert.   It was served in a heavy glass goblet, and he held the spoon up to my mouth for a bite.

"Mmmm," I said, smiling at him, my mouth still full.

Unexpectedly, he bent down and kissed me.   It was so different from the tone of the meal we'd just shared that I almost pushed him away, startled.   Instead, I made myself hold still, kissing him back tentatively.

This was the part that was easy between us, I thought.   None of the rest of it made any sense to me, but this part felt damned near too perfect.

He was lifting me onto a clear spot on the massive black table before I could blink.   His towel was gone, my dress pushed up in a flash.

"Are you too sore?"   His voice was a rough murmur against my lips.

"I can't imagine being too sore for this," I told him, reaching down his body to grab his thick arousal.   I stroked him with relish, and he thrust into my hand.   I ran my hands up his torso, along his muscular arms, then back up to his shoulders.

"You're body is perfect.   I can't believe you really are tan everywhere."

He smiled, enjoying my appreciation of his body. "My mother was half-Italian and half-Cherokee, though she had no family left to speak of by the time she was eighteen. It was quite the scandal, to my father's purely English family, when they married. My extended family all have the pasty white English skin you'd expect."

I laughed. "Pasty? What about me? Am I pasty?"

He bent down, nuzzling at my neck. "Your skin is creamy perfection."

I finally got a chance to touch him, stroking his back, his stomach, studying his incredible body with awe while I ran my hands across it.

He snagged one of my busy hands, pulling it up to his lips to kiss my wrist. He studied it intently, and I saw the imprint of rope marks there. The threads were a distinctive pattern, as though he'd marked me, temporarily, with his own special brand.

"I love seeing this on you," he murmured thickly against my skin.

He spread my legs wide, pushing me down flat against the table. He poised that overpowering erection at my entrance.

I shuddered as he paused, my eyes closed.

"Look at me," he ordered, his dominant voice surfacing again. It had faded to something softer and more charming since immediately after the first time we'd had sex. I'd missed it. I obeyed him.

"Watch me. I'll punish you every time you look away from me when I'm inside of you."

I nodded.

"Ask me for it," he ordered, his hand moving to stroke his impressive cock.

"Please, Mr. Cavendish, fuck me."   I loved saying his

surname, sounding out the three syllables as though they were a prayer.

He groaned, and he did. The first heavy thrust had my sore insides quivering, but it wasn't unpleasant. And as he pulled out, and plunged in again, a deep sound tore from his throat. I forgot about all soreness entirely, pleasure pulsing through my entire body and building at my core.

His gaze was ardent. "Does it hurt?" he asked without pausing in his punishing rhythm.

"It's perfect," I answered, my voice thick with passion.

He kissed me roughly. My eyes closed briefly, until he pulled back to watch me again. I didn't think I'd get a punishment for it, since he'd closed his, but I didn't really care at that moment.

"Come," he ordered me, and just like that, that all-consuming passion swept over me, my core rippling with an intense orgasm, my inner muscles clenching him impossibly tight.

I made a conscious effort to keep my eyes on him the whole time, and the effort paid off. It was exquisitely gratifying to watch his face as the fervor swept him, his piercing stare intensifying on me. It gave me an extraordinary feeling, being on the receiving end of such a stare. It made me feel like I was more important than air to him for a brief, profound moment. I felt enthralled in that moment. It was intoxicating.

"Stay the night. I promise I won't let you sleep in or be late to work," he said, catching me in a weak moment. "Just tell me what time I need to set the alarm for."

I closed my eyes, nodding slightly. "Okay."

He kissed my cheek in the sweetest way. "Thank you."

I didn't know what to say to that, so I didn't respond. He still hadn't pulled out of my body, and he didn't now, just wrapped me around him, and lifted me up. I gasped.

"You're still so hard," I murmured against his neck.

"Mmmm," he hummed, shifting inside of me.

"You couldn't...not again?" I questioned, surprised.

He answered by lifting me a few inches off of him, and thrusting fully into me again.

I gasped, and he chuckled softly.

"I've never wanted anyone this much in my life, Bianca. I could fuck you until I'm unconscious. I'd certainly be happy to try."

I didn't respond, couldn't. I could do nothing but whimper while he bounced me on his length and carried me up the stairs and back toward his bedroom.

"Let me know if you reach your limit. You should be sore and tender after your first time. I should be considerate and let your body recover." His voice was rough as he walked us down the hallway, the bounces becoming more pronounced thrusts the closer we got to his bedroom.

"Please, don't," I told him in a half-sob. He had me so close to the pinnacle again.

"You want me to finish you like this, standing up and impaled on my cock?" he asked. He stopped walking and began to thrust more intensely.

"Y-yes please. Oh, yes," I said, clinging to his shoulders.

One of his arms was braced diagonally across my back, gripping the top of my shoulder securely, the other hand gripping my butt hard, the sting of the contact adding to the pleasure. His knees were bent slightly, his legs braced apart as he began to thrust more powerfully.

"Come, Bianca," he told me roughly as the fervor took me. His voice was the trigger, and my body obeyed him by exploding into orgasm. I held onto his shoulders like a lifeline while I rode out the exquisite waves of pleasure.

He seemed surprised by his own release, his eyes wide. He shouted a low, "Fuck", as he emptied inside of me.

He lay me softly on the bed, pulling out of me this time. He moved about the room.

I closed my eyes. I knew that, despite my overlong nap, I

was going to drift away any second.

I came to for a moment when he placed a warm, wet cloth between my legs, cleaning me gently.

"Thank you," I murmured to him.

"Mmm. My pleasure," he told me.

He left and came back again. He rubbed some type of salve into my wrists and ankles, turning me effortlessly onto my stomach to knead it into my butt and thighs. He stroked some between my thighs tenderly from behind.

"Any other sore spots?" he asked me.

"No," I answered.

"What time do you need to wake up?" he asked.

I did some tired math. I didn't even know what time it was, didn't want to know. "4:30," I answered. Sleep took me.

I awoke in a sensual haze, in the most enjoyable way I could have imagined.

I was on my back on the softest bed. I was gloriously naked, spreadeagled, and the most beautiful man I'd ever seen was lapping at my sex like it was a particularly delectable dessert. I gripped his silky golden hair.

"Oh James," I moaned, and he looked up, smiling.

He rose, kneeling between my thighs. He brought one of my legs up to his shoulder, lining it up at his neck until it made a diagonal line across his torso. The other leg he straddled, lining his insatiable cock up at my readied entrance.

"Let me know if this is too much for you, k?" His voice was soft, and his words held a note of concern.

Was the dominant master present this morning? I wondered. It seemed like his other persona, the tender lover, was driving at that moment.

I nodded, and he pushed into me. The new position had him stroking new nerves that I hadn't even known existed. Yes, I was sore and tender, but I wasn't going to stop him. The soreness was a small deterrent to such pleasure.

He leaned his chest forward, pushing my legs farther apart and closer to my chest. Using a twisting motion inside of me, he thrust. *He's screwing me sideways*, I thought in a daze.

One of his skillful fingers began to rub my swollen clitoris, and I was lost.

He carried me into the shower after that. He washed us both.

I felt limp and couldn't imagine facing a fourteen hour work day after such an experience. I voiced the thought out loud.

He'd been spooning me from behind, washing the conditioner out of my hair. At my words, he froze.

"So don't. Take a day off. I'll reschedule my day, as well. We could spend the day in bed. I would make sure it was memorable for you."

I sent him a baffled look, laughing. *Rich people*, I thought, a little resentfully.

"I'm off tomorrow," I explained. "If I took today off, I wouldn't get paid. And dropping a shift so last minute could get me in trouble."

His arms tightened. He rubbed his chin on the top of my head affectionately.

"You could quit. Come work for me. I'd be a generous employer. You could be a flight attendant on my jet. We'd get all the time we wanted together, then. Or, if you want a change of careers, I could find you something else. If you don't care for the hotel industry, I have other companies you could work for. Or hell, just take some time off. Relax. I'd be more than happy to support-"

"Don't ever mention anything like to me again, please, or this is over, starting now," I interrupted him, my tone icy, my face composed. I was shaking a little.

The nerve of him, I thought. I had worked like a fiend since I was a young teenager, and he had just belittled every minute of it. It was an effort not to storm out of the shower with half-rinsed hair, and just leave.

His hands began to stroke my arms in a soothing gesture. "I meant no offense. It's just hard for me to see you struggle. Can you understand that?"

Struggle? I thought, a little wildly. Could he know the meaning of the word, if he thought that my life was a struggle? But then I remembered what he'd said about his parents, about how they'd both died when he was only thirteen. He hadn't led the perfect life that I had pictured. It was a hardship and a struggle getting over the death of a parent. We had at least something in common. It warmed me towards him some, and helped me to give him another chance.

I shook my head slightly. "Well, don't worry about me. And don't mention anything like that to me again. I mean it. It's a deal-breaker for me."

His face was stiff but he nodded.

I took a few measured breaths to calm down, then moved away from him, rinsing off and stepping out of the shower.

"I need to go. I don't even know what time it is, but I need to get ready for work." I wrapped one of his big soft towels around me.

"It's 4:40. I woke you up a little early. Sorry."

He sure didn't sound sorry, I thought, moving into his room to look for my dress. It was a crumpled heap on the floor. I picked it up tentatively, my nose wrinkling. I could see the stains on it from a foot away, and I wasn't about to smell it.

I glanced back at the bathroom.

James lounged in the doorway, leaning against the open door frame nonchalantly, his arms crossed. His face was expressionless, his eyes indifferent. He looked suddenly as forbidding as his opulent home. Perhaps I'd overstayed my welcome.

"Do you have a T-shirt or something I could borrow? It

doesn't matter what. I just need to drive straight from your driveway to my garage. And I'm not wearing this." I dropped the offending dress back on the floor.

He nodded, moving to his closet. He came out with a folded T-shirt and a pair of black boxer briefs.

"Will these work?" he asked, his voice toneless.

I nodded, grabbing them and heading into the bathroom. I changed and used the bathroom in less than a minute, coming back out.

"Do you know where I left my purse?" I asked him.

"In the entryway. By the stairs. You left your sandals there, as well," he told me without hesitation. I didn't even remember leaving them there.

I nodded thanks, striding out of his bedroom in a hurry. I had my shoes on and purse in hand before I turned back to him. I'd felt him following my every step.

"Um, bye," I told him, feeling very awkward and out of my depth. I had certainly never had one of these goodbye scenes before. I was sure he couldn't say the same. At least it wouldn't be much of a walk of shame, since I was going straight from his front door to my garage.

He stepped closer to me, but without touching. He still wore just his towel. I kept my eyes firmly on his face. He handed me something, and I looked down at a small silver box. I blinked. He wrapped my hands around it.

"It's a gift. It was just something that I hoped you would like. You can open it later."

He grabbed my hair suddenly, giving me a hard kiss on the mouth. He pulled back almost immediately.

"I'll call you," he said.

I just nodded and hurried to my car. I didn't have time to open his gift, or to worry about it. As it was, I'd have to rush to make it to work on time.

As I steered out of his drive, I wondered where he and I

stood. Everything had moved so fast, with so many ups and downs, both of us moody with each other. He had said he would call me, but I knew from a lot of my girlfriends that men said that most of the time, whether they meant it or not. The thought that I would never hear from him again was a knot of sick tension in my stomach.

CHAPTER SIXTEEN

Mr. Incredible

I rushed home, getting dressed in a hurry. My hair was still damp, my face bare of makeup, when Stephan walked in my front door.

He called out a greeting, showing up in my bedroom an instant later. I knew I looked like a hot mess.

"Have a good night?" he asked me with a mischievous grin.

"It was memorable, that's for sure. It isn't fair for a man that perfect to be loose among the public."

He laughed. "Let me drive today. We need to go, and you can do something with your hair and makeup on the way."

He noticed the silver box I had thrown on my bed. He gestured at it. "What's that?"

I grimaced. "A gift from James. I haven't had time to look at it."

He grabbed it, tossing it into my flight bag and slinging the bag over his shoulder.

"We can check it out when we get a break. Let's go, Bee."

I braided my damp hair as Stephan drove us to work. I put on the minimal makeup that I could manage in the car. I even had a moment to spare before we got to work.

I realized how sore I was as I finished my rushed makeup job. Every shift on my seat made aching muscles protest in unnamable places.

Well, he *had* offered to take it easy. Now I could see why, though I still couldn't regret our enthusiasm. I doubted he would either, if he realized that every time I shifted in my seat today I would have to think of him.

The marks on my wrists had faded into the faintest of pink marks. My old watch covered the mark on my left wrist, and I didn't think the exposed marks on my right wrist were enough to draw attention. But still, they were all reminders of himself that he'd left with me.

Part of me thought I wouldn't see him again. He'd been intense and passionate, but that may be how he was with every lover. For all I knew, he'd already had his fill of me. I was already bracing myself for the possibility.

We checked in for our trip and headed for the crew bus.

"Should I check real quick and see if we can pick up a turn tomorrow?" Stephan asked me while we waited. "I wouldn't mind taking the day off, either. We've been working so much lately, we *are* due for a little break. It's up to you."

I grimaced. "Let's see how today goes. We could always check on the flip side."

He just nodded. Neither of us were usually chatty in the morning. And I hadn't even had a cup of coffee yet. *I really need to remedy that soon*, I thought.

I made coffee as soon as we got to our plane, downing a large cup fast enough to burn my tongue. But it helped. I felt like I could survive the day after that.

The first few hours of the flight passed by in a flash. We had a full flight, and we didn't get a break to eat until we were only an hour and a half from DC.

No one had wanted the breakfast offering of greek yogurt, so we both ate that instead of our crew meals.

"Ok, open that box James gave you," Stephan said immediately after he'd finished eating. "We have a minute, and I'm dying of curiosity here."

I'd completely put it from my mind. I winced as he reminded me. I was dreading opening it. It made me uncomfortable to get a gift from someone whom I barely knew, and for no reason.

It's better to just get it over with than to stew about it, I told myself.

I almost just told Stephan to open it for me, but I had the sudden embarrassing visual of him pulling a pair of nipple clamps out of that little box. I could well imagine James doing that. Or giving me something even more kinky that I wouldn't recognize. In fact, the more I thought about it, the more I thought it was likely that it was some sort of kinky sex toy.

We didn't date. We had mind-blowing sex. If he was giving me a gift that he'd thought I would like, wouldn't it have something to do with what he liked to do with me?

I definitely needed to give it a quick glance before Stephan looked at it. The picture I'd suddenly painted in my head would be mortifying in person.

I strode to my bag, pulling the box out and opening it slowly, tilted towards me, half-dreading what I would find.

Well, it's certainly nothing kinky, I thought, stunned. It was a lovely, elegant watch. It looked like a very high end version of the one I needed to replace, silver in color and sporting a pale turquoise face. Of course this one's blue face was circled by diamonds. Even the hour markers were little diamonds. I hoped for a moment that they were just cubic zirconia, but then I saw the label. I knew absolutely nothing about expensive watches, but even I recognized *that* label.

"Oh, god," I said, a hand covering my mouth in shock.

Stephan took the box from me, giving me a puzzled look.

"Whoa," he said instantly when he got a look at the gift. "Holy shit, a Rolex?" He grinned at me. I smiled weakly back, though it was an effort. "Somebody is smitten with my Buttercup."

I didn't think that was it. I suddenly had the horrifying thought that this was his parting gift, his 'thank you for a good time' gesture. *Did he have a stack of these somewhere for all of his one night stands?* I wondered morbidly. I suddenly felt sick to my stomach.

"I need to use the restroom," I told Stephan, rushing into the tiny lavatory.

I splashed water on my face, then had to carefully wipe the mascara from under my eyes.

I had known that it was coming, but I'd thought he'd stay interested for at least a few memorable nights. I told myself sternly that this was for the best. If I was this upset about him dumping me after a night, I couldn't imagine what a week or a month would do. But I would return that damn watch. It was too much. I wasn't sure how much a Rolex cost, but I was very certain that it wasn't something I could have bought for myself.

I took a few deep, calming breaths, and went back out.

Almost at the same time, Melissa flounced through the curtain. "1A is a hottie. He's built like a linebacker. He's wearing Armani, too. That's never a bad sign." *Oh lord*, I thought to myself, more annoyed to see her than usual. She was trolling first class again.

Stephan still had the Rolex box open, and was still admiring it as though he hadn't looked away since I left. Melissa zeroed in on the jewelry immediately.

"What do you have there?" she asked, bending down to look before either of us could answer. She gasped more dramatically than either of us had. "Where did you get that?" she asked Stephan, her voice raised.

He grinned at her, and it was unmistakably smug. "It belongs to Bianca. James gave it to her. He's smitten."

She snatched it out of his hand suddenly, her face looking strangely furious. She sent me a scathing look, then studied the watch intently. She lifted it out of its case, looking at the back of the watch, and then the sides.

"God, it's real." She cursed. "It's a platinum president datejust. Holy fucking shit." She glared at me. "Do you have any idea what this is worth? Do you even know anything about Rolex's?" Her tone was condescending, and I just kind of snapped. I was whipping my old busted watch off before I could think about it.

I snatched the watch out of her hand. I held my wrist and the watch to Stephan, so he could put them on me. For all I knew, James would be giving Melissa a call tonight, but until then, I was going to wear this Rolex, and she wasn't. Stephan clasped it onto my wrist without a word, but I knew he was smiling.

"I don't need to know much." I waved my now weighted wrist at her. "Just how to wear one."

She eyed me top to bottom, sneering in an ugly way.

"I don't get it," she muttered, storming back through the curtain. Maybe I would keep it, I thought pettily, if all I had to do was wave a hand now to make Melissa leave.

"What a crazy bitch," Stephan said quietly.

I sent him a surprised look. He usually never spoke so harshly. I knew he was overprotective of me, and she had apparently raised his hackles as much as mine.

We got back to work after that, and thankfully, I was too busy to dwell on James for the duration of the flight.

I brought another bottle of water to 1A. The man that Melissa thought was a hottie was actually very polite and pleasant. He'd eaten everything I put in front of him, but only drank water. He had the feel of an Air Marshall to me, though he wasn't one. Or rather, if he was, he wasn't on duty.

He was constantly alert, glancing around the cabin often, and watching me a lot. However, I didn't get even the slightest impression that he was interested in me on a personal level.

"Are you sure I can't get you a glass of ice or a lemon with that?" I asked him, smiling. I was always more at ease with men who weren't attracted to me.

He smiled back. "This is fine, but thank you."

I continued down the aisle, checking with everyone to make sure they didn't need anything. I could feel his eyes on me the entire time. He'd had a small laptop out for most of the flight, but it seemed like he was watching the cabin more than the computer screen.

Strange, I thought absently.

Stephan and I sat down for landing a short time later. We were both staring down at my wrist.

"I know it's embarrassing for you to talk about, but was he good to you, your first time? Did it hurt very much?" Stephan stunned me by asking. But his tone was serious and concerned, so I felt a need to answer him.

I met his concerned gaze squarely.

"There was pain," I finally answered carefully. "But it was good. He was good. He's incredible in bed. He does things... they aren't necessarily normal things. Things that I love, though I'm not sure that I should." I'd been deliberately vague, but I still somehow felt I'd shared too much, and I blushed, looking down.

He patted my hand. "There's probably a reason you didn't feel the need to be with a man until him. Maybe those things he does fulfill a need for you. It's nothing to be ashamed of. We're all shaped by our childhoods. Accepting your preferences is not the same thing as being a victim. As long as you like what he does, and it doesn't harm you, I say let go and enjoy yourself. You deserve it."

I rested my head on his shoulder.

"You always make me feel better," I told him. I wondered, with a startling amount of panic, if I would even get the opportunity to enjoy myself in that way again.

"Ditto, Buttercup."

CHAPTER SEVENTEEN

Mr. Desperate

We landed early. It seemed likely we would actually make it home on-time as the plane emptied.

My hopes were short lived, however, when we were informed that we were delayed for weather for at least an hour. Thunderstorms were blanketing our route home, though the weather in DC appeared nice and calm.

The main cabin flight attendants decided to venture out into the airport to kill time. We suddenly found ourselves with too much of it, whereas a minute ago we'd been in a rush.

I declined the invitation to join them, wanting to just sit down and check my phone in relative privacy. The pilots joined them. Stephan stayed on board with me, sitting in the first class seat next to the one I was lounging in.

I had my flight bag open on the ground in front of my feet. With trepidation, I dug my phone out, turning it on. I had one missed call, one voicemail, and two texts. I checked the voicemail first.

I had to force myself to keep breathing as James's voice sounded in my ear.

"Hey," he began. There was a long pause before he

continued. "I don't want you to think I'm a stalker or anything, but I'd like to hear your voice if you get some time to call me when you're on the ground. I can't stop thinking about you. I know you're flying and your phone is off, but I still couldn't seem to keep myself from calling."

"I want to see you tonight. I'm sure your'e sore." His voice thickened suddenly. "I need to kiss every part of your body that I left hurting today." He cleared his throat. My hand was trembling. "I hope you think of me every time it hurts you to sit down. I miss you." The message ended, and I lowered my phone shakily. Apparently he wasn't done with me, after all.

My sudden and profound sense of relief was mortifying, but impossible to ignore.

Stephan was bent over writing next to me. He liked to be on top of his flight paperwork.

"Everything ok?" he asked me without looking up.

"Yeah." I said, my voice small. I looked back at my phone to check my messages. They were from James, as well.

James: How are you? Did you like your gift?

James: Thinking of you. You were incredible last night. Absolutely perfect. I can't stop thinking about it. I'm having a hard time getting any work done. I've never been this distracted in my life.

I was reading his second text for maybe the sixth time when my phone rang in my hand, startling me. When I saw that it was James, my hand went to my pounding heart. I answered after a moment of agonizing indecision.

"Hello," I said, my voice breathless.

"Bianca," James breathed, his deep voice sounding delighted. "I didn't think I'd be able to reach you. How are you feeling?"

"Good," I answered. I glanced at Stephan, then got up to

pace to the back of the plane.

"Are you hurting?" he asked.

"I'm very sore," I told him. I heard his breath catch.

"Can I come to your house tonight?"

I sighed regretfully. "We're delayed in DC. There's no telling what time I'll get home, so tonight's no good. I have to run some errands in the morning, but I should be free tomorrow night. We were going to pick up a turn tomorrow, but I guess that's not happening with this delay."

"Just call me when you're back in Vegas. I can come over late."

"I'll be tired and cranky."

"I'm coming over. Call me when you land in Vegas," he said, his dom voice coming out, making it an order. "What errands do you need to run in the morning? Maybe I'll tag along."

"Ones in public," I said, taking a jab at his insistence that we meet only in private.

He made a tsking sound over the phone. "My driver can take us. I'll turn the car into my office for the morning and get some work done while you do your shopping or whatever you need to do."

I snorted. "That's silly. I'll just call you when I'm done. I'm going with Stephan."

"He can come. I'm sure he wouldn't mind if we used my car. Just ask him. Did you like your gift?"

His tactic to change the subject worked, and my eyes shot down to the exquisite watch on my wrist.

"It's lovely. I have your watch on one wrist, and your mark showing on the other," I told him quietly, just knowing it would make him crazy. The low rumble that bled into my ear was gratifying. "But I can't keep it. I don't know a thing about watches, but even I know this thing is way too expensive."

His tone was firm and commanding when he responded. "It's a gift. You need to pick your battles, Bianca, and you aren't winning this one. I won't ask you to work for me or to let me support you again, but I'll give you as many gifts as I damn well please. The price of that watch is nothing to me, but picking out something that you think is lovely makes me very happy."

I stewed that over for a long moment. *Could I just give in?* I mentally steeled myself to do so. I was having sex with a man that had an obscene amount of money. I was going to have to compromise sometime. And I would just return anything he gave me when we stopped seeing each other. That thought made the concession easier.

"Okay. Thank you. The dial is the color of your eyes. Did you do that on purpose, so I would think about you all the time?"

He laughed, a relieved, joyous sound. "I'll use every dirty trick in the book to stay on your mind. But that didn't occur to me. I like it, though. Think about looking into my eyes as I make you come, every time you read the time."

"Oh," I breathed, caught up at the image.

"Are you wet?" he asked, his tone changing from playful to serious in an instant. Moody bastard.

"Yes, Mr. Cavendish."

"Are you alone?" he demanded.

I glanced to the front of the plane, then moved into the aft galley. Stephan hadn't moved, and there was no one else on the plane.

"Relatively. I'm in the back galley, and Stephan is in first class. Everyone else left the plane to get food."

"Does that galley have a curtain?" he asked, almost idly.

"Mmhmm." My voice was a needy hum.

"Shut it behind you," he ordered. I shut it. "Now lift up your skirt, and stroke the petals of your sex lightly." I gasped, but used one hand to obey. I was tender to the touch but so wet from his voice that it still felt good. "Now, slip two fingers in." I did, gasping. "Does that hurt?"

"Yes, oh yes. It's very tender."

"Oh, baby, I want to kiss it. Pet yourself softly. Keep it warm for me." His voice was getting rougher and rougher, and I wondered if he was touching himself.

I asked him.

"Yes," he bit out. "But I'm not going to jerk myself off. I'm saving it all for you. I'll wait, even if you're out of commission for a few days. Stop touching yourself now. You're such a hair trigger, and I don't want you coming until you see me again."

I complied, making a little sound of protest in my throat.

"I need to keep my cock out of you for a few days while you heal up, but there are plenty of other things we can still do. I'll eat you out until you beg me to stop. And I have this fantasy about coming between your lovely tits. You won't be sorry that I insisted on coming to your house tonight, I promise."

I made a little noise in my throat. Whether it was a sound of agreement or frustration, I couldn't say.

"What day do you fly back to New York?" he asked after my breathing had calmed. He sounded as though we'd been talking about nothing particularly personal just moments before.

Mercurial son of a bitch, I thought.

"Thursday night. I have three days off after today, but I need to pick up at least one more shift like the one we're working today, probably on Wednesday."

He made a sound of disapproval, but just said. "So you have two days off after today?"

"Yeah. When do you head back to New York?"

"Thursday night."

"Oh." I was surprised. "On my flight?"

"Yes. The redeye, correct?"

"Yeah, same as last week. How long can you keep doing that?" I asked, referring to his recent habit of following me around the country.

"Well, I have good people working for me, so I should be able to get away with it for a time. I can work wonders with just a

134

phone and a computer nowadays. There are a few perks to being the boss. And desperate times call for desperate measures."

"Desperate times?" I questioned.

"Oh, yes. You make me absolutely desperate, Bianca. I had never stalked a woman before I met you. I'm carrying a sliced up pair of your panties in my pocket right now."

I was afraid to even ask him about that.

I heard voices, and glanced between the curtains. The crew had returned, toting bags of food and coffee.

"The crew is back," I told him, readjusting my skirt and then the curtain to how it had been. "I probably need to go."

He made a frustrated sound in my ear. "Call me when you get back in Vegas," he told me. He cursed. "The waiting will make me crazy."

"Bye," I said, hanging up quickly as Brenda approached the aft galley. She looked surprised to see me there.

I held up my phone. "Just taking a call. I have a tendency to pace while I talk on the phone."

She smiled. "I do that too. You might still have time to go grab something in the airport, if you hurry. They're estimating an hour and a half delay now."

I groaned.

She sat in her jump seat, pulling a sandwich out of a paper bag. She waved the sandwich. "This place is good. It's right across from the gate."

I nodded a thanks, and started towards the front of the plane.

My phone beeped a texting noise at me. I looked at the screen. I sat down in one of the main cabin seats to read.

James: Hanging up on me will earn you a punishment as well.

Bianca: Sorry. Instinctive reaction to seeing coworkers

in the middle of a kinky conversation. Are you going to punish me tonight, then?

James: No. You're off the hook until I'm sure that you've recovered from all of the hard fucking we did last night. Did you like the crop?

Bianca: I'm partial to the crop. How many lashes will I get for hanging up on you?

James: 10.

Bianca: I love the crop, but I want you to use what you want on me. I want to please you.

James: You do. Don't doubt it. And I will use what I want on you. I can't wait to get you into my New York apartment. I have a playground for us there.

Bianca: Your bedroom in Vegas seemed like a playground

James: It was just a taste, Buttercup.

I didn't know what to say after that, so I put my phone in the pocket of my vest, heading back to the front of the plane.

CHAPTER EIGHTEEN

Mr. Possessive

When all was said and done, we didn't leave DC until we had well over a three hour delay on our hands.

Eventually, Stephan and I did get off of the plane briefly to grab ourselves a sandwich and a cup of good coffee. The plane coffee was drinkable, but only if nothing better was available.

I saw the man from 1A still hanging out near our gate. I nodded at him politely, but thought it odd that he was still there. We were delayed, but he was already at his destination.

What was he doing, still hanging out at the gate hours after we'd arrived?

He was speaking to another man who was near to a carbon copy of himself. They were roughly the same size, both with dark hair, and even wearing similar suits and ties. They reminded me so much of law enforcement that I nudged Stephan with my elbow.

"We getting air marshals on the flight?"

He followed my gaze, sizing up the large men. He shook his head.

"If we are, I haven't been informed of it yet. And with the

delay, I can't imagine I wouldn't know by now. They sure do look like FAMs, though. Probably just traveling FBI agents or something."

That made sense, so I put it from my mind.

However, I almost bumped into them as I picked up my sandwich order. They had been in line behind me, and I hadn't even known.

I nodded politely at them as I passed by. They both nodded back, one of them with a phone to his ear.

"Fine, Sir, she's just fine. No problems at all. Yes, Sir," he was saying.

We headed back to the plane after we'd gathered our goodies. The crowd that we passed was large and restless. Delays never made for a pleasant flight. There was nothing any of us could do about the weather, but a lot of the passengers would feel personally wronged for the inconvenience, and tempers would not be in our favor on the long flight home. I took the thought in stride. It was all part of the job.

It was a relief to finally take off and have something to do aside from waiting and checking my phone for messages.

James hadn't texted me again. Finally, about an hour before departing, I'd just turned my phone off, so I would quit checking.

The first three hours were a busy blur of activity. The man in 1A had been replaced by the man he had been speaking with in the airport. He behaved in a nearly identical manner, even eating similarly, taking all the food we served, and drinking only water. Once, he deviated, ordering a black coffee, but that was the only difference in the passengers.

Stephan noticed the odd Agent exchange as well. "The guy who was in 1A is in the back of coach now. Which is where this guy sat on the last flight."

I gave him wide eyes. "Should we be worried?"

He grimaced. "It is odd. But they are very calm and well behaved, so far. If that changes, I'll talk to the pilots. Who

138

knows, maybe they were delivering something in DC. Or picking something up."

We had a small break, then got busy again. I was just securing my last cart when I felt the wheels of the plane coming down for landing.

"Come on, Bee," Stephan told me, already buckled in. His voice held a faint plea. It always made him nervous if I pushed it and buckled in last minute. Mr. Safety.

I had told him about James's plan to drive us on our errands in the morning. He'd seemed excited about the idea, which was a relief. If Stephan liked James, it made everything easier. No matter how short a time the arrangement lasted.

We had deplaned and were on the crew bus before I remembered to turn on my phone.

I'd missed three calls, and one text. The calls were made sometime before departure, the text at some point during the long flight.

James: Why did you turn your phone off an hour before you pushed back from the gate?

My brow furrowed. I had done that so I wouldn't be tempted to check my phone every five seconds, but how did he know that? I supposed he could have tracked the flight easily enough online.

Stalker, I thought, texting him back.

Bianca: Quit stalking me. I hope this doesn't wake you up, but we're back in Vegas.

He responded almost instantly.

James: I'll meet you at your house. I told you to text me as soon as you got to Vegas.

* * *

Bianca: Working here. You don't get to boss me around at my job.

James: How wrong you are. Try me. I'll spank you in your galley.

I put my phone away. That was going nowhere that I needed to go on a bus full of co-workers. I ignored the next two dings that indicated a text.

Stephan drove us home in companionable silence.

"I'm sleeping in tomorrow. Text me when you wanna run errands," he told me, as he pulled into his drive.

"Sure thing," I said, getting out of the car.

I froze as I approached my own house. A black SUV was parked in front of it, engine running softly. A cold chill ran down my spine.

"Stephan," I called out, my voice a little panicked. I could hear his prompt running footsteps as he caught up behind me.

James stepped out of the back of the SUV, and I felt nearly weak with relief. Stephan cursed fluently behind me.

"God, I thought for a second that..." Stephan trailed off.

I just nodded, not looking at him. I knew what he'd thought, what we'd both thought, for a terrifying moment. I tried to shrug it off as James approached us.

"Everything ok?" he asked.

We both just nodded.

He nodded at Stephan as he walked up beside me, putting a firm hand at my nape.

He likes that spot, I thought, leaning a little into his hold. He gave me a warm look in response.

"Goodnight, Stephan," he said politely as he led me away.

"Goodnight," Stephan called back.

I let us into my house, hurrying through my security code and the locks.

"Nice. I like your security," James said behind me. I'd thought he would.

"I like to feel safe in my home," I said lightly.

We walked in, and I headed straight to my bedroom, where I kept my flight bag when I was at home.

"I like your house," James called out from the living room that doubled as my entryway. I re-joined him after stashing my bag.

I smiled, though it didn't quite reach my eyes as I accepted his compliment. It probably seemed like a closet to him.

"It's small, but it's mine."

He glanced back at the collection of watercolors I had arranged above my fireplace mantle.

"These are exquisite," he said, studying the paintings intently.

"Thank you," I said, flushing.

I hadn't displayed my own paintings all over my house ever intending for someone like *him* to see them. The ones he studied were a collection of desert landscapes, focusing on colors. There were enough of them, and they were small enough, that I'd arranged them into a sun mosaic of sorts. The bulk of the paintings were of some of the mountains that surrounded the Vegas valley. I had exaggerated the colors, making them deeper and richer, almost a kaleidoscope. In others, I had painted close-ups of individual plants with the same rich colors.

"You did these?" he asked, sounding astonished.

I nodded, walking to the table by the couch to straighten some books that were messily strewn there. I hadn't cleaned for company, though living by myself, I tended to keep things neat.

"I'm impressed. Do you have more?"

I shrugged. "It's just a hobby. You'll see my house is full of them. I know they're amateurish, and simple, but it's a cheap way to decorate my house. And painting is a good stress reliever for me."

"I don't think they're amateurish. I think they're enchanting." His voice was quiet, and I wanted to believe him, but I told myself he was just buttering me up with lavish praise that he probably didn't mean.

"Hmm thanks," I said, uncomfortable. I didn't want to like him any more than I already did.

"Can I see more?" he asked, smiling at me warmly.

"I'm beat," I told him, hesitant to show him anything more. I was starting to wonder why I had accepted his spending the night here so readily. This was already starting to feel too strangely intimate for my liking.

He frowned. "Of course. I'm sorry. I can see them in the morning. Let's get you to bed."

I was already heading to my bedroom, undoing my tie as I went. I went to the closet, stripping off my work clothes and hanging them as I went.

I could feel James watching me from behind. He had seen everything already, but I still felt strangely embarrassed.

I ignored the feeling, stripping until I stood in my stockings. I undid my garter belt, slipping the stockings down carefully. I hated to snag them. They could be expensive if I didn't treat them carefully.

James was still fully dressed, arms crossed, when I finished. He was just watching me.

I felt horribly awkward. Should I put something on for bed? Or was that silly? I unsnapped my bra, letting it fall to the floor. I wore nothing but a black lace thong then, and I couldn't read James's steady gaze.

I brushed past him, not used to his passivity. It gave me the strange urge to goad him into action.

I removed my new watch and small stud earrings, placing them in a safe drawer in the vanity set up just outside of my bathroom. I washed my face, then moisturized.

He still just watched me intently.

I brushed my teeth and climbed into bed. I lay on my back, and he came to stand over me, still just staring. It was positively agitating.

I cupped my breasts, pinching the nipples. I watched his face for a reaction. He hissed in a breath. He pulled off his dark V-neck shirt in one smooth motion.

"What did you want to do to these?" I asked him, becoming almost rough with my breasts as I fondled myself.

"Fuck," he cursed, undoing his pants. "Keep doing that."

I did, and he had himself naked in record time. He climbed on top of me, straddling my rib cage, his erection huge and hard between my breasts. His hands went over mine roughly, and he pushed my breasts around his cock, thrusting between once, twice. I gasped. I hadn't known that people even did this, but I was wildly turned on by it.

There isn't an inch of my body that he doesn't want to fuck. It was a heady thought.

He drew back, crawling down my body, and I protested.

"Quiet," he told me, throwing my legs over his shoulders, and burying his face between my thighs. He started licking softly. He lifted his head after only a few strokes of his tongue, propping his face on my pelvis. "Does that hurt?"

"No," I gasped.

He got back to work, licking every fold until I was gripping his hair and on the verge.

He spoke into my core. "Come," he told me, stroking my clit with a talented finger. It was a gentle touch, but it was enough. I came, crying out hoarsely. He had my body tuned to his touch like an instrument. It was intoxicating, and alarming.

He rubbed his erection along my sex very carefully. He crawled back up my body, placing his now wet member back on my chest. He handled my breasts, his eyes inscrutable.

"I'm going to fuck every part of your body. No part of you will

143

be left untouched by me."

"All tonight?" I gasped.

He laughed, giving me a wicked grin. *Capricious man.*

"No. There's no rush. I plan to take my time, violating every inch of you." With that ominous pronouncement, he began to thrust steadily.

My eyes ran over his beautiful body while he moved, his muscles working extraordinarily. His abs flexed with each movement, his arms bulging as he held my breasts in position for his cock.

I didn't know where to put my hands, so I ran them everywhere, drinking in his hard flesh with my fingertips.

"Look at me," he told me when my eyes had wandered for too long.

"I love your body," I told him.

He came on my chest, not even trying to contain the warm seed that coated my breasts in spurts. As he finished, he moved down lower to straddle my hips. He studied my wet breasts, then began to rub, coating my chest and ribs.

"Mmm," he murmured, still rubbing. "Mine."

It didn't take long for the unfamiliar liquid to start to turn sticky.

"Don't move. Time to clean you up." He left and returned quickly with warm, wet washcloths, cleaning me thoroughly.

He must have found the small towels under my bathroom sink, I noted in a disconnected kind of way. He was making himself right at home, digging through my things without asking. I didn't have the energy to care, and besides, his efficiency was too convenient not to appreciate in the moment.

I closed my eyes, ready to pass out.

He lay down beside me, pulling my back to his chest and throwing his arm over me.

"Mine," he whispered in my ear. I floated into a pleasurably deep sleep.

CHAPTER NINETEEN

Mr. Relentless

It was fully light out when I awoke. I stretched, feeling sore but good. I was alone in bed, but I could smell coffee.

I threw on the first thing I saw in my closet. It was the thin cotton shift of a nightgown I'd worn in the hotel the first night I'd spent with James.

I made my way slowly into the kitchen. It was empty, so I passed through into the small adjoining dining room. I leaned in the doorway to soak in the sight that greeted me there.

James wore only a pair of snug dark gray boxer-briefs.

Even his underwear looks expensive, I thought.

He held a coffee mug in one hand, his other arm running restlessly through his sandy hair. He was studying the paintings I'd arranged on the walls. I studied his flawless back. It was tan, of course. And it bulged with well-defined muscles. But it was also elegant, somehow, like the rest of him. His ass looked carved from stone. Unaccountably, I wanted to bite it, but I stifled the strange urge.

I licked a finger as I approached him, then rubbed it hard on the skin of his shoulder.

I knew a lot of girls that did spray tans. If his coloring was sprayed on, a little vigorous rubbing would reveal his secret. The lovely golden shade didn't rub off.

James shot me a baffled look over his shoulder. "You having fun back there?" he asked.

I lowered my hand, smiling sheepishly at him. "Sorry. Don't mind me."

He took my strange actions in stride, turning back to study the wall again.

He turned to look at me. His eyes were intense.

"Do you sell these?" He waved a hand at the wall of art.

I shook my head. "No. It's just a hobby."

He just raised a brow at me, raising his cup of coffee. "I made coffee."

I nodded. "Thank you."

I moved into the kitchen to make myself a cup.

He crowded behind me, kissing the side of my neck.

"How are you feeling?" he murmured against my skin.

"Good," I answered, taking a long draw of the dark liquid.

"It was torture, pulling myself out of bed with you lying there. I wanted you to wake up with me inside of you. But that will have to wait. You're still too raw."

I rubbed my back against his chest.

"How do you know?" I asked him.

He stilled. "I suppose I don't."

He sighed, a heavy sound, then stepped away. "Are you going to give me the tour? I want to see your house."

I shrugged, the thought making me self-conscious. I loved my house, and it was relatively new, and in good shape, but compared to what he was used to, it had to seem pretty shabby. Still, I showed him around.

The dining room and kitchen connected, and the living room doubled as an entryway, so it was a very quick tour. I had my paintings hanging everywhere, and he stopped for long pauses to study all of them.

"I'm not sure I like how many pictures you have of another man hanging all over your house," he told me with a raised brow.

I blushed, but only because I had remembered the picture I had begun of James on an easel in my backyard. I had forgotten to bring it inside, and I worried briefly that the weather had ruined it in the day I'd been away. I didn't want him to see it even more than I didn't want it to be ruined, though.

I'd check on it later, I decided quickly.

As for his comment about the handful of pictures I had of Stephan hanging around, I just ignored it. I wouldn't deign to respond to comments about Stephan and I. Either he was teasing, or he was jealous. Neither would matter. If he had an issue with Stephan, I would be showing him the door.

"Are you two somehow related?" James prompted, fishing in a way that made me tense up.

"Not by blood. He's my family, though. My only family." I was strung tight as I watched his face for a reaction. This was a deal or no-deal moment for us.

He just nodded, looking thoughtful, but making me relax instantly.

"I like him. It seems like he protects you," he finally said.

I felt so relieved that it scared me. I hadn't wanted to show him the door in the worst way. *That* thought made me panicky.

"You have no idea," I told him.

His eyes sharpened, and he tensed up. "What do you mean? I would like to have an idea, please."

I just shook my head, mentally kicking myself for saying something so untactful. The idea of having no idea would drive a man like him crazy, so I came up with a palatable answer.

"Just that we've been together since we were fourteen, and he's always been protective of me, since the day we met."

"Together? What does that mean, exactly?"

I shrugged. "You know, inseparable. Best friends."

He reached up and gripped the back of my neck lightly. His touch was light, but his eyes were hard and searching.

"What would I have to do to get you to open up to me?" he asked softly.

I didn't like this line of conversation. My mind worked furiously to try to get out of it.

"I would imagine you're as closed off as I am, Mr. Cavendish. So, you tell me. What would make you open up to someone?" I asked, thinking the tactic should work well.

I imagined that James's answer would be the same as mine. *Nothing.*

"For you, I'd take an exchange of information. You share something, I'll do the same. Sound fair?"

I eyed him uneasily. Unwillingly, I was tempted. Within reason.

"Do I get to choose the information I give?" I asked him cautiously.

He shrugged. "I'll take it if that's all I can get. I'll do the same. I'll start. My parents died when I was thirteen. I was left with an older cousin as a guardian. I detested him. He died a year and a half later, and it was one of the best days of my life. I disliked my next guardian, my Aunt Mildred, but she was a saint compared to the first one."

My eyes opened wide in shock. It was a random and strangely personal revelation, giving me some insight into James. I sincerely hoped that he didn't expect the same thing from me. I thought hard of something to tell him that I could bear to reveal. I sighed heavily when I realized the best way to distract him.

"I started painting a picture of you. It's in the backyard. It's embarrassing, but I couldn't seem to stop myself," I told him. It was a lesser evil by far, of all of the things that had popped into my head.

He grinned, and it was a heart-stopping grin. "So you do think about me, at least a little, when I'm not pursuing you relentlessly." He headed to my bedroom, where there was a sliding glass door into the backyard.

"One second. I need to punch in the code," I called, quickly doing so.

"Have I mentioned that I like your security?" James told me as I joined him in my bedroom.

He was opening the barred door that went over my sliding glass. It was an eyesore, but one that made me feel secure, and the bars had become popular in Vegas due to excessive break-ins, so it was fairly commonplace to see them. It didn't even make my house stand out. I had the thick bars mounted on my bedroom's sliding glass door, and covering all of my windows.

"Happy to please you," I told him, and he sent me a hot look.

"You have no idea, Bianca," he repeated my earlier words back at me. I stifled the urge to respond that I would like to have an idea.

He moved directly to the easel without asking. I just followed him. It was really a small price to pay for the knowledge he had given me. He was an orphan like me, and he'd had a rough time of it. Not homeless, but perhaps more alone. He hadn't been blessed to find a Stephan, like I had.

He studied the painting like he did most everything. Intently. It was only a rough outline of him so far, just his face and part of his torso, wearing a V-neck as he sometimes did. He hummed low in his throat.

"It's very good. Were you going to give it to me when you finished?"

I shook my head. "I was going to hang it in my bedroom to masturbate to," I told him, only half-joking.

His reaction was gratifying. He sent me a look that was pure heat and appreciation.

"You ever want me to pose for you, you let me know."

I brightened at the offer. "Yes, I do. I get much better results when I paint with my subject at hand."

I gestured at the view of the mountains behind my house. "It's why I have so many paintings of those." I tried to get the courage to ask him to pose nude, but couldn't quite do it.

"You have an extra bedroom you haven't shown me. Show it to me."

I wrinkled my nose at him. He was relentless, it seemed to me, about exploring every detail of my life.

He touched my nose with a finger. "It's so cute when you do that."

My nose wrinkled more, but then I tried to smooth it out. Being called cute by him just didn't do it for me. In fact, it kind of annoyed me.

How many cute girls does he go through in a week? As many as he wants, I supposed.

"My guest bedroom is tiny, and just storage at the moment. It basically holds all the paintings that I don't have room to hang."

He started moving instantly at that. "I'd love to see them."

I let out a frustrated noise, but the man always did what he wanted.

I leaned in the doorway while he rudely rifled through my guest room. There was a small guest bed, but even that was covered by some boxes and paintings. The room embarrassed me. I really needed to get it organized.

James made a sound of pleasure and pulled a canvas out from one of the many stacks of paintings leaning against the wall.

That was yet another reason I usually did watercolors. They took up very little space when finished. Just a piece of paper unless I framed them, whereas my numerous acrylics and few oils were on canvases that had taken over this room, my far more numerous watercolors occupied one small chest in the

150

corner.

It was a self-portrait, I saw, as he admired it. I cringed slightly. Self-portraits weren't my favorite. I usually only did them when I lacked for inspiration. I had painted this one a few years ago.

I'd used a picture Stephan had taken when I wasn't looking. I was wearing my cool, composed face, and it had interested me to paint myself that way, so enigmatic. I tried to behave that way, knew people viewed me as inscrutable, but I rarely felt it. It had pleased me that other people perceived me that way, and so I had painted it.

In the painting I was leaning against a counter, the one from our old apartment. My arms rested on the counter, my head tilted up and slightly away. But my eyes were a clear, pale blue.

We'd been having a party in our small apartment, I recalled. The picture had been Stephan's way of trying to draw me into the fun. I hadn't even noticed him until he'd taken several shots of me. I'd used the first picture to make the painting.

"I want this," James said softly. "Can I buy it from you?"

I gave him a very level stare. "Thats ludicrous. You can have it, if you want it. I never hang self-portraits. I can't imagine why you would want that, though. Where would you hang a thing like that?"

He just grinned. "Plural. As in, you have more?"

I rolled my eyes. "I do. They're in here, somewhere. As you can see, I don't have it organized. I have no idea where any specific painting is."

James just started rifling through my things with more focus.

I sighed, resigned to indulging his strange mood to dig into every part of my house.

"I'm going to make breakfast. You can have any pictures you want, but please don't take them if you're just trying to flatter me." I left before he could comment.

CHAPTER TWENTY

Mr. Accommodating

I made ham and eggs.   I needed to go to the grocery store, so it was the only thing in my fridge.   I had to keep a very clean kitchen, buying only things that I could use immediately or things that lasted for weeks before they went bad. It was one of the necessities of my job.

I made a huge portion for James, and a more reasonable plate for myself. I knew from my long experience with Stephan that a man James's size, no matter how fit, would put away a lot of food.   I was pleased to find a small block of extra sharp cheddar to top it with. Simple fare, but good.

I brought the plates and some bottles of cold water into the spare room.

James was digging through the mess with as much concentration as ever.

I saw that he had found four more pictures to add to his collection. The one on top was an oil picture of a lilly. I thought it an odd choice for him, but I just set his plate on the bed above where he crouched, digging.

I tried not to stare at him as I sat down on another cleared spot on the bed to eat, my plate balanced on my lap. He still only wore his boxer-briefs. It was beyond distracting.

"I made ham and eggs," I finally said, when he just kept digging. "It's nothing fancy, but it's getting cold."

He turned, sitting cross-legged on the floor and grabbing his plate. He grinned at me almost boyishly.

"It's like Christmas for me in here. It's not often that I find something I want that I don't have."

I can well believe that, I thought. Though what I couldn't imagine was why he would want my paintings. I still just wanted to think that he was trying to flatter me to get into my pants. Which was obviously unnecessary at this point. That, I supposed, was why it confused me so much.

He cleared his plate in short order. I still wasn't half done with my own when he took his last bite.

"That was fantastic. Thank you," he said, then got back to work.

I finished eating, then looked at the pictures he'd selected so far. Three of my self-portraits, and the lilly. As I was studying them, he found my chest of watercolors. He flung it open as though he had every right in the world. For some reason, I didn't even attempt stop him.

He added two more pictures to his selection almost immediately. More self-portraits, I saw.

I started to get antsy as he searched the chest. I was recalling a rather embarrassing self-portrait that I'd buried at the bottom. To hide it.

"I need to go run errands soon. I have absolutely no food for lunch, sooo…"

"Mmmk," he mumbled, but just kept digging. He singled out two more of my larger watercolor paintings, setting them on his pile. They were landscapes of the Vegas mountains, much like the ones I had in my living room. I actually liked them better than the ones that had ended up above my mantle, but they'd been too big for the mosaic.

I knew when he found the painting I was worrying about. He pulled out a smaller painting, and stilled, sucking in a sharp breath. He looked at it for so long that I walked to him, checking to see if my suspicions were correct. They were, of course.

It was on a not quite printer-sized piece of watercolor paper. My only fully nude self-portrait. Looking at it, I wasn't quite as embarrassed as I'd thought I would be. At least it was a better picture than I had remembered.

I had sat on a chair in my bedroom, in front of my full length mirror. I was sitting up very straight, and had even painted the paintbrush in my hand and the easel and board I was working on. My breasts were fully revealed, though my legs were closed modestly. Modestly for a nude. Just the barest hint of what lay between was revealed. My gaze was steady, though wide. My free hand lay on my thigh, clenched. My bare feet were arched, my toes pink. My hair had hung loose, though it didn't cover a thing.

"Exquisite," James said, tracing a fingertip along the page. "I don't know where to hang it. I should burn it, so no one else can ever see it, but I just couldn't do that. It's too perfect."

His hand shot to my leg where I stood to his back and side. I jumped, startled.

"You're too perfect. I need to travel with this one personally. Do you have a folder I could carry it in?"

I reached into the chest. His hand remained on my thigh, gripping it firmly even when I took a step forward. I pulled out a navy folder. I had them everywhere. They were handy for storing watercolors.

"Here. But if you take that painting, it's only fair that I get to paint a nude of you."

"As you wish, Buttercup," he told me, turning to plant a hard kiss on my stomach before hiding the nude in the folder.

"Go shower. I'm going to arrange for these paintings to be

transported and framed." He held up the folder. "Except for this one. This one I carry." He strode out of the room.

Unaccountably, I was a little bit shaky, but I headed to the shower without another word.

I was in the shower for a good ten minutes before James slipped in behind me. I had already washed, but he soaped me up again without asking, touching me everywhere. His rock-hard erection pressed against my back. I rubbed against it, and he pushed my hips away gently.

"Not until I check to see how raw you are," he said roughly. But he continued to touch me, rubbing my breasts gently for long minutes. My head fell back, and my mind went feverish.

"These must be sore, too, but I can't seem to keep my hands off. My self-control is apparently shot where you're concerned. I've never had this problem before." His voice was a rasp in my ear, as though he were telling me a dirty secret. It got me unbelievably hot. He shut the water off.

He toweled me off, quickly drying himself and wrapping the towel around his hips.

"Get on your back on the bed," he ordered me.

I moved to the bed, and felt his large presence behind me with every step. I sprawled on my back on the bed, my wet hair fanned out above my head.

He pulled my legs apart as he dragged my hips to the very edge of the bed. He was more masterful than rough as he handled me. He knelt between my legs, using a light touch to study me. I should have been embarrassed, but I was beyond it.

"I don't care if it hurts," I told him. And I didn't, not right then, though I had been extremely sore at work the day before.

"Quiet," he told me, his voice harsh. "My control is hanging on by a thread, but you're just too chafed. I rode you too hard that first night, and that morning. Fuck, I can't believe I did all of that to a virgin. I feel like a bastard, looking at all of that injured pink flesh." His fingers were still gently touching my petals as he examined my sex. "But I still want to fuck you so badly I can't see straight."

I wriggled against his fingers. "Just fuck me, then. Please."

He slapped the side of my butt, hard.

"Don't." He looked at me with troubled, beautiful eyes. "I'm going to need to be more careful with you. I didn't realize you could take so much without protesting, so I just kept going. Fuck. I shouldn't have taken you after that first time, but I'll remember that night for as long as I live. It was so perfect."

His words were bringing me to a fevered pitch. I stroked my breasts as he ranted. He gave me a hard look. Hard, but hot.

"Well, we'll have to do something about this." A wandering finger found my backside. I stiffened instinctively. He chuckled, withdrawing. "Not that."

Without another word, he buried his face between my legs with a purpose. He had me gasping out his name with an orgasm in less than a minute. He crawled up my body to kiss me wetly. I ran my hands everywhere I could touch.

"I love your body. I never get to touch you enough. I want to," I murmured into his mouth as he pulled back.

He fell back into a sprawl almost instantly, accommodating my whim. He folded his tan muscular arms behind his head, smiling. He was definitely all tender lover this morning, only glimpses of the dominant in him showing.

"Have at it, Love."

I didn't hesitate, using both of my hands to stroke his chiseled abs. Those starkly ridged abs made Brad Pitt in his prime look sub-par.

I kissed his abs as my hands moved higher, licking. He sucked in a breath. I moved up to his chest. His small nipples drove me wild, a shade of brown darker than his perfect skin. I stroked and licked up to his neck. Everything about him was just so long. His arms, his legs, his torso.

My gaze traveled south, to his quivering arousal. It was long too, and so hard and thick. I wanted to taste it the most, but knew my exploration would be over if I so much as touched it.

I went back to his neck, moving down to the defined line between his pecks. I nuzzled there, lingering.

I loved this spot, felt almost comforted when I buried my face there. I let myself linger there for long minutes. Reluctantly, I moved away.

I sucked at a nipple, biting down lightly. When he didn't protest, I bit harder, then sucked hard.

He moaned. My hands kneaded at his arms as I went back and forth between his nipples. He was so hard, but his skin was unbelievably smooth. I was getting so turned on that I kissed a path directly to his cock. I'd lost the control to stay away.

I cupped his scrotum, putting wet lips on his tip as I shifted for a better angle. He grabbed my thighs, moving me until I straddled his face. I was shocked when his tongue started licking me from that angle. His hand moved to the back of my head, pushing my surprised mouth back to his erection.

He spoke against me, his voice a low, vibrating rumble. I shuddered at the feel of it, and at his words. "Don't orgasm until I say. I want us to come at the same time like this."

I didn't answer, couldn't, as I sucked him into my mouth hungrily. The more he licked and nuzzled at me, the more furiously I sucked at him. I stroked his shaft hard with both hands, as he'd shown me, taking as much of him into my mouth as I could.

I came up for air once, breathing on his deep red tip when he sucked on my clitoris. His cock surged up at me furiously, and I took him back into my mouth.

"Come, Bianca." He breathed the words into my core.

I did come then, sucking him hard, my lips pulled over my teeth. He poured into my mouth at the same moment, and I swallowed as shudders wracked through me.

CHAPTER TWENTY-ONE

Mr. Bossy

He turned me onto my stomach. His fingers brushed lightly over my thighs and ass as he studied me.

"This healed well. Your skin loves a good spanking." A hand wandered between my legs, stroking, whisper soft. "You'd be in good shape if I hadn't been so rough. The ways I fucked you, on your first time…I can't stop thinking about it, but I still can't believe I didn't have more self-control."

I closed my eyes, just enjoying his touch. "I loved it. I wouldn't have wanted it any other way."

He stroked my hair at that.

"That's because you were made for me. But I still need to give you a few days to recover now, and that's regrettable." He suddenly slapped my ass.

"Get dressed, Buttercup," he told me, moving to the overnight bag he'd left by my bedroom door.

He dug into it, pulling out boxer briefs, then moved into my closet. I hadn't realized he had clothing hanging in there. And much more than a night's worth, which I found curious. Maybe he just liked to have his pick of clothes, I mused.

He moved from his clothing to my own, grabbing a white

sundress with sunflowers on it. He handed it to me. "Wear that," he told me. I didn't protest. It was comfortable enough. I grabbed a bra and some panties out of my dresser. He followed me there, digging through the drawer without asking. "Nice," he said. "I ordered you a few dozen more pairs. The last line of defense between me and your pussy is bound to take some casualties."

I laughed at the visual. *Strange, controlling, funny man,* I thought.

I went into my bathroom to get dressed. James was too distracting.

After I'd changed, I texted Stephan that we were almost ready, and that I'd come knock on his door when it was time.

Stephan always looked like a model, but he never needed more than ten minutes to get ready. I found it both convenient and infuriating, depending on the time of the month.

I sat down at my vanity and used the blow-dryer for about a minute on my hair. I would let it air dry the rest of the way. It would be pin straight when it dried, so I wouldn't worry about it. I put on just a touch of makeup.

James had dressed quickly, and sat on my bed, watching me, his hair damp. He wore a pair of navy cargo shorts that let me admire his long, muscular calves. He paired it with a light gray V-neck shirt that was tight enough to be distracting. It was the most casually dressed I'd ever seen him.

He combed his fingers through his hair and seemed to be ready to go.

I glared at him. "It's not right, someone looking that good with so little effort," I told him.

He just smiled at me.

I put my watch on, though I usually didn't wear a watch anywhere but work, where it was required. I thought it would please James. I was right. He rubbed my shoulders, his eyes warm as he studied me in the mirror. I leaned into the caress, closing my eyes.   His hands were positively magical.   He stopped, pulling me to my feet by my hands.

"Let's go."

An SUV stretch limo was parked outside, and I shot him an arch look. "Isn't that a bit much for errands?" I asked him.

He shrugged.   "I need to do some work while you guys run inside. I thought it would be more comfortable."

He pulled on my hand, tugging me to Stephan's house.   He knocked, and Stephan pulled the door open almost immediately.

He grinned at us, stepping out and locking up. He wore some plaid cargo shorts and a light blue polo.   He was in his full Abercrombie glory today.

Stephan kissed my cheek in greeting.   "Good morning, beautiful.   You are positively glowing today," he told me, and I blushed.

James squeezed my hand.

We headed to my favorite art supply store first. It was across town, so I stocked up on supplies when I went there, since I didn't make it often. James was practically plastered to my side in the limo, an arm thrown around my shoulders.   Stephan sat on a seat that faced the side of the car, lounging comfortably.

"I could get used to this.   Thanks for driving us, James," Stephan said with a happy smile.

James just nodded pleasantly, a hand absently stroking my hair. It was a little awkward at first, but I made myself relax into his hold.   It wasn't that I didn't like his touch.   In fact, my reluctance had more to do with liking it too much.

Stephan's phone dinged a text at him, and he took it out, muttering, "Excuse me."

He gave a little whoop when he read the message.   "Nice. Damien and Murphy have a line that mirrors all of our New York trips this month. I knew they were trying for it for the last few months, but they kept getting bumped. Their new bid starts this week, so they'll be on our layover this weekend."

I smiled. "Nice," I said.

I saw James looking a question at me. I tried to interpret the flight attendant speak into English for him. "Damien and Murphy are pilot friends of ours that always fly together. They just got a new schedule, and we'll be doing all of our New York layovers with them."

"Melissa will *love* Damien," Stephan muttered, texting furiously.

"And we won't have to watch her hooking up with that married captain anymore," I said, studying James. I didn't want him to feel left out of the conversation.

"Why will she love Damien?" James asked Stephan, his voice bland.

"Well, he's a captain, so he makes a decent paycheck. Also, he's hot. He has an australian accent and looks like Colin Farrell." As Stephan spoke, he never once looked up from his phone. *Was he tweeting about it? Who knew?*

I laughed. "He actually does. I never thought of it."

"Melissa will be chasing him like a bitch in heat."

I blanched a little at Stephan's harsh choice of words. It wasn't like him, but I knew why he disliked her so strongly. She'd brought out his protective side with the way she'd treated me.

I looked at James. His eyes were cold. Something had upset him. *Was he upset that Melissa would hook up with Damien? Was he interested in her? Had she given him her number, like she'd said?* I didn't want to ask him, so I looked away.

We were turning down Ramrod Street when I explained to James. "We might take awhile in there. They have a station where you can build your own frames, and Stephan needs to frame a picture."

James just nodded, getting his laptop out of its case. "Do you have a grocery list?" he asked.

"Yeah."

He held out a hand. "I'll give it to Clark. He can grocery shop next door. Stephan, if you have a list as well, I'll take it. I'll cover the groceries."

I started to protest. James just held up that hand. "You'll be cooking for me for the next few days. It seems a fair trade to me. Stephan, will you come have dinner with us tonight?"

Stephan accepted the invitation happily. I sent James a warm look. He knew how to butter me up, that was for sure.

"Do you both like sushi?" James asked.

We both nodded.

"Good. There's actually a very good place about five minutes from here. We'll stop by there when you've finished." With that, he gave his attention to his laptop, dismissing us.

We got out of the limo, grinning at each other.

"Your boyfriend is bossy," Stephan told me teasingly.

I grimaced. "He's not my boyfriend. We've only known each other for a few days. And I don't think he does the girlfriend thing."

He raised a brow. "So what does he do?"

I waved a hand at the limo. "He does this thing. I think he furiously pursues short, private, physical relationships."

Stephan gave me a slightly troubled frown. "And how do you feel about that?"

I shrugged. "I'm not sure. I don't want to think about it too much. The thought of something permanent terrifies me, so maybe this will be ideal for me."

He reached for my hand, looking sad. "Don't get hurt, Buttercup."

I shrugged. "Life hurts. As long as it doesn't kill us, we weather it."

He swallowed, nodding. I knew he wanted to say more, but he held his tongue to keep the mood from getting dark, as it could.

163

I stopped on the sidewalk before entering the store, looking at him squarely.

"I think he's good for me, in a way. I can't seem to resist him, and I have to face my fears when I'm with him. I find it liberating, if a little terrifying."

I paused, taking a few deep, even breaths.

"I think I'm going to do it. I'm going to the police. I need to tell them what I saw," I told him quietly, referring to the decade old incident that still haunted me.

His gaze searched mine. He knew what I meant, but he wanted to know why.

"I just need the closure. It's always somewhere at the back of my mind. And I'm tired of living with the fear. If I testify, maybe that monster will be behind bars where he can't touch me. And some sort of justice might bring me some semblance of peace."

He nodded. "Just tell me when. I'll be there with you."

"Soon. Maybe after this James thing blows over. A week or two."

His hand tightened on mine. "I get why a relationship would terrify you, of all people. But that doesn't mean you don't deserve more than a fling with this guy, or that you shouldn't try for something more."

I just shook my head. "I can't even entertain the notion right now, Stephan. Not with James. Trust me, I'm fine with what it is. I would feel better, though, if you approved."

He put his arm around me, squeezing. "I approve of anything that makes you happy. But if you're hurt at the end of this, that rich bastard is gonna have to sue my ass, because I *will* beat the shit out of him."

I was shocked by his words, though his tone was almost light. I studied him intently. He, like me, had a long and sordid history with violence.

Stephan had been raised with a strict mormon upbringing. He was an old-fashioned gentleman because of it, which I always found irresistibly charming.   I was also convinced that this was what had made him a hopeless romantic, always thinking everyone should get a happy ending, with their one true love.   This charmed me as well.   He had so many deeply ingrained, good, wholesome qualities that I had always believed stemmed from his deeply religious beginnings.   But he hadn't quite fit into the mold his parents had designated for him.

Stephan had been nine when his uncle had begun to abuse him sexually.   The sicko had been his father's brother.   He'd also been a pillar of their religious community, holding a position a few steps higher than Stephan's own father.

Stephan's father had looked up to his older brother, and when a ten-year-old Stephan had tried to talk to his father about it, he had been sharply reprimanded.   Stephan had told me that there had been no violent abuse from his father before that time.   But there was plenty after that.

His father had called Stephan a liar, while still blaming him for events he wouldn't even admit ever happened.   He'd begun to take offense at every little thing Stephan had done, calling the young boy 'wrong', and 'queer'.

The beatings had increased and escalated until Stephan had begun to fight back.   He was big from an early age, and he had told me he'd made a decent attempt at defending himself against his father, after a time.

Stephan put up with the near-constant abuse until he was fourteen, when he said he'd become so fed-up he didn't even care if he lived anymore.   He had confessed to his parents then that he was gay.   His father had beaten him severely, taking nearly as much damage himself from a then strong Stephan, then ordered him to leave.

Stephan had always hated violence, but his bastard of a father had guaranteed that he was good at it from a young age.

I poked Stephan in the ribs with an elbow. "You hate to fight," I told him.

"Yes, I do.   But I'm good at it.   And I'm guessing Mr. Cavendish never had to fight in a ring to keep from starving."

I flinched, remembering those days. "It won't come to that, ok? I'll be just fine at the end of this thing, and you won't even think about throwing a punch."

Stephan nodded, but I wasn't entirely convinced.   I finally dragged him into the store.   We'd spent enough time dwelling on unpleasant things.

CHAPTER TWENTY-TWO

Mr. Doting

Stephan headed straight for frames while I went with a shopping cart and replenished my supplies. I stocked up well.

I was in a mood to create. I grabbed several varying sized canvases and even more watercolor paper. I selected a few new acrylic colors carefully, finding a blue that was absolutely perfect. Painting was all about color for me.

I grabbed half a dozen tubes of watercolors that just needed replacing. I stocked up on some cleanup supplies that the paint shop had cheaper than everywhere else. The prices at the eccentric shop were what drew me from across town to resupply.

It took me a good five minutes to locate a tiny sable brush that I used for details. It was a brush I had to replace often. When its bristles started to soften, it didn't do me much good. I bought two, and some new oil paints, since I would be saving money now at the grocery store.

It was a nice feeling, quite a relief really, to be able to get a few extra goodies for my coveted hobby. I tried not to feel guilty for allowing someone to help me out in such a way. But it had been hard not to refuse the offer. The order, rather.

My cart was uncharacteristically full when I finally sought out Stephan, who still agonized over his frame choice. He was very particular about his home decor. That made it doubly flattering to me that he chose to decorate nearly all of his walls with my paintings.

He showed me the five choices he'd narrowed it down to. I zeroed in on a heavy, dark, roughly carved pattern immediately.

"This one," I told him.

He gazed at me, sending me his best 'Puss in boots' pleading look. I smiled, starting to put the frame together for him. I had planned to, anyways. Stephan would butcher it, and I had the touch for this sort of thing.

I got wrapped up in the process, using the picture Stephan had brought to double check my work. I hammered the V shaped nails in lightly and slowly, which was the trick. Stephan tended to hammer them straight through to the other side with one strike.

When I finally finished, I held the finished art up to Stephan, smiling. He beamed back. He had been engrossed on his phone nearly the entire time I'd worked, which was his habit. He was the social butterfly of our duo, constantly texting someone, updating his Facebook page, or throwing out Tweets.

I went first through the one open checkout line. I was starting to feel a little remorseful about splurging as the price began to rise even higher than I'd anticipated. I really didn't want to have to put some things back. That was an embarrassment I hadn't had to suffer for years.

It would be a close thing, I realized, as the price grew higher. But as I got my debit card out, the checker held up a hand.

"It's all been paid for, Ma'am." I was speechless as she bagged the last of it. I felt grateful and helpless all at once.

Probably his intention, I thought absently.

Stephan's purchases were covered as well, though he hadn't

wracked up anywhere near the bill that I had.

"It's wrong to allow him to do all of this, isn't it?" I asked Stephan.

Stephan shrugged. "Why? He's doing something nice and thoughtful. It's not a crime to let him dote on you."

Clark met us halfway through the parking lot, taking the shopping cart solicitously. He managed to both push it to the car and get our door opened before we could reach it.

I nodded at him, smiling warmly. "Thank you, Clark," I told him.

He gave me a surprisingly shy smile in return. He was a large black man with a bald head and big dark shades. His suit looked expensive and professional. He looked so intimidating, but had the nicest smile. He nodded back politely.

"My pleasure, Ms. Karlsson," he said, surprising me by knowing my last name.

I slid onto the cushy seat next to James. He was on the phone, his computer open. He didn't look at me or speak, just placed a possessive hand on my knee as I sat next to him.

Stephan bounced into his seat, grinning. I could tell he loved getting the royal treatment, as we were today.

It went a long way towards silencing my protests. Denying myself something was easy. Denying Stephan, on the other hand...

James stayed on the phone as Clark started driving. He was giving short, crisp, cold answers to the poor soul on the other end. His hand would occasionally tighten on my leg, as he tensed. "If I need to find new management for my New York offices, I will do so. I expect a level of competency that you're not proving to me at present." He paused, gripping my leg.

He glanced at me absently, and his grip turned into an apologetic stroke.

Clark stopped the car, getting out and heading into a Sushi place. It must have been the one that James had been talking about. James just stayed on his phone, listening and squeezing my leg.

Clark was back in the car surprisingly quickly, his arms full of takeout bags. He began to drive again. I assumed we were headed home.

"How is it that I can be absent from every other property for weeks or months at a time, and things still run smoothly? It seems obvious to me that this is a management issue." James's voice was growing in agitation. I shot Stephan a look. He was on his phone, of course.

My hand covered James's experimentally, then ran up to his arm, carefully avoiding the spot on his wrist with the thin lines of scars. I was avidly curious about those scars, but of course I wouldn't ask. It would be inviting similar inquiries about myself.

I clutched the back of his bicep, rubbing tentatively. I wasn't accustomed to this touching thing.

I leaned against him, putting my cheek to his back as he leaned forward. I moved my hand to his leg, the other to his shoulder to massage tentatively.

He froze at my touch. I started to pull back. He moved his phone away from his face.

"Don't," he told me, putting my hand back on his leg. Neither of us was used to me doing the touching, but it didn't seem unwelcome.

I rubbed his leg lightly and he seemed to relax, bit by bit.

"Make it happen. This is your chance to prove yourself, for better or worse." He ended the call, shutting his tiny laptop and stowing both into the bag near his feet.

He spared a brief glance towards an occupied Stephan. He grabbed the back of my head, gripping my hair firmly and kissing me. It was a hot kiss, and I tried to draw back. This was no way to act in front of Stephan. He gripped me tighter, sweeping a tongue into my mouth. I had just started to soften when he pulled back.

"It makes me wild when you touch me," he whispered roughly. "Remember that the next time you touch me in front of other people. Having an audience or even being in public won't stop me from touching you back. This is my only warning."

He sat back, but pulled me hard against his side.

Was he somehow staking his claim in front of Stephan? I just couldn't tell with him.

"How was the shopping?" he asked.

"Great. Thank you for, um, for buying everything."

He surprised me by kissing me again roughly.

"Thank You. For all of those wonderful paintings that you so generously gave me, with no thought for recompense."

I flushed. I wasn't that comfortable with compliments in general, and praise for my painting was a novelty, since so few people had witnessed it.

Stephan finally put down his phone. He'd kept his painting in a bag and brought it into the car with us. He pulled it out, showing it proudly to James.

"Isn't she amazing?" he said proudly. "She even built the frame."

James studied the painting. "She is."

"My whole house is covered in her paintings. Should we eat over there, so you can check it all out?"

James agreed readily. "Yes, thank you. And I have a favor to ask you, Stephan." James arm tightened around me as he spoke, almost as though he was afraid I would try to get away at his next words.

"Sure, man. What's up?"

"I've studied Bianca's paintings extensively, and I think she has enough accomplished work for a gallery showing," James began.

James casually covered my mouth when I tried to speak. "I have a gallery in New York. I can have my people handle all of the details. As you can see, she's going to resist the idea. I need you to help me talk her out of her reservations." He uncovered my mouth, but I was suddenly speechless.

"I've been collecting art since I was a teenager. I have an eye for it, and I know she has a rare talent." James continued when neither of us spoke.

Stephan looked shocked, then ecstatic. "Yes, she does. You have to do this, Buttercup. I will have an absolute conniption if you don't."

I said the first thing that came to my mind. "Most of them are desert landscapes. There is no way that would go over well in New York." Of all of the things I found impossible about his proposal, I didn't know why that detail was at the forefront of my thoughts, of all things.

James smiled, a triumphant smile. It was mesmerizing. The smile of a savage conquerer. And I'd just given him what he wanted.

"You never know, they might like a change of scenery, but that will be for my gallery people to decide. I have a gallery in L.A as well, and even a small one on the strip here in Vegas. The Vegas one is mostly a tourist attraction, though. I wouldn't consider it for a showing."

"All I need you to do is to set aside anything you don't want shown, and to name the pictures that you'd like named. I'll send a sampling to both galleries so they can give me some feedback before we set up a showing. Also, I think some of the work you have displayed around the house could sell really well as prints, if you'd consider something like that."

I thought back to all of the pictures he'd set aside. "So that's what you were getting? Samples for the galleries?"

He looked at me like I'd gone insane. "No, of course not. Those are for my own collection. You and I will decide together what to send as samples."

I felt a wave of insecurity. "I have no training. I-"

He covered my mouth. "None of that matters, Love. You've

either got it or you don't. And you have it. Now tell me you agree."

I didn't agree or disagree, but just sat for awhile, stunned. I did want this, wanted it badly, though I'd never even considered that something like this could happen. And I knew that it wouldn't have, if a billionaire hadn't taken a sudden, obsessive interest in every aspect of my life. I supposed that was my biggest reservation about the whole thing; the fact that this was all just another way for him to dote on me.

"Will you take a cut, for your trouble, if I sell anything?" I finally asked.

He raised a brow at me. "I wasn't planning on it, no." He managed to sound insulted with the small statement.

"I would feel better if you did. The gallery will at least charge for putting on the showing, right?"

He sighed. "That is usually the standard procedure," he said carefully.

Stephan burst out suddenly, his tone thick with exasperated annoyance. "Oh, for God's sake, Bianca! How can you say no to this? You have a rare opportunity here, and if your work sells, it sells. If it doesn't, it doesn't. What's the hangup?"

He was using a certain tone he had, a tone that asked 'Where's your backbone?' without him having to utter the words. It made my spine straighten, which was the point.

I nodded. "Okay, I'll do it. When should we select the samples?"

James pulled me into his lap, kissing me way too passionately for anywhere but the privacy of a bedroom.

"Thank you, love," he murmured against my mouth, then started kissing again. His hands stayed firmly on my hips, holding me tight in his lap. But his mouth was positively obscene.

I couldn't forget that Stephan sat just a few feet away, but I also couldn't keep from responding. I tried to stifle a little moan as his tongue stroked into my mouth.

He bit my lip, hard.

I gasped, my hands gripping his rock-hard shoulders. I could feel his conspicuous erection against my hip. As his tongue swept in again, I sucked on it. That made him pull back, giving me a hot but censorious look.

"That will get you fucked in a hurry, Love," he whispered, but I figured Stephan could still hear us, in such a small space.

I glared at him. "You started it."

I heard Stephan stifle a laugh.

James just grinned wickedly.

CHAPTER TWENTY-THREE

Mr. Volatile

Lunch was a happy affair. James and Stephan seemed to be getting more and more chummy. They joked comfortably while we ate sushi at Stephan's dining room table.

James had been right, of course. The sushi was great. And the selection Clark had collected was vast. It was literally enough to feed ten people.

I gamely insisted on using chopsticks, picking out a Philadelphia roll and some shrimp tempura to start, dipping it generously into soy sauce mixed with chili sauce.

"You joining us at that bar in New York again on Friday night? Same time, same place," Stephan was saying to James.

James reached over, placing that familiar hand at my nape. "I was actually hoping Bianca would come see my apartment on Friday. Could I steal you away for a night, Love?"

I swallowed my mouthful of shrimp tempura. I was more than a little curious to see the playground he had mentioned. Equal parts thrill and trepidation coursed through me just thinking about it.

"Yes, you could," I said simply. James sent me a scorching look, then went back to chatting with Stephan.

After lunch, James got a tour of Stephan's house and again studied every piece of my art like his life depended on it. He took several pictures with his phone.

We stayed at Stephans until late afternoon. The two men found a surprisingly great deal to talk about, from politics to sports, to movies, to cars. I was silent for a good deal of it, simply taking in the novelty of the two men in my life interacting like it was the most natural thing in the world. When they finished talking, we watched TV.

I didn't have a television, so the only TV I did watch was at Stephan's house. We watched a few episodes of New Girl, a show Stephan had recently made me watch until I'd realized that I loved it. I was behind by at least a dozen episodes, but I was always behind on TV.

I laughed out loud at the show. James seemed to be enjoying himself, though he watched me more than he watched the screen. He smiled and touched me constantly, keeping me close to his side. I loved his touch, so I didn't protest, although the whole thing was a little surreal for me.

When the third episode ended, I stood.

"I need to cook dinner," I told them. It was already nearly 4:30. "I was going to grill some chicken, and cook some asparagus and couscous. That sound okay to everyone?" I asked. I was cooking one of my healthier meals, trying to cater to James's preferences.

"Sounds great! I love that blackened marinade thing you do on grilled chicken, Bee," Stephan said.

"I can't wait," James said.

Stephan was still watching TV. "You need any help?" he asked me.

"Nah. It's an easy meal. I'll text you when it's ready."

"I need to make some calls," James told me as I let us into my house. He was carrying the bag with his laptop. "Where would it be most convenient for me to set up shop?"

I shrugged. "Anywhere that's not directly in my way while I'm cooking."

He set up in the dining room, watching me cook while he worked, talking on the phone nearly constantly, taking call after call.

He cursed suddenly, and I looked back, startled.

"I forgot that was Friday," he was saying. His tone turned dry. "It slipped my mind. Fuck." He listened for a few moments, looking agitated. "Yes, yes, set it up. I know. Drop it. I said set it up."

He looked at me, trouble in his eyes. He ended the call, then closed his eyes and cursed fluently.

I went back to cooking. It had been deeply ingrained in me at a young age not to pry, so I didn't. If he wanted to tell me something, he would. But the curiosity was killing me.

"I forgot about a charity event that I can't miss on Friday evening," he told me, his tone careful. "I don't have to be there until maybe ten, so we'll have until then to spend together. You can, of course, stay at my place while I attend. I'll duck out at the earliest possible opportunity."

My spine stiffened at the realization that this was what the 'no dating' part meant. He would leave me at home like a dirty little secret while he met with his peers.

"That's alright," I said in a carefully neutral tone. "I'd rather stay at my hotel room. It's an early morning for me. I'll just leave your place when you do on Friday night."

"I would prefer that you not leave," he said in his most polite, cajoling voice. "I promise you won't be late in the morning."

I shot him a level stare, but quickly went back to prepping the chicken. "If you're leaving that night, then so am I."

He sucked in a breath.

"Are you upset?" he asked, sounding alarmed.

"I'm not," I told him.

"Why won't you stay with me on Friday, then?"

"I don't want to stay there if you're going out. I'll leave when you do," I repeated.

"What can I do to change your mind?" he asked, his tone turning seductive.

"You can't. Don't bother trying. We have an arrangement based solely on our preferences. This is what I prefer." My voice was cold and getting colder. I wasn't angry, but I was... resigned. Resigned to the idea of him disappointing me. And even more resolved not to give him more than I was willing to lose.

"What if I made it an order? Or a condition?" he asked, his tone getting hard.

I made my face into its best expressionless mask and looked at him. "Then this association may end even sooner than I had realized."

His jaw clenched, a tick starting up in his cheek. "I can't back out of this. It was my mother's charity, and I'm expected to attend, even to say a few words."

I didn't miss the fact that asking me to come with him hadn't even occurred.

"I don't know why you're pressing the issue. So I'll sleep at my hotel. What is the problem?" My words were growing clipped with frustration.

"I can't head back to Vegas until Monday. We won't see each other for days," he said, as though that explained his reaction.

I shrugged. "Just call me when we're in the same city. What is the issue?"

My voice had become so brisk that I could hear a hint of my mother's long ago accent surface. It usually only came out when I was deeply shaken. He had an affect on me that I didn't want to acknowledge, even to myself, but even my voice seemed to know it.

He had moved in behind me, and he gripped my hair softly, breathing warmly on my neck as he spoke. "Are you so unaffected by me?"

I was breathing hard now, but I answered calmly enough. "I went twenty-three years without sex. A few days certainly won't kill me. What do you think I'll do when we're finished? I doubt I could find another lover right away." My accent thickened slightly as I realized at the end that I was *trying* to goad him.

It came back to me way too easily, the accent I had heard and affected for most of my young life. It surfaced only with strong emotions. It both terrified and titillated me, what I would found down the road of his fury.

He growled, literally growled, into my neck. "I'm going to punish you for that."

"Yes, I know," I breathed, dreading and wanting it in equal parts.

He wrenched himself away, sitting back in his chair in the dining room. He seemed too big for the room suddenly, his eyes livid and wild.

"You're playing with me," he said raggedly.

His assessment of the situation surprised me. I sent him a questioning look.

"Is that how it seems to you?" I asked, stunned by the notion.

He ran a hand over his face and scraped it through his golden-streaked hair.

"You're tying me in knots, yet you remain unaffected yourself. Are you just waiting for a reason to end this? That's the impression I'm getting at the moment. And that drives me fucking crazy, since I don't have a clue what will tip the scales against me."

I finished prepping the chicken, putting the marinating dish in the fridge until I was ready to grill it. I moved to the asparagus.

"I don't know what to tell you, James," I finally said. "Perhaps I can't give you what you want."

"I want you!" His fist made me jump as it struck the tabletop with a jarring boom.

"If you ever use your fists on me, that will be a reason," I told him quietly, watching that clenched fist and trying not to flinch.

He looked instantly remorseful, and I knew from his reaction that the stark terror that always resided somewhere inside of me had revealed itself, at least a little.

He approached me, and I tried not to cringe away. I was determined to face the fear, not to curl into a ball as I had as a child. He hugged me very carefully from behind. I let him, because I would have felt like a coward if I ran.

"I would never do that, you have to believe me. I would never use my fists on you. I'm so sorry if I scared you."

I shrugged. It was a jerky motion. "As long as we're clear."

"I never saw it before, but I scare you, don't I?" he asked, a strange edge to his voice.

I tried to concentrate on washing and breaking the asparagus.

"Is this an information exchange again? Are we sharing?" I asked archly.

He blew out a frustrated breath. "What do you want to know about me?"

A question popped immediately into my head. I hated it, but I hated not knowing more. "When was the last time you had sex, before the first time with me?"

He cursed. "I don't think you want to know that. I don't think that's good for our relationship, to tell you that."

I shrugged a tiny shrug, and he cursed again.

"That damn shrug is the most infuriating thing I've ever seen! What does it mean? That you don't give a damn, one way or another?"

I shrugged again. "It means tell me or don't tell me. But if you want my information, you'll give me yours."

"About eight days, I think. The day before I met you," he said, and I felt him watching my face like a hawk.

So it was as I had suspected, I thought, keeping my face

blank. *He does this all the time. I was right to place no stock in this.*

I just nodded, though unaccountably, my chest hurt a little.

"Yes, you scare me," I told him, after a very long silence, while I processed his answer. "But I'm irrevocably fucked up, so you excite me in equal measures. I find it liberating, to let someone control me. Someone who makes me tremble with fear. I've spent a great deal of my life running from the things that scare me, so this has been illuminating for me." My voice was quiet, but that damned accent was back.

He stiffened and backed away from me, looking aghast.

I glanced over my shoulder, surprised. "Is that unusual? Isn't that how this little game is played? I just assumed that most of the women who liked pain with pleasure were like me. But I suppose you are probably a far bigger expert than I am about that."

I studied him closely. His face held a harsh sort of tension, though I could see that he was trying to hide it.

"I don't want you to fear me," he said, his voice raw. "I want to make you nervous and skittish and submissive, but not scared. I want you to trust me."

I blinked at him, at a loss. "I'm sorry."

I went back to cooking, and he fell silent.

CHAPTER TWENTY-FOUR

Mr. Charming

"You get a faint accent sometimes. What is that?" he asked, breaking the long silence.

It was almost a relief to have him do something other than just stare at me, brooding, though I didn't care for the question. I would have preferred that he not notice my slip.

"Another exchange, so soon?" I asked cooly. "I would have thought the last one was enough for one night."

He didn't speak for a long time, though I knew without looking that he was angry.

"Fine. Ask me anything," he said through clenched teeth.

"How many women have you slept with?" I asked, and immediately wanted to kick myself. If I was going to reveal my feelings so recklessly, I would have preferred a better question.

"A lot. I haven't been counting. More than I'm proud of. Mostly submissive's in the last five years or so, and, for the most part, very short acquaintances."

"Have you ever had a serious relationship?" I plowed on, hoping he wouldn't make me reveal two things as well, though if he tried, I was ready to point out that he hadn't technically answered *my* first question.

"No. I was basically a slut in college, if I'm honest. I fucked any hot woman I saw. And after that, I found girls with very specific tastes, but it was never about anything but sex and dominance."

I sighed, not knowing if I was relieved or appalled. I'd have to examine my feelings later.

"I was born in the states," I began. "My parents, however, were both from Sweden and spoke with heavy accents. I had a slight accent myself, until they were gone. Then I tried to lose it. It comes back sometimes. I don't know why."

"It's lovely. I don't know why you would make an effort to disguise it."

I gave him my little shrug, not looking at him. "Stephan and I stood out enough already. We attended a few high schools together. We were inseparable even then, but I didn't want to make us stand out even more with a strange accent. We were already the only two ridiculously tall blonds at every school we went to. We were a head taller than everyone else there."

I glanced at him.

He was focused on me with that certain look on his face that made me think he was soaking up every scrap of information I fed him.

I fell silent. He had actually gotten me to chat about myself. I was a little dismayed at the realization.

Eventually James went back to answering his phone, and I went outside to put the chicken on my tiny charcoal grill. I texted Stephan that dinner would be ready in twenty minutes.

He brought a bottle of red wine, revealing it with a flourish.

I gave him a wry smile. We both knew he would be the only one drinking it. He grinned back, going directly into the kitchen to open it and pour himself a glass.

"Would anyone like some?" he asked politely.

James shook his head, ending his phone call quickly.

I refused, and James sent me a warm look. The man did not

like alcohol, it was clear.

I served dinner as soon as it was ready, and there wasn't even a hint of awkwardness while we ate dinner, chatting amiably. I enjoyed it while it lasted. Both men complimented the simple meal lavishly.

"So Bianca tells me you two went to high school together here in Las Vegas. And that you towered a head above everyone else there."

Stephan laughed, sending me a surprised but pleased look.

"Yes," he said. "Everyone called us Barbie and Ken. They all thought we were a couple, since I carried her backpack and walked her to every class."

James smiled a cheshire cat smile.

Sneaky bastard, I thought. I saw his plan clearly now. He was going to get some free information out of Stephan.

"Bianca wouldn't admit it at the time, but the nickname embarrassed the hell out of her," Stephan continued.

James was all charm and smiles now, a man getting everything he wanted through a clearly easier route. "And what about her other nickname? Where did Buttercup come from?"

"Remember that old movie, Princess Bride?" Stephan asked James, not even hesitating to open up.

James nodded.

"We used to love that movie. This..." Stephan's glance shot to mine as he paused, "place where we used to hang out a lot used to show it on movie night. It was the *only* movie on movie night. Ever. We could both quote you every single line. So I took to calling her Princess Buttercup. You have to admit she kind of looks like the actress in the movie, the one that played the princess. And as a teenager, she even kind of acted like her, very haughty and proud, but still so sweet to me. She was annoyed with the nickname at first, but it grew on her when it became just Buttercup."

"Good movie. Now I want to watch it again. I haven't seen it since I was a kid," James said, still smiling.

Stephan smiled brilliantly. "I can't think of anything I'd like to do more. I have the movie at my house. And ice cream. What do you say, Buttercup? Dessert and a movie at my place tonight?"

I agreed readily enough.

Stephan headed next door to find the movie and get his house ready. We stayed behind to clean up dinner.

James insisted on helping, clearing the table and washing dishes while I put the food away.

"This is not exactly what I pictured when you talked about not dating," I told him carefully. "Hanging out with my best friend and watching movies feels pretty personal."

He turned to me, looking baffled. "I never said anything about not getting personal. I intend for us to get very personal, Buttercup."

His answer perplexed me, but I chalked it up to him being too rich and spoiled. Even his most casual affairs had to have a rich eccentricity to them…

We watched the movie and had ice cream and then popcorn at Stephan's house. It was a highly enjoyable day overall, I thought, even with some bumpy conversations in the road.

We got ready for bed in silence later, and my body sang with anticipation as I lay down to wait for James, who was still in the bathroom.

He joined me a few minutes later, sliding in beside me and spooning me from behind. I tensed, waiting to see what kind of a move he would make, but he just nuzzled against my hair and settled down to sleep.

I tried to turn to him, but he kept me securely in place, placing a soft kiss on my temple.

"I'm letting you recover for a few days, Love. Just sleep. I'm content to hold you for tonight."

I was in that house again. I lay in my hard, tiny bed. I was hugging my knees to my chest, rocking and rocking, and trying to ignore the harsh shouts just a few thin walls away.

If I stayed in my room, it would all go away. They would forget I was even here and in the morning my Dad would sleep all day and leave us in peace so I could tend to my Mother.

But that wasn't meant to be. Not this time.

The yelling grew louder, my mother's shouts turning into terrified screams. When I couldn't stand the horrible noises a moment longer, I crept quietly through the house to investigate.

In spite of my overwhelming fear, my need to at least attempt to aid my mother almost always thrust me into the violent thick of things.

I looked down at my thin bare feet, wishing I knew where some clean socks were. I was so cold, an achy kind of cold, down to my very soul.

My parents were speaking in Swedish, and I pieced together some hysterical words as I got closer to the kitchen where they fought.

"No, no, no. Please, Sven, put that away."

My father's voice was an angry roar. "You've ruined my life. You and that brat. I've lost everything because of you. My fortune, my inheritance, and now, my luck. You've taken everything from me, just by living. Tell me why I shouldn't take everything from you, you silly cunt?"

"When you're sober, you'll regret it. We have a child together, Sven. Please, just go to sleep. If you sleep on it, you'll feel better."

"Don't you dare tell me what to do! Fuck sleep. Fuck you. And fuck that little brat. Look at her, hovering in the door, frozen like a frightened little mouse." His cold eyes went to me.

I was frozen in place, as he'd said.

He changed his tone when he spoke to me, and it turned into

a mockery of a gentle tone. "Why don't you join us, sotnos? Come be with your pretty Mama."

I moved to my mother, having learned a very long time ago not to disobey him when he was in this mood.

He sneered at the two of us when I stood beside her.

I was in my early teens and tall, already taller than my mother, but he towered over us both.

My mother didn't look at me, didn't reach for me. I knew she didn't want to draw more attention to me. She tried to protect me, as I did her, though she did a better job of it than I did.

"Look at my pretty girls. The daughter is even prettier than the mother. What use, then, is the mother? Tell me why you're useful, Mama?" he asked her.

I didn't hear her answer. My gaze was focused solely now on the object he was holding at his side. It was a gun. My gut clenched in dread. The gun was a new and terrifying addition to this violent scene.

My gaze flew back to my father's face as a laugh left his throat. It was a cackle of a laugh, dry and angry. I began to back away, shaking my head back and forth in denial.

"Wrong answer, cunt," he said.

He waved the the pistol in front of her. "You can't take your eyes off of this. Do you want it? Would you like me to give this to you? Take it, if you want it. You think I can't touch you with a gun in your hand?"

My mother watched him, her eyes almost blank with terror. She must know, as I did, from the mocking tone of his voice, that he was testing her. She would pay dearly if she took the gun from him, even if he had told her to.

He laughed. "I insist. Take the gun."

Unexpectedly, and horrifyingly, she did. She pointed it at him with hands that shook.

"Get out," she said, her voice tremulous and awful with her terror. "You can't do these things, especially in front of our daughter. Get out, and don't come back." She was sobbing, but she managed to pull the hammer back.

He laughed again. With no fear and no effort, he grabbed her hand. His hand covered one of hers, ripping the other one away. He turned the gun, slowly and inexorably pointing it away from himself and pushing it into her mouth.

I had backed myself against the wall as I watched their exchange, but when I saw his clear intent, I suddenly rushed forward, sobbing.

"Mama," I cried.

I stopped as though I'd run into a wall when my father pulled the trigger, covering us, and the entire room, in bright red blood and gore.

My horrified eyes met my father's. His showed no expression at all.

I screamed, sitting up.

I was out of the bed and in the bathroom as fast as my body could move. I began to scrub at my face, over and over again. My breath was shaky and gasping.

The light turned on behind me.

"Are you alright?" James asked, his voice soft with concern.

I couldn't look at him. I especially couldn't look at my reflection. I hadn't had that dream in a very long time. I usually couldn't look at myself for days after I had that dream.

"Yes. Just an old nightmare. I need to be alone, please."

I turned on the shower, knowing that the sink could never get me clean enough to wash off all of that blood and gore.

I stepped into the shower without checking to see if he'd listened. I got under the still cold spray, shivering and hugging myself. I sank to the bottom of the tub as the water turned warmer.

I didn't realize that I'd left my thin shift on until James was pealing it off of me.

"Don't," I warned. He ignored me, sitting behind me to curl himself around me. "I just need to be alone," I told him.

"Not anymore, Love," James murmured into my ear.

I didn't cry. I didn't break down. I just washed myself, again and again, until James took over the chore, turning the scrubbing into soft strokes.

"You ready to dry off and go back to bed?" he asked, after several minutes under the spray.

I nodded.

He dried me and carried me back to bed, cradled like a child. He wrapped me in the covers, then wrapped himself around me. He stroked my hair comfortingly until I drifted back to sleep.

We passed the next day together pleasantly, James staying almost glued to me the entire day.

I woke up first, watching him sleep for awhile, marveling at his beauty. The sun streamed into my bedroom, touching pieces of his skin. It looked flawless even in the bright sun, his tan set off darkly against my pale blue, washed-out sheets.

I made myself get out of bed. I was infatuated, and it wasn't a condition that I planned to cultivate.

I threw on a thin cotton sundress, not bothering with any kind of underwear. I slipped quietly from the room.

I mentally beat myself up as I brewed a pot of coffee. I was feeling things that I was too smart to be feeling about a man like that.

At the end of this, I must at least keep my pride, I thought. *And my heart*, I added to myself, cringing, because I knew I already felt too much for the mercurial man.

James joined me not long after I'd made myself a cup of coffee.

I leaned against the counter, sipping it.

He made himself a cup and perched a hip on the counter at my side. He was wearing only black boxer-briefs, and they were tight enough to show me his clear, heavy arousal.

I looked deliberately away from the sinful display, my eyes fixed sightlessly on the cupboards.

He took a sip of my coffee and winced. I laughed. I made my coffee strong. It wasn't for everyone. He took another drink, trying to adjust to the harsh flavor.

"You walking around like that should be illegal," I told him, without looking at his body again.

He smirked, eyeing up my tiny sundress, and my conspicuous lack of underwear. I was way too busty to get away with going braless and not have it be obvious.

"I could say the same about you."

"You're a tease," I told him.

"I am not that. A few days won't kill us. Besides, I need to prove to myself that I can exercise some self-control where you're concerned."

This was news to me. "Why?"

"Your...pain threshold is a concern to me. I need to know that I can put your welfare before my own impulses. I would hate myself if I went too far with you. I know I'm a bastard, but even *I'm* not that much of a bastard.

My brows shot up. He had been so much more caring than I had expected him to be. I was surprised he thought of himself that way.

"Why do you think you're a bastard?"

His expression darkened. "I know it's all consensual, but the fact is, I like to hurt women during sex. There's a reason you fear me. My strongest impulse is to control and to dominate, but make no mistake, I'm a sadist. It doesn't exactly make me a good guy."

I was sad for him, and the weak part of me wanted to ease his torment.

But how could I? I had my own demons that I didn't know how to control. My need to comfort him won out. The need to comfort us both.

"Even masochists need lovers," I told him, my tone gentle. "What would a girl like me do without someone like you? Perhaps everyone is good for someone."

He leaned down and kissed me. "Thank you. What a beautiful thing for you to say to me. Just when I think you don't care for me, you give me some hope."

I looked away, embarrassed.

We picked out samples from my paintings for hours in the morning. James seemed endlessly patient and didn't pressure me to choose.

I held up the two small paintings I was debating about.

"Which one, do you think?" I asked.

He pointed at the desert flower. "This one for the sample."

His finger moved to the other picture. It was of the cat that seemed to live in my backyard part-time. It was fat, and loved to sleep on top of my tall concrete barrier on its back. The picture captured just such a pose. "But this is good," he added. "It should definitely be in the gallery showing. It seems like a good candidate for print sales, as well. People are really into cat pictures right now. Especially quirky cats."

I smiled. "I love that cat. I don't know who it belongs to, but it can't be a stray if it's that fat. Though it does try to come into my house half the time when I open my back door."

"I saw the other picture of it in your kitchen. Fat cats are cute," James said, meeting my smile.

"You're determined to make me like you," I told him playfully.

He looked a little hurt by the comment. "You don't like me?" he asked.

I thought back to my words. I hadn't realized how rude they could be taken when they were coming out of my mouth. "I didn't mean it like that. I was just teasing you. You've just been so well-behaved, so charming. It's like you're trying to make me become attached to you."

He studied me intently, like I was a particularly fascinating novelty to him. "Well, yes, I want that. I don't know how to show you any more clearly that that is *exactly* what I want."

I just raised my eyebrows at him, staring for a long minute.

"It seems rather pointless and selfish to me that you would want to make someone become attached to you, while you remain detached yourself," I told him quietly, raising my chin almost defiantly.

He never looked away from me as he spoke. His eyes were snapping with intensity as he caught my hand, pulling it to his chest. "You silly girl, I'm caught fast. I've been attached from the start. How can you doubt it?"

I pulled my hand away, skeptical and uncomfortable.

Is this some game to him? I wondered.

"I can doubt just about anything, Mr. Cavendish. I am, by nature, a skeptic."

He raised a hand to my cheek, stroking it with a featherlight touch. "How can someone so young and innocent also be so cynical?" he asked me.

"Life hasn't taught me to be anything else. Forgive me, but I wouldn't even begin to know how *not* to doubt someone I barely know."

He pushed me down onto my guest bed, its surface recently cleared. He loomed over me.

"Then I will make sure that you know me, Bianca," he said, and kissed me with bruising intensity.

CHAPTER TWENTY-FIVE

Mr. Shameless

I finally settled on the samples I wanted, and James had sent them off before I even knew that was his intention.

He gave me a wry smile. "It's not in my nature to procrastinate. I tend to get things done right when I think of them."

I shook off his whirlwind behavior, chalking it up to more rich people quirks.

He started making phone calls and working on his computer again, so I went out back to work on the painting I'd begun of him. He came out and sat in one of my cheap plastic chairs, still on his phone. He covered it briefly.

"Will I disturb you if I sit with you?" he asked.

I shook my head, still working. It helped, actually. Though he wasn't posing, it still helped to look at him frequently as I painted him.

I worked for several hours and he stayed where he was, working and watching me. I distantly noted that he ordered food, but I just kept working. I had no idea what time it was and didn't really care.

"Food is here," James said after awhile, getting up. He left and came back, carrying to-go bowls from my favorite tex-mex restaurant.

I smiled at him. "I love that place."

"Sit and eat," he told me, pointing at the chair across from him.

I did, taking one of the bowls from him. It wasn't what I normally ordered, but it was good, maybe even better than my usual.

I ate quickly, trying to be polite about it. My mind was still on the painting. I had eaten nearly the entire bowl before I realized it.

I went back to painting, not speaking. James went back to working and watching.

I was nearly finished with the painting when I quit. I always liked to finish a project with a fresh perspective.

I would step away from it for a few days, then come back and see it with new eyes.

James was on the phone and I started to clean up my supplies when I thought better of it. I started to prepare new watercolor paper.

"Would you pose nude for me?" I asked him when he ended a call.

He looked surprised.

"Out here?" he asked, glancing around my backyard.

I laughed. It was tiny, but the barrier *was* high, giving it a fair amount of privacy.

"On my bed?" I asked cautiously. I couldn't believe that he would do it, but I was starting to feel hopeful.

"Okay, but I need to make one more phone call."

I nodded, grinning, very happy at the prospect of such a painting.

"I'll be in my room, setting up."

He came in several minutes later. He was still in his boxers.

"Where do you want me?" he asked, eyeing up my small room.

"Just on the bed.   On your side, I think, though I may experiment a little."

He slid out of his only piece of clothing and complied.   He lounged on the bed, looking relaxed. Well, most of him anyway. His cock was *not* relaxed, jutting huge and erect between his legs.

I licked my lips.

"Should I paint it like that?" I asked, pointing at him. "Or will it get soft?"

He laughed. "You might as well paint it like that. It won't be getting soft any time soon. It has a mind of its own."

I licked my lips again. "Can I do anything for it? For you? Before I start painting. I could take you in my mouth."

His eye got a little glassy at the suggestion. "No. I need to prove to myself that I can abstain for a few days."   But he stroked himself roughly with his hand.

I moved to him, but he waved me off, letting go of himself.

"No," he told me firmly.   "It's important to me that I know I have control of what I do to you."

I swallowed, but respected his wishes. Whatever the reason.

I began to paint him without any of my normal prep work. It was a joy to work on him, and I lost myself in the process for the second time that day.

It was unusual for me to get so engrossed in two projects in one day, though it did feel like more of a continuation of one project.

"I love painting you," I told him.

He watched me tirelessly, his hard jaw propped against his fist. "That works out well, since I love watching you paint. You have such dreams in your eyes. It's mesmerizing."

I gave him a warm look, thinking that he could be almost unbelievably sweet.

"What are you going to do with this painting?" he asked after a long period of comfortable silence.

"Hang it right next to my other painting of you, as part of my spank bank," I told him, trying to make him laugh.

It worked. He clutched his stomach, falling onto his back as he laughed.

"What on earth do you know about a spank bank?" he asked me with an infectious grin.

I smiled back, still painting. "My best friend is a guy. I've heard the term often enough, though I never really related to it before."

He moved back into his pose, an irrepressible smile still on his face.

"I'm surprised you can sit still for so long. I wouldn't have guessed you had it in you. You seem like a constantly on the move type of guy," I told him.

"It is unusual for me. I like your house. It's a peaceful, happy place."

I couldn't help it. I beamed at him. "I'm pleased you like it. I like it, too."

"I hope I'm invited back often."

I just smiled, working on the painting intently.

We'll see, I thought.

He let me paint him for hours before I finally quit, needing a break.

He had taken to reading a Manga from my bedside table. It was a Shojo Manga, and I blushed a little when he found it, embarrassed for him to see that I was interested in something so romantic and silly.

He was smiling at something as he turned a page. It was a library copy, the only kind I could afford. I hadn't read it yet, but it was #15 in a series I'd been following for years. I'd been on the library's waiting list for it for almost six months.

"Don't give anything away," I warned him. "I haven't had a

chance to read it yet."

He looked up with a toothy grin. "You're that into this? I have to say, that almost gives me hope. It's so sweet and romantic."

I gave him my little shrug. "I don't know what it is, but I'm totally infatuated with manga and anime. It's all very funny to me. And I love the characters."

He wiggled his brows at me as I finished putting my supplies away, coming back into the room, where he was still reading the manga.

"So let's watch some anime. You watch it on your computer?" he asked.

I nodded. It was the only place I watched anything at my house, since I didn't have a television.

"I want to see your favorite," he told me.

My old computer was set up in a small nook in my living room. James pulled my love seat close to the computer, and I set up an episode of a vampire anime that I had watched several times. I loaded the first episode.

I couldn't imagine that James would enjoy it. It was kind of screwed up, and I thought that the target audience for it must be girls. But it was the first anime I had thought of when he'd asked me to play my favorite.

We watched it for hours. James cuddled me against his chest, but seemed glued to the screen, transfixed by the anime. I had always found it fascinating, as well. I got caught up in it again.

"So we're voting for her to choose the silver-haired guy, right?" James asked me as we finished a cliff-hanger episode.

I scoffed at him. "No. The dark-haired one. She totally adores him. She's been in love with him forever."

He threw up his hands, laughing at me. "We just found out that that one's her brother!"

I glared at him, feeling defensive about my beloved characters. "He was just raised as her brother. He was reincarnated, or whatever." It had a convoluted plot, which seemed to happen a lot in the animes I loved.

He laughed harder. "So that makes him her great-great-great-great grandfather? And that's somehow better?"

I poked him in the ribs with my elbow, but couldn't help but laugh as well.

He nuzzled against my ear, then pinned me down beneath him, holding my wrists above my head.

"You're a perverted girl, aren't you? I bet you like hentai," he teased me, referring to the X-rated version of anime.

He began to tickle me. I slapped at his hands, giggling helplessly.

"Say it," he laughingly insisted. "Say, I like hentai, you naughty girl."

I said it, and he kissed me, but it was a quick kiss, since we were both still laughing.

"You can call me Grandpa, if that does it for you," he teased.

I laughed, tugging on his hair.

I'd never had so much fun watching anime, especially since I usually only ever watched them by myself. Stephan didn't care for anime. He said they never had happy endings. He thought even the silly, funny ones were a little sad. Whereas, I thought even the saddest ones were a little silly and funny.

I made a quick trip to the bathroom, but froze when I saw what James was looking at on my computer when I re-emerged. I blushed harder than I'd ever blushed in my entire life.

I didn't look up porn often. Hardly ever, in fact. But I had felt a strange urge to look up some sites with very specific BDSM content the night I'd come home after meeting James for the first time on a flight.

I had always had an unwilling fascination with BDSM, and even with the small interaction James and I had had on that flight, that fascination had been triggered, to the point that I'd come home and looked up the things that I fantasized him doing to me.

I still didn't know why, even with my inexperience, I had known so certainly what he wanted to do to me. There had just been something in his eyes, a hint of the dominant in him so clear to me that I couldn't deny it.

He was watching one of the videos I'd found that night. A bound and gagged woman was being flogged rather vigorously by a huge man who stood behind her. She was wearing a black leather corset that still left her breasts bare. Her lips were bloody red, her hair raven black.

The man was dark-haired and burly, with coarse hair matting his barrel chest. He was a crude beast of a man, especially compared to James. It had simply been the closest thing I could find to the things I pictured James doing to me, the things I had imagined he *craved* to do to me. I had turned out to be very right about him. In fact, my fantasies never could have done him justice.

"You looked at my history," I said softly, moving to step up behind him. If he had looked up my history, that meant he knew just when I had been watching the raunchy video.

He just turned and looked at me, his eyes very knowing.

"Yes," he said without shame. Then he smiled. It made my breath catch. "You were quite the busy, kinky girl the night we met. You never fail to surprise and delight me, Bianca. But I do hope this brute of a man is not your type." He waved his hand at the screen.

I shook my head vigorously, my eyes wide. "I never had a type until I met you, James. And now I suppose my type would be impossibly beautiful men with honey colored hair, turquoise eyes and an unexplainable, perpetual tan. There wasn't any BDSM porn available with that 'type'."

He lounged back in the small computer chair, running his tongue over his teeth just so.

I clenched my thighs together, feeling a rush of heat between my legs.

"You know what I did that night when I got home?" James asked, his voice very low, his eyes so warm on my face.

I shook my head.

He smiled. "I jerked myself off three times in a row just thinking about that little blush you got every time our eyes met. You were so composed, so professional, but I knew you would submit to me perfectly in bed. Just one look at you, and I was lost."

I blushed, my mind flying back to that first meeting.

I had been called in to do a charter flight from Las Vegas to New York. Our CEO had personally requested for me to work the flight on my day off, so I could hardly refuse. I had been baffled when Stephan hadn't been asked. I hadn't looked forward to the trip, even though it was good overtime, because our CEO tended to be a little too friendly, slimy even, with female flight attendants.

But I had gone. The plane had been nearly deserted, and I had been the only flight attendant to work first class. Three flight attendants worked main cabin with less than twenty passengers to tend to. I had only had two. James and the CEO.

James had arrived first, and we had frozen at the sight of each other. He had just been stepping into first class when our eyes met. I had been paralyzed, and he had been, well, intense.

I had forgotten the job I was supposed to do, the things I was supposed to say, as we just stared at each other for long minutes.

I told myself I was imagining all of the things I saw in his eyes, that they were just wild fantasies about an impossibly beautiful man in an impeccable suit.

I had looked into those eyes and seen a man who I wanted to submit to on the most basic level.

We hadn't moved until my CEO's voice boomed from behind James, prompting him to take a seat. I had shaken myself and gone back to work, but every interaction, every glance his way, had made shocks of awareness shake my body, heat rising to my cheeks every time I met his incredible turquoise eyes.

We had never even had to touch and he had dominated me on that flight. I had thought I'd never see him again after that, but still I hadn't been able to get him off my mind.

James closed out the window of the crude porn, rising and walking to me. He hugged me to him, pushing my face into his chest. He kissed the top of my head almost sweetly.

The rest of the evening went smoothly and I was marveling at our drama-free, sex-free day when my phone dinged a text at me during dinner. It was in my room. It had gone off a few times during the day, but when I checked it and saw that none of the texts were from Stephan I had ignored them.

"Excuse me," I said to James, who was eating leftover chicken as though he did so everyday. I would have bet it was the first leftover dinner he'd had in awhile, if ever.

I grabbed my phone, heading back to the table. The text was from Stephan. I hummed as I read it.

It had been such a perfect day. James hadn't even asked me about my nightmare of the night before.

If this was what it was like to be in a relationship, I could get used to it. I shocked myself with the thought.

"Who's texting you? What does it say?" James asked. He was nosy and had no shame about it. I wondered how he would take it if I was so nosy with him.

"Stephan. I have to work tomorrow. Just a turn, so we'll be back the same night, though late."

James brooded after that. I knew he had assumed I would keep all of my days off this week. He couldn't seem to understand that I needed to work overtime to pay my bills.

"I can't imagine you eat leftover chicken for dinner very often,"

I said, smiling at him, trying to draw him out of his sudden dark mood.

He had never even put a shirt on, just wore his boxers around like the shameless hedonist he was. Though he had stayed strong in his resolve not to have sex with me. I wasn't particularly pleased with his success.

His eyes were cold as he raked me with a glance. "Are you done eating?" he asked in a bland voice.

I nodded.

"Go get on your bed," he ordered.

I did, thinking that he was an unpredictable tyrant with every step.

"Lay on your back," he ordered.

I did, and he yanked my hips to the edge of the bed, shoving my nightgown up to study me. He parted my legs, then put my feet up on the edge of the bed with his hands gripping my ankles. He removed one of his hands almost instantly and touched the petals of my sex with light fingers, examining every inch of me. It made me squirm.

"Stop that," he told me in a hard voice. I did.

He slid a finger inside of me ever so slowly. It smarted a little, but not too much to bear. It was a delicious kind of soreness.

"Are you sore?" he asked, still pushing.

I moaned, not answering, hoping that was answer enough. He cursed, pulling his finger out in one motion.

"Another day, at least, before we can fuck."

He began to work on me with his mouth, making me pant and beg in scant seconds. After coaxing a quick, intense orgasm out of me, he rose.

His face was still hard and cold, even wet with my passion. He went into the bathroom and closed the door. I heard the shower running.

I began to get my things ready for the next day, packing up my flight bag and setting my alarm.

He came out with a towel around his waist and I could tell with one look on his face that he was still in a dark mood.

"Is there something I can do for you? I feel bad being the only one to get pleasure out of an exchange."

He just stared at me for a long minute. "No, I'm fine. When do you have to go to bed?"

"I should probably get to bed as soon as possible. Are you taking off?" I asked, assuming from his demeanor that he was planning to.

His face darkened even more. "Are you kicking me out?"

The idea startled me. "No, of course not. You can stay, if you like, but-"

"Yes, I like. Let's go to bed," he said, going into the closet to slip into a new pair of boxer-briefs.

He sprawled on the bed, closing his eyes without another word.

I got ready for bed, lying beside him awkwardly. It took me a long time to fall asleep beside him. It wasn't like any of the other times we'd slept together. No parts of our bodies were touching.

CHAPTER TWENTY-SIX

Mr. Withdrawn

My alarm went off. I turned it off quickly, trying not to disturb the sleeping man wrapped around me tightly. One of his hands was cupping my breast, even in deep slumber. He had apparently thawed out a bit in his sleep.

I pulled free of him slowly and with effort, padding softly into the bathroom to shower.

He was sitting up on my side of the bed when I re-emerged. He ran a hand through his hair when he saw me.

"Will you call me when you get home?" he asked.

I nodded, and went back to getting ready. He got dressed as well, though he didn't pack his things. I suspected he was going to leave them there without asking me if it was okay. I decided not to make an issue of it. I didn't want to rile him just then.

"I'm off for most of Thursday. You know we don't fly out until late in the evening," I told him, trying to draw him out of his mood.

He just nodded, and I worried that I'd been too presumptuous, assuming he'd want to spend another day with me.

"I'll come here again after you get off of work, unless you object to my company," he said.

It was the closest he would get to asking, I thought.

"Sounds great." I smiled at him, but he remained expressionless.

He was ready before me, but waited patiently, dressed in a pale gray suit, with a dark gray shirt and a crimson tie. It was beyond stunning to see him fully dressed after spending so much time with him nearly naked in my house.

"That's a lovely suit," I told him.

He thanked me for the compliment, but stayed withdrawn.

I realized that his withdrawal made me want to cling to him. I squelched the unhealthy urge.

He walked me out. He didn't say goodbye until Stephan approached my open garage. James gripped the back of my head, giving me a hard kiss on the mouth.

"Call or text me the *second* you get back in town," he told me gruffly, moving out of my way.

He didn't get into his own car until we started to drive away.

Stephan gave me a careful look. "That man is intense," he said quietly.

I heard the implied question there, but I just nodded. He was worried about me, but I still didn't know James well enough to confidently reassure him that everything was fine.

Both of the flights we worked were agonizingly slow.

The only interesting thing about the day was that the Agents were back, following exactly the same routine that they had on the previous turn. Stephan reassured me that he would fill out another report on the strange behavior, just to cover bases, but we decided, after some debate, that the two men must be investigating the airline.

I didn't call or text James during our short time on the ground. I wasn't sure he wanted me to, so I decided to err on the side of caution. I had no missed calls or texts, so I figured that was the safest bet. Though my ear had picked up a strange line of conversation from one of the Agents as he was exiting the aircraft. "Yes, Sir, she is well. There were no problems. No one bothered her at all."

I began to get an inkling of a paranoid idea, but I immediately brushed it off as batshit crazy.

Even eccentric, filthy rich people aren't that insane, I told myself.

Agent #2, whose name on the manifest showed James Cook, gave me a warm smile when I handed him his fifth bottle of water.

"Here you go, Mr. Cook," I said, smiling back. As strange as this pattern was, he was really a very pleasant passenger.

"Thank you, Ms. Karlsson," he responded, and I froze. He would know my given name, but there was no reason in the world why he should know my surname. It wasn't on my name tag.

I looked at him squarely. "How do you know my last name?" I asked him frankly.

He looked a little sheepish, as though it had been a slip. "It's my job, Ma'am."

I told Stephan of the exchange. He looked baffled. "Do you suppose *we* are being investigated?"

"I think it might be James..." I said quietly, revealing my paranoid theory.

Stephan grimaced. "I'd like to say that was impossible, but I can actually picture James doing something like this. Are you going to ask him?"

I sighed. "At some point. I'm not sure I want to deal with the answer. I'm not ready to break things off just yet."

Stephan gripped my shoulder. "Breaking things off isn't the

only solution, Bianca."

We stared at each other for a long moment, but I didn't agree or disagree with him.

I texted James almost immediately when we landed in Vegas, turning on my phone while we taxied in.

Bianca: We're back in Vegas. Taxiing in right now.

He responded almost instantly.

James: Good. I'll be at your house when you get there.

And he was, not startling me this time when he stepped out of the dark SUV, since I recognized it now.

I waved goodnight to Stephan. James met me at my walkway, his hand going possessively to my nape. He was uncannily silent.

I let us in, kicking my shoes off at the door and putting my flight bag back in its spot on a small table by my bedroom door.

James was still a silent presence behind me. I felt a shiver of fear stroke down my spine. In this mood, would he really hurt me? What had I gotten myself into, becoming so intimate with such a stranger? Furthermore, becoming intimately violent. I had gone too far to go back. *Hadn't I?*

I felt disgust with myself for even considering it. I would regret it if I never discovered what lay down this path, a path that had always secretly fascinated me. But the fear was strangely persistent with such a silent, cold man at my back.

My father had always done the most damage when he was done screaming and became the cold monster that haunted my nightmares. A picture of his expressionless face, covered in blood, flashed into my mind, making me shiver. His cold blue eyes flicking to me with an almost absent-minded warning. And how sick was I, that James, in his cold, dominant persona, was the most irresistible to me?

I made a note to get back in touch with my neglected therapist. But even with all of my dark musings and spine-chilling fears, I never even considered asking James to leave.

I wanted to face this, to feel brave when so often my bravery had fled me, and I had simply run in terror, leaving someone else to take the damage.

"Get on the bed. On your back." James's voice was hoarse when he finally spoke.

We had been standing in the dark for long minutes in total silence. I did it, and just the act of submitting made me relax a fraction in relief. It was all in his hands now.

"Lift up your skirt," he told me. "More. All the way to your waist. Good."

He turned on the light and approached me, dragging my hips to the edge of the mattress and positioning my heels there in what seemed to be his examination routine.

He knelt, his still, stony face lowering between my legs.

I shivered.

He made a little tsking noise when he saw the moisture there. He touched me, holding up two wet fingers.

"Is this all for me?" he asked blandly.

I swallowed and just nodded.

"I'd like a proper answer."

"Yes, Mr. Cavendish," I tried, not really knowing what he wanted.

"Tell me if you feel any tenderness at all," he ordered, sliding a finger inside of me slowly. All of the soreness was gone, leaving only an achy pleasure, and I squirmed.

He slapped the side of my ass, hard. "Don't move." He continued to stroke me, touching every inch, circling his finger.

"So fucking tight. Unbelievable," he muttered. It was the closest to thawing that I'd witnessed from him since he'd gone cold at dinner the night before. A second finger joined the first, stroking along every part of my walls, looking for any rawness.

"Any soreness here?" he asked, shoving in deeper a little roughly.

I gasped. "No, Mr. Cavendish."

He pulled out abruptly, still studying my sex.

"Good. Now I'm going to punish you. Go put that fuck-me nightgown on." He straightened as he spoke, and I watched in fascination as he sucked on his fingers, then loosened his tie.

"It's dirty," I told him. It was on the floor of my closet.

"It's about to get filthy. Go put it on."

I did, hanging my work clothes up with shaking hands.

When I came back out of my closet, he had taken only his jacket and tie off, rolling up the sleeves of his dress shirt. His arousal was obvious in his snug, pale gray slacks. And his eyes were still chips of ice.

"Get on the bed, face down. Put your hips directly on the wedge in the center of the bed."

I noted the strange pillow on the bed only when he mentioned it, but I complied without a word. It was like a miniature version of the ramp he'd used in his house. *Travel-sized*, I thought.

My head snapped up as I felt a rope being tightened around my wrists. He was bending over the bed, binding them together. My bed didn't have a real frame, just a flimsy headboard, but James was prepared for that, using a long rope and tying it completely around the underside of the bed to hold my wrists in place.

I watched him a little numbly. Being bound for the second time should have been less terrifying, not more so, but my mind just wouldn't process that information.

"Do you remember your safe word?" he asked. He dropped to his knees to rig the rope under the bed casually, as though it was the most normal thing in the world. He even managed to look dignified while he did it, totally unruffled by having to crawl around on his knees.

"Yes, Mr. Cavendish," I answered, trembling.

He tied my feet efficiently, pulling them slightly apart rather than together.

I tried to turn my head to look, but he covered my eyes with a black blindfold, tying it snugly. I wanted desperately for him to touch my face, any sign of affection, but he remained stoic and cold as he prepared me for punishment.

Soft music began to play from the small speakers that my phone plugged into. It was unfamiliar music, but beautiful, a woman's voice singing a haunting melody accompanied heavily by violins.

I could feel him simply staring at me for long minutes after he'd finished tying me. I squirmed a little.

"Mr. Cavendish, please," I implored him. For what, I wasn't entirely certain. He didn't respond.

I gasped when a hand finally touched me, touching the back of my thigh lightly. He lifted my nightgown up from mid thigh to my shoulders. I heard some rustling. Cloth? Something thicker. And then another touch. It felt like his hand, though not like his skin. Had he put on a glove?

Several more minutes ticked by in an agony of waiting, and all I knew was that he watched me.

The first strike caught me by surprise, a harsh slap from his gloved hand to my butt. I gasped. It hurt. I could feel one of his thighs touching mine as he leaned in close to my side. The first hit was followed by another slap to a spot just below, and then he began in earnest, hit after hit on every inch of my butt and thighs.

I gasped and shifted a little, trying in vain to get away from the harsh contact.

Why does his hand hurt so much more than the riding crop? I wondered. He must have been holding back a lot before. But he wasn't holding back now.

I lost track of the number of quick-fire slaps, my mind going into a kind of numb state that was all too familiar but seemed to be changing inexorably into something else...

He hadn't even paused in the blows when I heard him gasp and curse. Suddenly, he was shoving into me, burying himself to the hilt with one brutal stroke. I was so wet that it didn't hurt, and I clenched deliciously around him. The fullness felt overwhelming for a moment, though, and I screamed, a sound that none of his slaps had solicited from me.

I was in an oasis of pleasure amidst all of the pain as he started pumping inside of me relentlessly. He worked hard at it, my tight passage fighting him with its involuntary clenching.

He grabbed my hair with both fists, pulling my head up as he thrust.

"Come," he said in the roughest voice I'd ever heard out of him. His cock dragged along just the perfect spot as he pulled out of me, and I came with a scream. He didn't stop, didn't even pause, grinding against me with ragged, intoxicating gasps.

He brought me to orgasm twice more before I felt him emptying inside of me with a harsh groan. He leaned along my back, covering me completely, his mouth at my ear. He was still thrusting in a small motion inside of me, even spent, as though he couldn't stop.

"My Bianca," he whispered into my ear raggedly.

He lay on top of me like that for long minutes, still buried inside of me, his lips against my neck now, kissing me softly. He seemed to have exercised all of that cold fury out of his body, and I was left again with the tender lover.

He lifted himself from me eventually, examining me with light fingers. My thighs and butt were sore to the touch. He fingered my sex, wet now from both of us.

"Tender?" he asked in a hoarse voice.

"No, Mr. Cavendish," I answered from my sightless position. He thrust two fingers inside of me.

I wriggled and gasped.

"I wonder how many times I could make you come in one night," he mused idly. "You're such a hair trigger. I'd test you, but I think you'd pass out before you asked me to stop."

I thought he might be right.

He spread something cool and soothing along every part of me that he had hit, applying it with the softest touch.

He untied me eventually, and I lay there passively until he turned me onto my back, pulling my blindfold off.

He arranged me on my back, even fanning my hair out above me, staring at me with the softest eyes, a stark contrast to those glacial eyes that had studied me coldly when we'd entered the room. "You're an exquisite angel, Bianca. I've never touched anything so fine in my life."

My eyes were growing heavy as he bent down and kissed me reverently on the forehead. He was still fully dressed, with just his slacks undone.

"Now go to sleep, Love."

CHAPTER TWENTY-SEVEN

Mr. Tender-Lover

I awoke as James pushed inside of me. He had my wrists clasped in his hands and pinned above my head. Our naked chests rubbed together and he was kissing me softly and sweetly, murmuring endearments. I was wet and so aroused that he slipped into my tight passage smoothly.

"Morning, Love." He smiled against my mouth.

"Mmmm," was the best reply I could get out of my throat. "Ahhh," followed quickly.

He moved so slowly inside of me, stroking with long, hard strokes that seemed to go on forever. "I want to wake up like this every morning," he murmured between kisses.

"Mmmm. I could get used to this," I mumbled back, gasping as he withdrew, dragging along my most sensitive nerves.

"Good. I want you to," he said with a smile. "Get. Used. To. This." He said, thrusting to drive home each word.

"Wrap your legs around my waist," he told me.

I did and he thrust hard, making new nerves quiver inside of me. His beautiful eyes were glued to mine, intense and tender.

"You're so beautiful," he told me. "Your eyes change color. I swear they're almost green this morning. Have I told you yet today how perfect you are?"

"First he's sour, then he's sweet," I murmured back to him, quoting an old line from a commercial about sour candies.

He laughed, then began kissing me passionately.

I felt like I was drowning. I was too inexperienced to resist such a seduction. He wanted all of me, even my emotions, and in spite of myself, he was getting it.

I felt things as I looked into his intense gaze that I hadn't thought to feel for anyone, let alone someone I'd met just over a week ago.

"What are you doing to me?" I asked him in a rough whisper.

His nostrils flared and he drove into me hard, picking up speed. "I hope it's something like what you're doing to me. I want you to feel what I'm feeling, Bianca. I want you to feel this uncontrollable need. I can't stand the thought that you're indifferent to me."

As though in answer to his words, I came, crying out, tears seeping from the corners of my eyes from the exquisite rapture. Shudders wracked me and I cried out his name, again and again.

His eyes went so soft with his own release, and he released my wrists, cupping my cheeks. He held my gaze as the ecstasy took him.

"Bianca," he called. It was the most intimate moment of my life, shivers of my release still running through me as our eyes exchanged our charged, raw, emotional need. I wondered if every woman he did this to fell in love with him.

How not? I thought, my mind rolling helplessly back into an exhausted sleep.

I awoke to the smell of breakfast and the sound of soft cursing in the kitchen. Short minutes later he served me breakfast in bed, and I sat up, eating the simple fair as though I were starving.

"How do you get women to leave you alone after this kind of

treatment?" I teased him, smiling into his beautiful eyes. "I'm surprised you don't have a mob of them following you everywhere, just for a taste."

He smiled back, but his eyes held a hint of trouble. He smoothed my hair back from my face, kissing me on the forehead affectionately.

"You think I'm like this with everyone?" he asked, mild reproof in his voice. "Don't you know? You're special, Buttercup."

I just gave him a wry smile. It sounded like a line to me, so I shrugged it off. "So what's the plan today?"

"You wanna work on those paintings?"

"I'd love nothing more. I'll need a brief nap in the late afternoon. It's a long night without one, since I can't sleep on the redeye, obviously."

And so we shared another idyllic day, me painting to my hearts content, him working and posing as I worked on the two paintings.

Amazingly, I finished the first painting of him, a record for me. It usually took me weeks to finish a project. I pinned it up in my room proudly, deciding that it would definitely be getting a frame as soon as I had a chance to make one.

James seemed to love the prospect of having his image marking my room whether he was present or not. He grinned as I hung it, then dragged me to the bed for another bout of love-making. The tender lover was driving for that one, with just a dash of the master. I wasn't particular. I had quickly grown to adore them both.

We napped for hours, far longer than I was usually able to sleep for my usual pre-redeye nap. I worked on his nude briefly before getting ready for the flight. "I can only hope that this one will get done anywhere near as fast as the first. I usually don't work this quickly. It can take me weeks to finish a piece."

He helped me dress for work, buttoning my blouse and

straightening my tie. He fondled and kissed and made me wish we had ten more minutes by the time I needed to leave.

"Don't you have to catch a flight?" I asked him archly as he walked me out.

"Why, yes. I'm leaving now, Love," he said, kissing me shamelessly in the driveway while Stephan waited in his car. "I don't exactly need to pack. Remember, I live in New York most of the time."

I hadn't remembered, and the thought saddened me. This thing we were doing, where he invaded my house and lavished attention on me, would end soon. Even if we didn't end everything right away, it would soon be dwindling down to a one day a week affair, I was certain.

He seemed to notice something on my face. His eyes pinned me. I tried harder to make my face expressionless.

"Don't worry, Love. I have obligations there, but I will certainly make an effort to be here more. This hotel is one of my larger properties. It makes perfect sense for me to divide some of my time here."

I gave myself a little shake. He wanted me to depend on him for some perverse reason, and I had started to give in to him a little. I determined to make a better effort at keeping my head on straight.

"I'll see you soon," I told him, walking away.

It was going to be a particularly dead night at work. I studied our paperwork briefly and saw that the flight was only booked to 60 out of 175, with only 3 passengers in the first class cabin. I usually hated flights like that, with too much time and not enough to do, but tonight I was relieved.

Perhaps I would get some time with James. And some time with Stephan, to talk about James.

We met up with our pilots on the crew bus. Damien and

216

Murphy both embraced me.

I hugged them stiffly back. I genuinely liked the two pilots, but I was loathe to let the other pilots on the crew bus get the idea that I was receptive to any kind of touching. In my experience, pilots were always looking for an excuse to touch. I preferred to be seen as untouchable, particularly at work.

"You look amazing, Bianca," Damien said, smiling as he pulled back from his spontaneous hug. "Beautiful as always. I can't tell you how happy we were when we found out that you were our layover crew."

Damien was very good-looking, with shiny black hair and friendly brown eyes that had charmed many a flight attendant right out of their clothes. He was at least six one, and I could feel the hard play of muscles on his arms and torso when he embraced me. To top it all off, he had a strong Australian accent that acted as slutty girl Kryptonite.

I smiled back. "Yeah, when Stephan told me you were our New York pilots, I knew it was going to be a fun month," I told him.

I was always friendly with him, but I also felt the need to be a little reserved. He had hit on me when we first met, but when I declined, he'd been nothing but platonic. However, I still got the feeling sometimes that he was just waiting until I changed my mind. Even if I had been interested in dating, which I emphatically wasn't, I wouldn't have dated him. He was a shameless womanizer, had in fact slept with some of my friends, and no part of me wanted him as anything but a friend.

Murphy, the first officer, was a heavy-set blond man with rosy cheeks and a constant stream of jokes that had had me rolling many a time. His endearing face wore a perpetual grin. I couldn't ever even recall a time when his happy face wasn't smiling at least a little.

"Damien made a deal to be born the anti-christ just to be on your route, Bianca. HIs poor mother wasn't too happy about it, either," Murphy told me by way of a greeting.

The entire bus laughed. He just had that infectiously happy nature, always bringing everyone in on the joke.

Melissa was the happiest I'd ever seen her when she met our new pilots. Perhaps her romance with the married Captain Peter had grown stale already. I'd be shocked if she and Damien weren't sharing a room by the end of the layover.

I sent a glance Stephan's way, and he beamed at me. "What happy times, Bee. My girl is finally falling for a great guy, our crew is practically a dream team, and I've got a date tomorrow."

Stephan was a staunch optimist. Despite everything bad that had happened to him, he was always finding the silver lining. He never failed to make me want to be a better person. A person more like him. I couldn't be, but I always tried not to bring down his happy moments with my own doubts and fears, so I just beamed back at him.

"It's bound to be a great month," I agreed.

We had a crew briefing when we got on the plane, leaning against the plush first class seats. It was a jovial affair, the seven of us joking and laughing and making plans for the next evening.

It was easy enough for everyone to decide on Melvin's bar, since it was on the corner by the hotel, and Stephan suggested it. Melvin had arranged for us to get a crew discount, as we did in many bars, so drinks would be cheap, and of course, there was the karaoke.

"Oh, Bianca, say you'll sing for me," Damien teased.

I just smiled.

"She can't come tomorrow. She has plans," Stephan said, frowning a little as he looked at Damien. "Let's hope she'll come next week."

I nodded. "Sure. Sounds good," I said. I couldn't ditch Stephan two weeks in a row, so I didn't have to consider it long to know I'd be there.

Damien made a mock begging gesture. "Too cruel, Bianca! We haven't seen you in months, and you ditch us?"

"Have mercy on the man, Bianca! You're going to turn him into a cutter if you ignore him much more!" Murphy joked.

I saw Melissa giving me none-too-friendly looks behind their backs. The only thing she hated more than someone else getting the man was someone else getting the attention, I had observed.

"We need to prep for boarding or the gate agent is gonna kill us," I said, trying to shift the attention away from myself. It was effective, since we really had been chatting for too long, neglecting our work.

I was prepping my galley as Murphy and Damien took turns poking their heads out of the cockpit to joke with me.

"I'll take a gin and tonic," Damien said in his attractive accent.

I just laughed, and he ducked back in.

Murphy poked his head out. "I'll take a vodka martini, shaken, not stirred," Murphy joked, butchering his own version of an Australian accent.

"James Bond was British, not Australian, or whatever accent that is you're trying to do," I told him.

He looked shocked and wounded.

I was giggling in spite of myself as I checked my carts.

He gave me a mock stern look. "Okay, I didn't want to have to do this, Bianca, but you leave me no choice. Here's my final offer. I'll perform Tina Turner's 'Private Dancer' for you at Karaoke, if you come. Take it or leave it. Well, okay, you twisted my arm. To sweeten the pot, I'll take my shirt off and do my Chris Farley Chippendales dance to the beat. Final offer," he warned, then ducked back in without waiting for an answer.

I was laughing too hard to give him one. I'd seen that performance before. It was as funny as it sounded. I'd even heard tales that it had gone viral.

Damien showed up again. "Okay, picture this. Murphy is

Chris Farley and I will play the Patrick Swayze part, and in a thong. And we'll make it a duo. Final offer, Bianca."

I still just shook my head, laughing as he ducked back into the flight deck.

"Would it be possible to get a drink of water when you're done flirting with those pilots?" a frosty voice asked from behind me.

I turned, my laughter dying, as I took in a furious James.

CHAPTER TWENTY-EIGHT

Mr. Personality

I reached into one of my carts, handing James a cold bottle without speaking.

He took it, watching me with narrowed eyes. Cold Mr. Cavendish was back in full force.

What had I done now? I wanted to touch him. I wanted to ask him why he was angry, but I didn't. I just watched him without speaking until he turned and strode to his seat.

I hadn't even known we were boarding. Normally Stephan both made an announcement, for those of us in the galleys, and then came and told me personally.

Of course, with Damien and Murphy in the cockpit, things ran a little bit differently. He didn't have to pull pilot duty for me, so he hadn't had to come up to the flight deck.

Damien poked his smiling head out again, then came out completely, standing a little too close to me, his voice pitched low. "Who was that asshole?" he asked.

I just grimaced. I wasn't about to talk about it. I was already distracted enough.

"Could we get a couple of waters, as well? I'll try not to be a dick about it, though, like Mr. Personality there," he said with a smile.

I gave him a slight smile back, though I had to stifle the urge to tell him that it was Mr. Beautiful, thank you very much. I handed him two bottles.

"You guys need anything else?" I asked politely.

He dipped his head. "Thank you, beautiful. We're good to go." He disappeared back into the cockpit.

I shook my head. *He's in an odd mood today.* It was poor timing, to say the least. James would take exception to even harmless flirting, I was quickly learning.

I headed into the cabin briskly, to tend to my three passengers.

I stopped at James first. He was in his usual seat, looking tense, his features hard as he sat and twisted his unopened bottle of water.

"Can I get you anything, Mr. Cavendish? May I take your jacket?"

He stood, crowding me back a step when he moved into the aisle. He moved closer, and I stood my ground that time. His chest brushed mine as he shrugged out of his pin-striped suit jacket.

I saw the Burberry label clearly as I folded the garment carefully against me.

"He calls you beautiful. How much of your beauty has he seen, Bianca?" he asked, his quiet voice intense.

I gave him a perplexed, unhappy look. "I have no idea what you're talking about, but now is not the time to do so. I'm working, Mr. Cavendish."

His jaw clenched. "Whatever you were doing up there with those pilots looked more like play than work to me."

His anger didn't make me want to cower, as I might have expected. It made me want to fight.

"Don't be ridiculous. I was working, and they were being friendly. You don't get to control me outside of what we do in the bedroom, James." My voice was quiet, but furious. "And you especially don't have any control over anything to do with my work."

He shut his eyes tightly, then opened them again, looking a little more controlled than he had just an instant before.

"I hate that. You can't have any idea how much I hate that," he said quietly, moving back into his seat. He leaned his head back, closing his eyes.

I let him be, hanging up his coat. I checked on my other two passengers, who sat in the last row of first class. I sent an unmoved James a glance as I walked back into the galley to prepare two Jack and cokes.

He kept his eyes tightly shut even on takeoff. I watched him, my brow furrowed. Stephan glanced between the two of us.

"Everything okay?" he asked.

I gave my little shrug. "I don't know. He doesn't like me being friendly with Damien and Murphy. But I am, and I've only known James for a week. I don't understand him at all."

Stephan sighed. "I told Damien that you were involved with someone. He took it well, but he was obviously bummed about it. You know he's always liked you."

My eyes widened. "He always likes every woman he meets. What does that have to do with anything?"

Stephan gave me a meaningful look, then shook his head. "Never mind. Once James realizes just how unreceptive you are to any interest on Damien's part, I'm sure he'll be more reasonable."

I rolled my eyes. Reasonable did not seem to be part of James's repertoire, so far as I had seen.

At ten thousand feet I rose and began my service promptly, in spite of the fact that it would only take minutes, and then I would have hours to kill.

I stopped by a still unmoving James, debating whether to ask him if he needed anything, or just to pass him by, pretending he was sleeping. I knew he wasn't by his hard mouth and clenched fists.

I decided to tend to the other passengers first, easily putting off the decision on how to deal with him.

I served the couple two more cocktails, and two waters, heading back to James. I sat in the empty seat beside him, but he still didn't open his eyes. I touched his hand lightly, then his arm.

"Mr. Cavendish?" I asked him quietly.

"Didn't I warn you what would happen if you touched me in front of other people?" he asked without opening his eyes.

I looked around. "No one can see us, so I don't think this technically counts."

He grabbed my hand, quick as a snake, placing it firmly against his rock hard cock. He was so ready to go. I was shocked. Just sitting here on the plane, fully aroused...

"Are you always hard?" I asked him quietly, almost more curious than anything else, though I was far from unmoved by his ardor.

He smiled, a pained smile. "Of course not. Just most of the time, lately."

He moved against me slightly as he spoke, and I gripped him without thinking. He groaned.

I pulled back and stood, realizing what I'd been doing and where. And how fast it would lead to something more. I couldn't believe my lack of control.

"I need to get back to work. Can I get you anything?"

He just gave me an ironic, arched look, his arousal obvious where he lounged, hands on his armrests now. "I don't need a drink, if that's what you're asking."

I left him hastily. Things were quickly getting out of hand.

I hand served the snack since I only had three passengers. James nodded that yes, he wanted the snack, then didn't move. I had to open his tray table for him, something I did often. But folding it open on top of his impressive arousal was definitely a new experience for me.

He gave me a very heated, heavy-lidded gaze as I moved on. *Damned temperamental, arousing man*, I thought in agitation.

I served the pilots next, then served the couple several more rounds of cocktails. They looked about ready to pass out, but still spoke quietly to each other and drank heavily.

As I re-entered my galley, I nearly jumped, my hand going to my heart.

"Damien, you startled me," I told the pilot. Stephan was helping in back, and I hadn't expected to find anyone behind the curtain when I'd swung it open.

He just smiled. "Sorry, beautiful. How's it goin'? Are you bored out of your mind with an empty cabin?" he asked, knowing that I liked to keep busy.

I nodded, smiling. "I may have to cut off the couple in first class. They're slurring their words, but show no signs of stopping. That'll add a bit of excitement, if they're the usual disgruntled drunks I'm used to dealing with."

He flexed an arm. "Lemme know if you need a hand. I'd be happy to throw my weight around for you," he joked.

I just laughed. "That won't be necessary. They'll probably just send me nasty looks for the rest of the flight, if I've judged them correctly."

"So Stephan tells me that you're actually seeing someone now. I thought you didn't date... And he told me it's pretty serious. Is that true?" he asked. *That line of questioning is inappropriately personal*, I thought. *And it came out of left field.*

My eyes widened in dismay at a number of his comments. I thought it was possible James could hear us from his close seating. I didn't want him to think that I was telling people falsehoods about our purely sexual relationship, so I was quick to correct the Captain.

"Serious? No, of course not. I've only known him for a week.

We're actually not even dating. It's...complicated."

Damien looked way, way too happy with my explanation. An explanation that I never would have given Damien if I didn't want James to be sure that I would correct any false assumptions about what we had going.

Damien was the type of guy I could be friends with, but he wasn't anyone I would have confided in about a rocky relationship. I felt like I had revealed way too much, by his reaction. He positively beamed at me.

"Ah, I see. So you're not gonna break my heart by going off the market, before I've even had a shot?" he teased, giving me a harmless smile.

I gave him a slightly stern look.

"You're incorrigible, Damien," I told him.

"It's a fact," he said, winking at me as he went back into the flight deck.

I moved into the bathroom almost the second he left. I started to shut the door behind me, but a hard body got in the way, pushing me farther into the bathroom.

James shut and locked the door behind us, his eyes wild. He grabbed my hands, placing them around the handle to the right of the mirror so that I was angled at the mirror with a clear view of myself with him behind me.

I gripped it automatically.

"Not serious?" he asked roughly, shoving my skirt up to my hips.

He pressed against me, hard arousal lined up against my cleft from behind through his slacks and my panties. He rocked against me slightly as his hands moved to the buttons of my blouse.

I'd removed my vest, so it was just my shirt he had to contend with. He tugged on my little neck tie, but left it intact. He unbuttoned my shirt just enough to grip it open, exposing my bra. He undid the front clasp, freeing the heavy globes of my breasts.   He fondled me roughly, pinching the peaks into hardness while those wild eyes watched every move.

"You have a strange interpretation of the word serious, Bianca," he growled at me as his hands and cock worked me to a fever pitch.

He moved one hand away from my breasts, and I felt him fingering my sex around my panties.   He abruptly yanked, ripping my thong off in one brutal motion.   He tucked the offending garment into his pocket, then went to work freeing his impressive erection with one hand.

He pushed against my entrance for just a beat, then thrust into me hard, and it felt so exquisite that my eyes closed as I moaned in pleasure.

"Open your eyes!   Does this feel serious to you?" he asked me.   He jolted into me.

I just moaned and moved against him.   He moved faster and harder, thrusting in and out, until the pounding was jarringly intense.

"Answer me.   Does this feel serious to you?" he asked again.

It was an effort to get the words out.   I didn't know how he did it.   My mind was in a hazy disarray that didn't allow for clear thinking.

"It feels like ser-serious f-fucking," I told him as he continued to ride me mercilessly from behind.

He growled like an animal and pulled my hair until the back of my head was forced to his shoulder.   It made my back arch impossibly back.   He bit my neck hard enough to leave a mark.

I came so hard that I thought I may have blacked out.   He was still riding me when my vision cleared, though his pace had slowed.

"If anyone asks, you're off limits.   I thought we made this clear from the start," he told me coldly, never pausing as he fucked me senseless.

"I-I-," I tried to speak and couldn't.   He was rubbing my clit now, building me towards another mindless release. "Wha-wha-," I gave up speaking after that.

He was merciless, bringing me to orgasm again and again, thrusting endlessly.

He's punishing me with pleasure, I thought through the haze.

"Please, no more," I told him finally, coming back down from another drugging spell.

"Tell me who you belong to," he ordered, no hint of softness in his tone.

James wasn't home. Only Mr. Cavendish could be this callously possessive.

"I'm yours, Mr. Cavendish. I was a virgin when I met you. Don't you remember? You took my hymen. If I'd wanted someone else, I wouldn't have been untouched." I didn't keep the desperation or the exasperation out of my voice.

He came with a growl, eyes still impossibly wild.

His cock twitched inside of me for long minutes after he finished, and he gave these impossibly sexy, involuntary thrusts as he rubbed out the rest of his long orgasm.

"If you are having trouble understanding, let me spell it out for you," he told me harshly. "This is serious, Bianca. I've never been more fucking serious in my life."

CHAPTER TWENTY-NINE

Mr. Affectionate

James began to straighten my clothes before he'd even pulled out of me. He fastened my bra, adjusting my breasts inside of the cups as though he did it every day. He buttoned up my blouse, straightening my tie and then my collar. He smoothed my hair, and then his own.

I noticed that he looked perfectly composed. His hair was perfect and even his tie was straight. Whereas I looked like someone had just tried to fuck my brains out. I said as much.

He laughed. It was a rich, dark sound.

"Not quite. I was more likely trying to fuck the serious *into* you," he said, obviously in a much better mood.

"Has anyone ever told you that you're a moody son of a bitch?"

He looked a little sheepish, and then thoughtful. "Not quite like that, but I can hardly argue with it." As he spoke, he pulled out of me. It was a drawn out process, and he watched me the entire time.

I shivered. "I need to get back to work," I said as he started to clean me, reaching around me to use the tiny sink.

He kissed my neck as he wet a paper towel.

"I want to fuck you again, Bianca," he murmured against my skin, but made no move to do so. "But I get to show you the 4th floor tomorrow, so you're safe until then. I would hate to ride you too hard before then and then have to take it easy."

My look was a question. "The 4th floor?"

His tone was off-hand as he cleaned me. "That's the location of our playground, Love." He straightened my skirt, smoothing it down. I shivered.

"I don't have panties now." It was an accusation.

"Yes, I know. They're in my pocket," he said blandly, straightening his own clothing and refastening his slacks.

I watched his every move, my eyes glued to his mouth-watering length as he pushed it back into its confines.

"I could use my mouth on you," I said, watching that instrument of pleasure disappear and licking my lips. I was impetuously ravenous to do just that.

He straightened, watching me like a hawk in the mirror. He brought a hand to my face, pushing his index finger into my mouth. I opened, sucking it in. He pushed his finger in and out of my mouth, a parody of the act.

"Harder," he told me, and I sucked him roughly. "Use your teeth, just a bit."

I did, and he made a sound of approval in his throat.

"I'm going to fuck your mouth tomorrow. But not until I've fucked your cunt into submission." He pulled his finger free as he spoke.

I squirmed at his coarse language, somehow never in the least offended by the dirty things he said. In fact, I was hugely turned on by it.

"You have a filthy mouth," I told him, my eyes heavy-lidded.

He smirked. "Is that an invitation? I could get it that way in a hurry." He ran a tongue over his teeth as he spoke.

My insides clenched at the sight.

I shook my head, trying to get my mind back on the fact that I was working and that I needed to actually do some work.

"I need to go."

He gave me a twisted smile. "If anyone complains, you can always say you were servicing a passenger."

I wrinkled my nose at his choice of words, opening the door to ease out of the bathroom. I shut it behind me, assuming he would wait a moment before following.

Stephan was in the galley when I opened the curtain, fixing more rum and cokes for the couple in first class.

"Sorry," I mumbled, going to the counter and leaning against it.

He glanced at me with a wry smile. "You don't do anything half-assed. You go from stone-cold celibacy to being too loud in the bathroom at work. You've got it bad, Buttercup," he said, but with good humor.

He swept from the galley to deliver the drinks and I was still blushing when he came back in.

James joined us, coming to hug me from behind, as though completely unconcerned about the fact that I was working.

I tried to pull away. "James, I'm working."

He just hugged me harder, kissing my neck.

"What has gotten into you?" I asked him.

"You guys should be fine, if you stay in the galley," Stephan piped in with a smile. "The plane is practically empty, the couple in first class just used the restroom in back, and they show no signs of moving at the moment. Canoodle away, lovebirds."

I glared at him. "You're supposed to be the voice of reason, Stephan."

He shrugged. "It's not as though it's a crowded flight. If nobody knows, there's no harm done."

As though taking those words as an invitation, James pressed against me harder.

I elbowed him. He didn't budge.

"What about the rest of the crew? Anyone could write me up for this."

James kissed the top of my head, putting his hands lightly on my hips. He hadn't said a word since he'd come out of the bathroom. I couldn't fathom what he was thinking. I could only tell that he was suddenly as affectionate as a baby kitten.

Stephan shrugged. "I doubt anyone would. Melissa doesn't like you, but I have way more dirt on her, so she wouldn't dare. Just relax. Flight attendants bring their significant others on flights all the time. You think you're the first one to join the mile high club?"

I wondered briefly about what kind of dirt Stephan had on Melissa, but we were interrupted before I could ask.

As though cued into our conversation, Murphy stepped out of the cockpit, grinning at us.

"Did you consider our offer, Bianca?" he asked jovially, taking in James without comment.

Hard arms wrapped just under my breasts from behind.

I smiled at Murphy, hoping that James wouldn't turn things awkward.

"Murphy, all you did was scare the poor girl away next week, as well," Stephan told him with a grin.

Murphy looked crestfallen. "Is it possible I'm not as sexy as I think I am?"

We laughed. I looked up and even James was smiling.

Murphy went into the restroom.

"See, Mr. Beautiful, he's not so bad."

His grin died. "He's not the one I'm worried about," he told me.

How could such a beautiful man be insecure? I wondered. It was baffling to realize that he was.

I hadn't *thought* James was worried about Murphy, but I was still totally bewildered that he was actually jealous of Damien.

"You're the most gorgeous creature on the planet. How do

you not know that you've completely ruined me for other men?" I asked him quietly, and he gave me a beatific smile.

He bent and ravished my mouth until I yielded. I was hesitant at first to share such a hot kiss outside of a bedroom. But it was hard to remember that in the moment. He swept a tongue into my mouth, and it went on and on.

I was moaning low in my throat when he pulled away.

"Tell me that again," he murmured against my kiss-softened lips.

"A male supermodel would look downright homely standing next to you. No man could compare to you. Why would I ever bother with another one?" I spoke the words quietly, and he was swiftly kissing me again.

I realized I had found a weak spot. The words were nothing but the truth, but I needed to remember to use them when I needed them. I doubted he could stay mad when I reassured him in such a way.

I had no idea how long we'd been necking like teenagers when he pulled back again. I looked up into the startled gaze of Captain Damien, and a sheepish Stephan.

"Oh, hey," I murmured through kiss-swollen lips. The two men looked like they had been trying to speak to us and I hadn't even noticed.

James wrapped himself around me from behind again, his arms under my breasts and dangerously close to brushing too close for decency. He kissed my neck, giving me a soft bite as he pulled away. It was way too sensual for company, but I knew he didn't give a damn.

He reached out a long arm to the shorter Damien. "Hi. I'm James Cavendish. Bianca's boyfriend."

Damien shook his hand, looking stunned. "Oh. Boyfriend? Oh, well, hi. I'm Damien. Nice to meet you. You must be a pretty great guy if Bianca gave you a chance."

James kissed my neck again, sucking hard enough to leave a

mark. He kissed the spot again as he pulled his face away.

I squirmed uncomfortably. Things were getting awkward fast.

"We were made for each other. It's as simple as that. Bianca told me just a moment ago that I had ruined her for other men." His voice was all charm, but I glanced up and behind and found that, unsurprisingly, his smile was all predatory challenge.

I elbowed him in the ribs. I couldn't believe he'd said that. I blushed profusely.

Stephan laughed, though it died away when he saw my look.

Damien coughed uncomfortably. "Well, okay. I'd better get back. See you later." He left.

I was fuming.

James began kissing my neck again.

I tried to stomp back on his foot and missed. "That was embarrassing and out of line, James. You can't take things I say and use them like that. It makes me want to never tell you things like that."

He murmured an apology against my neck. "I'm sorry. I just had to set him straight after the things you said to him earlier. I won't do it again. Forgive me?"

His teeth tugged at my ear, and it was hard for me to concentrate.

"You need to go back to your seat," I told him sternly, far from appeased.

His hands drifted up to my breasts, and I looked around, scandalized. But we were alone. I hadn't even heard Stephan leave.

"I love your breasts. I'm going to clamp them tomorrow. I would pierce them for you, if you'd let me. I would love to mark you like that."

I knew he was trying to distract me, but even knowing that, his tactic still worked. I was shocked. It sounded like such a hardcore, permanent thing to do. I had never in my life even considered doing something like that. And he said it as though he'd do it himself.

"You could do that? As in, you could do the piercing yourself?"

He murmured a yes against my shoulder, kneading my breasts with just the right pressure.

"You think I would allow anyone else to handle these? To do that to you? Fuck no. That would be a job for me." He pinched them roughly as he spoke.

"You've done that before?" I asked him cautiously, my back arching automatically. I wasn't really thinking of doing it. I was more curious about this odd skill of his.

He rubbed his hard erection against my butt. "I'm properly trained and quite good at it. It can't be painless, but I'll try my best to lessen the pain."

I noticed that he didn't exactly answer the question. I had a sudden vision of all of his ex-lovers sporting nipple rings for years after he was done with them. It did seem like a small price to pay, I supposed, considering how good he was in bed.

"Do you pierce all of your lovers?"

He snorted. "You have the oddest notions. No, I do not normally pierce my lovers."

"Just your favorites?" I asked, half-serious.

"I only have one favorite," he replied, nuzzling against me.

"What was her name?" I asked, getting annoyed that he wouldn't give a real answer to the question.

He pinched a nipple hard enough to make me yelp. "I was referring to you, you silly girl. And to finally answer your persistent line of questioning, I have pierced three of my ex-lovers. Now, I believe it's my turn to get some information from you. And, considering that you got to pick the question for me, I'll do the same to you. Have you ever gone out with Captain Damien?"

I couldn't have been happier with his question. I'd just been about to protest the exchange when he'd asked it.

"Nope."

"Has he ever asked you out?"

"That's two questions," I said smugly.

"I believe I answered more than one."

I sighed. "Yes, when we first started hanging out with them, he did. I said no, and he's been completely platonic ever since."

"Why did you say no? You seem to like him."

I turned my head just enough to give him an arch look. "I wasn't interested. Apparently it takes a very specific type of man to get my interest."

He practically purred against my neck.

CHAPTER THIRTY

Mr. Gratification

We were taking our seats to land before I remembered to ask Stephan about something curious he'd said earlier.

"What kind of dirt do you have on Melissa? And why is this the first I'm hearing of it?" I asked him. He didn't, as a rule, keep things from me, even minor things.

He flushed a little. "It was a very crude story, and frankly I wanted to shelter you from it. You're not a virgin anymore, but what I saw made me feel dirty, so I didn't want to unload it on you."

This did nothing but pique my curiosity even more, of course.

"What on earth happened?"

He grimaced. "I walked in on Melissa in the cockpit last week. She was, um, she was giving the captain, Peter, um, oral pleasure."

I gasped, a hand flying to my mouth. He just nodded with a disgusted look on his face.

"Where was the co-pilot?" I asked, not sure why that was the first question that popped into my head.

"He was just sitting there, looking uncomfortable. I think

Melissa thought he'd be into it, but he sure wasn't. And then, after she saw your watch, I overheard her talking to Brenda and Jake as I approached the back galley. She had the nerve to tell them that she was planning to write you up for accepting gifts from passengers. She had the gall to actually imply that James had been paying you for something that you did for him in the bathroom of the aircraft."

My jaw literally dropped.

"That lying skank," I said in disgust, reacting quickly with temper.

He held up a hand. "I handled it. First of all, I confronted her in front of the others, making sure they knew that she was a flat-out liar. They had no trouble seeing that she was just jealous of your watch. Brenda and Jake both know me better, and they trust me, so they easily took my word over hers. And then I made sure they all knew what I had caught Melissa doing in the cockpit. She at least had the decency to look embarrassed about it. I even spoke to the first officer, and he agreed to back me up if I needed to write a report about it. Melissa knows I won't hesitate to get her fired if she tries to hurt you. She's lucky I didn't get her fired for trying to spread nasty rumors about you. I still get furious just thinking about it."

I patted his hand comfortingly, mulling over the drama that had unfolded around me while I had just been going about my work, oblivious.

"She's a piece of work," I commented, then dropped the subject.

"James is so crazy about you," Stephan murmured to me quietly.

He's crazy, all right, I thought, but I didn't comment.

I considered sharing every scandalous detail about our relationship with Stephan, but decided against it. It would dispel his strange notion of James falling for me like some romantic hero, but it would also make him unnecessarily sad.

238

James was waiting just outside the door as we walked out of the jet bridge as a crew, finally done for the night turned morning.

"Drive with me," he ordered as he fell into step beside me.

I slowed until the others passed us.

"I can't," I said to him quietly. "We're supposed to drive with the crew, and I need to go check into the hotel to reserve my room."

He flushed, his pretty mouth curling as he reached to pull my luggage for me. "That's all unnecessary, Bianca. For the love of God, just stay at my place."

I set my mouth. "We're not going over this again."

He walked beside me in silence until we were nearly at our pick-up location.

"Fine. A driver will come pick you up at the hotel," he said finally, handing me my bag.

"When?" I asked, but he was already striding away.

It was an entertaining bus ride, with Murphy at his most amusing. I wondered, as he was telling a funny story, if Melissa would try to go down on Damien with Murphy looking on in the flight deck this week. Or would she go down on both? I didn't know how that sort of thing worked.

I was just discovering my own kinky nature in full, but taking on two men just seemed too sordid to me. No matter what kind of spell James seemed to have me under, I knew I could never be talked into something like that.

Murphy interrupted my scandalous thoughts by addressing me directly. "You can't tell me you're not gonna be sorry to miss out on us tonight! Admit it, you love us!" Murphy had adopted his atrocious mockery of an Australian accent as he spoke. He did so often, claiming that it if it worked for Damien, it could work for him. Damien always winced when he heard the butchering of his accent, which just made it funnier.

I smiled. "I made plans before I knew about yours, Murphy.

Don't take it so hard."

"Just have James join us. If he has a romantic evening planned, just tell him to save it for another night!"

I thought of how he was going out that night without me. I briefly considered meeting up with them after that. I knew, from other nights we'd gone out with these pilots, that they would have no problem staying out late and then getting up early.

"Maybe I'll swing by the bar later," I conceded. "I'll have to play it by ear."

Murphy whooped as though he'd won a victory. I met Damien's eyes, and he was smiling warmly. I felt a little uncomfortable, and couldn't place why. We'd gone out with these pilots many times and there was usually never an uncomfortable moment.

Am I just worried about what James would think? The thought troubled me.

We reached the hotel and got our room keys in short order. Everyone was lingering in the lobby, chatting with the hotel staff. Murphy was convincing them to join up at the bar after work. It sounded like he was succeeding. Murphy was nearly as charming as Stephan, in his own silly way.

"Ms. Karlsson." A quiet voice spoke behind me.

I turned in surprise. It wasn't the usual way I was addressed. I was a little surprised to see Clark standing there, both in New York and in our hotel. I hadn't realized that he traveled with James outside of Las Vegas..

"Hi, Clark. How are you?" I asked, smiling.

"Great, Ms. Karlsson. The car is out front. Please, allow me to take your bag." He did so without waiting for an answer.

Stephan kissed me on the forehead. "Have fun, Buttercup. Call me if you need anything."

I nodded absently, seeing the strange looks on the rest of our crew's faces as I made a somewhat hasty departure. I gave them all a quick wave as I departed.

James could have told me that he meant right away. He probably hadn't told me for a reason, thinking I would argue with him. He may have been onto something.

Clark had already loaded my luggage and had the door open for me when I caught up to him. He was very fast. I smiled at him as I ducked into the low town car.

Strong arms startled a yelp out of me as I was plucked immediately into the now familiar lap of James. He hugged me tight, burying his face in my neck, nuzzling.

"You love that spot, huh?" I asked him, referring to the neck he was kissing.

"Oh, yes," he murmured against me. "I love all of your spots."

I rolled my eyes. "We both need a nap," I told him, wondering at his plans.

"We can nap after. I'm dying to show you some things. All of my self-control has deserted me. And to think, I used to be a man who believed in delayed gratification."

I raised my brows at him. "Seriously?"

He laughed richly, and I couldn't help but smile at the sound.

"Yes, believe it or not. I can't seem to help breaking all of my rules with you, Bianca."

James's apartment was a scant five minute drive from my hotel, but there was a world of difference in those blocks. We were passing swank high-rise buildings when James addressed Clark. "Go through the garage, please. I don't wish to use the front entrance today."

It made me stiffen a little. He was hiding me away. In spite of myself, I felt hurt. He was embarrassed to be seen with me, and I was getting too involved with him emotionally to just shrug it off for long.

He must go on some dates, I thought. He was just choosing *not* to do so with me. A flight attendant was hardly in his league. I just tried to add my hurt to the list of reasons why this was going to be a short, if intense, affair.

Clark drove us into an underground parking garage that looked typical of New York. James pulled me quickly from the car when Clark stopped in front of an elevator, not even waiting for Clark to open the door.

"I'll see you out front at 9:45," James told Clark briskly, pushing the elevator button impatiently.

Clark slipped back into the car and drove away without a word.

The elevator door opened and James pulled me inside the expensive looking cab, using a key to push the penthouse button.

Of course it was a penthouse, I thought.

"I have something for you," James said. "I'm not sure you're going to like it at first, but I want you to give it a chance."

That sounded ominous, and I just blinked at him.

He grinned at me. "I know you're new to the whole BDSM thing. New to all of it. And I'm not sure how fair it is that I've shown you things rather than explaining them to you, but I'm not sorry for any of it. Perhaps I owe you more of an explanation for some of it, and I will get to that. But I had something made for you. It has significance for me, and I want you to wear it."

I just pursed my lips and looked at him. "Is it some kind of a piercing?" I asked him.

He laughed, pulling me against him. He fondled me. I tried to elbow him away.

"That's not an answer," I told him.

"No, it's not a piercing, though I'm not done trying to talk you into that, either." As he spoke, he kneaded my breasts.

"Well, I won't agree to anything if you don't tell me what I'm agreeing to."

"I want you to be mine, Bianca. Will you be my submissive?" he whispered in my ear.

My heart stopped. I wasn't exactly shocked by the submissive thing, but the formal way he asked it sounded almost like a romantic proposal on his lips.

"I don't entirely understand what that means, James."

"It means anything we want it to. What it means to me is that I want you to belong to me, and that you will submit to me, and trust me to dominate you how I need to."

I had no idea how to respond to that, but I didn't have to for a moment as the elevator opened and I was pulled swiftly into James's sumptuous apartment.

It was a frivolously open space, considering the usual New York cramped living spaces. I could see that it had at least three stories just from the entryway.

He had chosen a clean, modern decorating style, with floors lined in a stark gray hardwood and glass walls interspersed throughout. Heavy vases and expensive looking artwork added most of the color to the mostly gray, neutral space. The splashes of color were vivid, brought out exquisitely against the lack of color, as though the floors and walls were meant to be the perfect frames.

"It's lovely," I told him as he pulled me through the opulent space without pausing. As we passed through room after room, I marveled at the size of the place.

"Do you like it?" he asked, still pulling me along. He was glancing into doorways as though he was looking for something.

"Yes. You have impeccable taste."

He flashed me a grin. "Yes, I do," he said, giving me the warmest look, and I blushed. "I'm glad you like it."

He approached a large open dining room. It had a spectacular view of central park. He drew me to the window.

"Stay here," he told me, walking through a closed door to my left. I heard him speaking to someone in the next room. Staff of some sort, I noted, from the snippet of conversation I could hear.

I felt overwhelmed by his home, but still appreciative of its beauty. I ran a finger along the gleaming dark gray top of the heavy, colossally large table that dominated the room.

I admired the huge arrangement of flowers in the middle of the table. It was a mix of vibrantly colored orchids, displayed in a short, square, intricately carved crimson vase.

I was studying the extravagant view of central park when James reappeared a few minutes later, holding a thin square box and smiling.

CHAPTER THIRTY-ONE

Mr. Mercurial

He took my hand and began to lead me again. "I'll give you the grand tour later," he muttered, hurrying. He led me up both flights of stairs, then down a long hallway.

"I seem to only get to see very specific parts of your houses," I responded archly.

He sent me a conciliatory smile. "I'll make it up to you. Later."

He pulled me into a room that I could see was the master bedroom just from the monumental size of the bed. The blinds were opened to the same amazing view of the park as the dining room, just a few stories higher. The window lined nearly an entire wall of the room, floor to ceiling. The bed was a more modern take on the one he had in Vegas, with cleaner lines, but I was sure it had the same function by the cage-like top and thick, square posts. The hues in the room were a mix of bright, varying shades of green, accented with white, with starkly dark wood dominating all of the furniture and the floor. With an entire wall framing a spectacular view of the park, it had the feel of an indoor forest.

"It's amazing," I told him honestly.

He smiled, pleased with my reaction.

I noticed a small door with no handle near the open bathroom. It was conspicuous because there was a lit panel with a button beside it. I pointed at it. "Is that an elevator?"

His smile turned wicked. "Yes."

"I didn't realize the apartment had an elevator."

"It has a few, actually. But that one goes somewhere special. I'll be showing you soon. First, I want you to get on your knees and close your eyes."

I sent him a startled look. He had switched gears without blinking, as usual. It was hard to keep up with his changing moods.

I knelt, obeying him because we were in his bedroom, and it was just so natural to let him rule me here.

I closed my eyes. After a few heartbeats I felt something cool being placed against the very upper edges of my collarbone.

James straightened the collar of my uniform, shifting it around.

"Perfect," he murmured. "You can wear it to work." He tucked what felt like a slightly rough circle of some kind against my chest.

"Okay, open your eyes," he said finally.

I did, and he pulled me to my feet, leading me into a large, softly lit closet. The closet was twice the size of my bedroom, with expensive men's clothing lining the walls. It smelled divine, like James himself.

He positioned me in front of a large floor-length mirror, and began to undress me without a word. He undid my tie first, politely hanging it on a hanger. He showed me a large, bare rack in the closet. "This will be for your things. If you run out of room, I'll make more for you."

I was a little stunned at his assumption that I would be keeping things here.

"I would very much like for you to use my personal shopper to buy a wardrobe for you here in New York, so you don't have to move your things across the country. She should be getting in touch with you in a few days."

"That's silly. I don't want you buying me clothes," I told him, trying not to get angry. "It feels too much like being kept."

He sighed. "It's just clothing. I thought we had decided that you weren't going to balk at gifts."

I glared at him, and he saw my expression.

"Please, just consider it. You don't have to decide right now. We have other things to talk about, at the moment."

I lost my train of thought as he removed my jacket and vest, hanging them. His fingers lingered on the button at my throat. He undid my top four buttons, spreading my shirt open to reveal the necklace he had placed around my neck.

It was lovely, made of some kind of silver metal into what looked like one solid band, but was in fact soft and moveable, just a very seamless looking, tightly linked necklace. It sat right at the very top of my collarbone, at the base of my throat. He was right. It had been hidden just perfectly under my uniform. At the center of the thick choker sat a large diamond studded hoop. I fingered it, and he reached around me to hook his index finger into the loop, tugging lightly.

"It's lovely," I told him, but I was troubled. *What was its significance to him?*

"I had it made as a sort of workable version of a slave collar."

I froze at the word, instantly wanting to take off anything with such a name. He gripped my hands tightly, holding them down at my sides firmly, as though sensing my intent.

"Just hear me out. We already have a dominant-submissive relationship. It comes naturally to us. It is just who we are. But that can mean whatever we want it to mean. Do you understand? I want to find the best balance for us both."

I was already shaking my head at him. "That only comes natural to us in bed. I don't want this going anywhere else. You don't get to boss me around in any other part of my life. And I'm no slave."

He inclined his head, although he looked displeased.

"I'm not trying to boss you around anywhere else. I'm trying to have a *relationship* with you, something I've never done before, and I'll take what I can get. I want you to see that I will work with you. I will make...concessions for you, if there's something that you can't accept. I simply want you to give me all that you can. And not to run, if you get overwhelmed. And it's called a slave collar only because it denotes ownership. It is a symbol of your commitment to me, to give your body only to me and no one else. To submit your body only to me. There is a lock and a key that only I will be the owner of, but I won't lock you in until you agree. I want you to tell me when you're ready for that. Until then, you can wear it unlocked."

I stared at him for long minutes, my mind having a hard time processing what he was saying, when I was conflicted about so much of what he'd revealed.

He wanted a relationship? What the hell did he mean by that? I shook myself, trying to focus on the issue at hand.

"What if I'm never ready to be locked in?"

He gave me an almost sinister smile. "I will endeavor to convince you."

He began to unbutton the rest of my shirt. I didn't stop him, just stared at my collar, my mind racing.

He stripped me with quick sure motions until I was only in stockings and garters. He watched me for a long time in the mirror, wearing just that, but eventually stripped those off too. He tugged off my watch and even my small stud earrings. My first instinct when standing completely nude in front of him was to cover myself with my hands, but I stifled the urge with effort. I knew it wouldn't please him, and my overpowering urge to please him had only grown during our short, tempestuous acquaintance...

He reached into a drawer and pulled out a tiny scrap of see-through black cloth. He wrapped it around my hips, fastening it with a tiny silver chain. It fit perfectly, sitting right below my waist, as though I'd been measured for it. It seemed to show as much as it concealed, every curve clearly visible beneath it, but James seemed very pleased with the results, his eyes positively glowing as he stared at me.

I assumed by its ready location in the drawer that it was some sort of submissive uniform for him. God only knew how many women he had dressed in just this way. I tried my best not to think about that.

He pulled something out of his pocket. It just looked like a lovely silver chain at first, but I saw the little clamps as he straightened the chain into a smooth line. He used a tiny clip on the chain to fasten it to the hoop in my collar.

I gasped.

He wrapped it through the hoop several times until there was just enough of the chain left to reach my nipples with the clamps. He fastened them, his eyes hooded, while my breath grew rough in agitation. It looked like a sort of obscene halter top of metal. With a slave collar...

He smoothed my errant hairs into the chignon at my nape. He couldn't seem to stop touching me. He stroked my shoulders and my waist and hips, but his fingers always found their way back to my breasts. He was tweaking the clamps until I could hardly stand the wait.

"If you enjoy the clamps, you should be well suited to the piercings. The clamps actually apply more pressure than the piercings, after the initial pain." He continued to play with my tortured nipples, tugging until I moaned.

He pulled me by the hoop at my neck through his room and to the elevator. I could feel every step and pull in my achy breasts. I trailed after him, barefoot and nearly naked, him fully clothed in one of his mouth-watering suits. I looked back at his bed longingly.

"I want you to take me on your bed," I told him, a strange note of a plea in my voice.   It just looked so perfect, and I was suddenly so needy.

"I will, Love.   But, first things first, " he said, pulling me into the elevator the second it opened.

The elevator began to move, descending smoothly.

"How far down does this thing go?"   I asked him, after it seemed like we had gone impossibly far.

"Just four floors."   The elevator finally stopped, opening slowly.

James tugged me out. "Welcome to the 4th floor, Bianca."

We entered a plain gray hallway first. The floor was smooth gray wood. It was clean and flawless, but starkly monotone.

It feels like a dungeon, I thought with a shiver.

We passed by two rooms before we entered the door at the end of the hall. I wanted to ask what the other rooms were, but I was suddenly terrified, my mind running wild with strange possibilities, feeling transported into another century. *For all I know, he could have other women in them.*

The thought stopped me, and James had to tug harder to get me to follow him this time.

"This is not the place to be obstinate, Bianca."

"Yes, Mr. Cavendish," I said, a tremor in my voice.

What was the worst that could happen? I asked myself, trying to talk myself out of my sudden, disproportionate terror.

He positioned me in front of him, giving me a full view of the huge, dark gray room that he'd led me to. He waited patiently, giving me time to process what I was seeing.

It was indeed a playground. It was a BDSM wet dream, from what I understood of what I saw.   Chains, whips, shackles. Various torturous looking devices were set up in stations around the room.

My attention seemed to focus first on some sort of swing to

my right.   It was a series of leather straps and metal that fascinated me. I shifted towards it without thinking.

James followed my gaze and my movement. "So you like the swing? We can start with that. Since it's your first time on the 4th floor, I'll let you pick. I'm feeling generous today."

"Are you going to punish me?" I asked, my voice breathless.

He just tsked at me, pulling me towards the swing. "If you disobey me in here, I *will* punish you. Until then, consider this just a lesson. Do you understand?"

"Yes, Mr. Cavendish."

He positioned me just in front of the swing.

"Don't move," he ordered, grabbing my wrist and fastening it with a thick leather cuff. He pulled it tight with its belt loop fastenings. He tested it to be certain it was nice and snug. The material touching my wrist was soft as down, whereas the leather on the outside of the cuff looked stiff and unyielding. He fastened my other wrist with sure, economical movements. He placed my hands around a metal bar above my head.

"Lift yourself," he ordered.

I did, and he settled thick supportive straps against my lower back and my ass. He knelt down to my ankles, and I watched him fasten similar leather restraints to the ones at my wrists there.   He cinched restraints just above my knees, as well, though they were a softer, more pliable material. The area just above my elbows got the same treatment.

He straightened, then began to adjust all of the straps above me.   He seemed to know exactly what he wanted, his hands moving from one to the next with no hesitation.

Finally, he stepped back, shrugging out of his suit jacket and loosening his tie impatiently.

"Let go of the bar," he ordered.

I hesitated, feeling as though I would just spin to the floor if I did so.

"Now," he barked.

I hesitated just a fraction longer, but let go. I felt weightless as I fell back. The straps caught me in a strangely light embrace, the strap against my back and butt more comfortable than I would have imagined.

My arms were suspended nearly even with my shoulders. My back was arched, displaying my chest and stomach decadently. My legs were splayed wide, my sex exposed.

I tried to close my legs, at least a little, but it was impossible. The ropes held them tight.

James approached me, placing my feet into soft stirrups that parted my legs impossibly wider.

I whimpered low in my throat.

He just pulled at my nipple clamps lightly before stepping away.

I saw him unbuttoning his dress shirt impatiently as he strode behind me. I tried to turn my head to watch him, but I was suspended too tightly for that. I thought this must be what a fly felt like when it was caught fast in a spider's web.

CHAPTER THIRTY-TWO

Mr. Wonderful

I couldn't tell where he went from my prone position, but it sounded like he'd gone to the other end of the room.

He was gone for several agonizing minutes before I felt him behind me, stepping close enough for his now bared chest to brush my back.

"Just a taste. For not trusting me when I told you to let go," he whispered in my ear before adjusting the strap at my ass until my backside was fully exposed to him.

Something slapped against me hard enough to make my eyes sting with tears. He repeated the action twice before he readjusted the support strap until my butt was again covered, and my sex was exposed.

He circled around until I could see him again. He was shirtless and shoeless now, but his slacks remained on, his erection straining against his fly. The expensive cloth against his perfect, bare skin made his muscular physique even more starkly apparent, his muscles bulging as he folded his arms and stood, legs apart, just looking at me.

His eyes were hungry, but so stern.

He held a rectangular paddle in his hand casually.   It reminded me of the kind they used to say were used at schools for punishment, though this one was black.

He walked between my parted thighs. He bent and kissed my forehead.

"Exquisite," he said against my skin, then pulled back.

I writhed, becoming impossibly impatient in my need for his physical contact. He placed a hand on my inner thigh, just shy of my cleft. It was torturous, watching that hand touching just above where I needed it. The flesh beneath his hand quivered.

In a flash, he slapped my other thigh with the paddle just hard enough to sting.

He took a step back, grabbing my wrist and giving the swing a hard shove, sending me spinning in circles until I was dizzy. I gave an embarrassing little scream of surprised distress.

He stopped my spinning with a hand on my wrist, and he was suddenly between my legs, thrusting into me in a smooth but brutal motion. His hands kneaded the flesh of my breast around the nipple clamps firmly. Those were our only two points of contact. Cock to cunt, and hands to breasts.

He thrust in and out, only a half a dozen slow strokes, before he pulled out of me, stepping back and spinning me again.

He was stepping between my legs as I came to a halt, right onto his well aimed cock. He gave me a longer taste this time before pulling out. My head had just stopped spinning when he whirled me again.

He stopped me with a grip on my ankle this time, and thrust into me harder, working in and out like a jackhammer. He massaged my clit with one hand, the other getting rough with the clamp that held my nipple.

"Come, now," he ordered, and it worked, as it always did.

I came with a scream, my head thrown back.

He pulled out, flipping me around before my walls were even done clenching in orgasm.

He had me repositioned, face down, ass up, in a blink. He worked in slowly, and I shivered around him, still having little aftershocks.

"Fuck," he cursed. "Those little clenches are gonna make me come."

"Yes," I sobbed. "Come."

He slapped my ass, thrusting agonizingly slowly inside of me.

"I won't come until I've shown you more of the delights this little swing has to offer." He wrenched out of me, sending me spinning again.

I whimpered.

He jolted into me hard when I stopped this time, moving with a purpose now. He reached around me, his talented fingers collaborating to bring me to my next release.

I sobbed out his name as I came again.

He flipped me in a flash until my face was only inches from the floor. He began to suck at me with his mouth, the soft contrast to his previous treatment making me beg brokenly. For what, I wasn't sure.

He pulled his mouth away, and a moment later he was working his stiff cock into me again. It was a slower process in this position. He had to squeeze in inch by inch. I heard him cursing. I was stuffed so full that I held my breath in alarm at the sensation. He made little rough strokes for only a moment before pulling out.

He rearranged me upright, taking several minutes to suspend me just above him. Our mouthes were on a level for the first time.

He kissed me passionately as he thrust into me, letting loose and thrusting wildly.

I was keening in my throat. I couldn't touch him with my restraints, but he touched me.

His hands were everywhere, caressing and pinching and soothing with incredible skill.

"Fucking come," he said between gritted teeth, as his head fell back with his own release.

It was mesmerizing to watch him lose it like that, and so my eyes never left him as I came at his command. I moaned his name.

"Fuck, fuck, fuck," he cursed, again and again, as he poured into me.

He unfastened me masterfully and cradled me in his arms. He carried me to an oversized bed in the corner. He laid me on top of the spread, sprawling at my side.

I saw that he was completely naked, a fact that I had somehow overlooked before.

He must have stripped out of his pants while I was spinning, my dazed mind noted.

He removed my nipple clamps, sucking gently at the red flesh. He took his time, giving equal attention to each abused nipple. After long moments of drawing on them with special focus, he straightened to study my face.

He loomed over me, a hand pressed flat to my lower belly, just watching my face for long minutes. He kissed my forehead. He seemed to be waiting for something.

I asked him what.

"I was waiting to see if you were falling asleep. Are you in the mood for an information exchange?"

I stretched, feeling languid and exhausted, but strangely, I was far from sleep. I thought about his question. It was strange, but the thought of answering his questions wasn't troubling to me at that moment. I supposed a half a dozen orgasms had something to do with that. I figured he probably knew that. He was far more familiar with post-coital feelings than I was.

I felt oddly open to him, uncharacteristically free of my usual reserve. I hoped, in a distant kind of way, that this was a temporary insanity, and not yet another symptom of my growing obsession with this man. I gave the little shrug that drove him crazy.

"Fine," I said, running a hand along the chest that loomed over me. "Ask me something."

He smiled at me softly, then bit his lip as though he was nervous.

I watched the action in fascination. I'd never seen him do such a thing. James doing anything that vulnerable just didn't connect in my head.

"I found out what sotnos means. I want to know why a term of endearment became your safe word."

I wasn't shocked. I'd known by the look on his face that it would be that, or something just as personal. The words were leaving my mouth before I could talk myself out of it. I wanted to know him, so perhaps it wouldn't hurt to let him know *me* a little.

"My father used to call me that," I said. It was true, and it was the simplest answer.

His brow furrowed. He had been hoping for more of an answer, I could tell. "That doesn't really explain anything to me. Why would an endearment from your father be a good safe word for you?"

"You're gonna owe me one hell of a revelation after this," I told him, poking his chest.

He nodded solemnly, and with no hesitation. It reassured me, for some reason. I took a deep breath to begin.

"He used to beat the shit out of me," I began.

James tensed, and my hand stroked him absently.

I continued with a sigh. "Not spankings, or a slap on the wrist, or whatever normal kids get. He beat me senseless. He would wail on my mother and I with little thought for the consequences. And there were none, not for him. The only reason I knew that he had even an ounce of control was that he didn't hit our faces. He thought we were pretty, and he was proud of that. He wanted us to stay pretty, I guess."

I stole a glance at his face. It was ashen, his pallor suddenly gray. But I continued, feeling a weight lift as I let out some of the gory details. "He was a cold brute of a man. And huge. God, he was so huge. As a child, I thought he was a giant. Stephan fought him once. You wouldn't know it, since he hates violence, but Stephan is a hell of a fighter. Stephan managed to overpower him, but only barely. My dad has to outweigh him by at least fifty pounds, and it was a close thing. But Stephan was a quicker and much more experienced fighter. Stephan used to literally feed us by fighting, and he was barely sixteen at the time. My dad was only used to beating on women and children, I suppose. But seeing how those beefy fists nearly sent a large man like Stephan to a hospital, I can't imagine how my mother and I survived them for so long..."

I shook myself out of my musing, and got back to the point. "He was not an affectionate father. He was just cold, and then brutal and angry when he lost his temper. But even his rages were cold. He often addressed my mother and I with the endearment sotnos, in this cold, mocking way of his. So when you asked me to pick a safe word, for when things went farther than I could handle, I just thought of it. Nothing terrified me more than those words on his lips. It seemed perversely appropriate."

"Fuck," James muttered with feeling, looking distraught.

I grinned wryly. "I told you I was fucked up," I told him.

"How did he die?" James asked in a hoarse voice, his hand stroking my belly.

I didn't mention the score we were keeping on our information. Apparently I was in an answering mood, because I just answered. "He didn't," I said softly.

His eyes went a little wild as they shot from my stomach to

my face. "But you said-"

"I lied. About him, but not my mother. She's dead."

"How did she die? And where is your father?"

"She killed herself." The lie slipped from my lips with no effort or remorse. It was an old lie. And a necessary one. "And I have no idea where he is. I ran away from home just after my mother died. I was nearly fifteen, and I never stopped running. He found me, a few times. The foster system was actually unhelpful enough to reunite us. But by then I had Stephan. He would always protect me, and we would run again."

"So you were in foster care? That's how you met Stephan?"

I gave a swift shake of my head. "We had some run-ins with foster care, but no. We were homeless runaways. I met Stephan because some homeless old man was trying to rape me, and he beat the pervert to within an inch of his life. You can thank Stephan for helping to keep my virginity intact. We were inseparable after that. We never even discussed it. We just became family."

I saw a fine tremor rock his body. I touched his jaw softly with a fingertip. "

I want to kill somebody," James whispered. I traced his jaw. "I can't bear the thought of the man who beat you as a child running loose. I can't believe that someone like you was made to live on the streets, unprotected."

"I had Stephan," I said simply. He had made all of the rest of it worth it. Having someone like him at my back had made my life bearable during the horrible times.

"I love that guy. Remind me to buy him a ridiculously extravagant gift. I know he likes cars..." he trailed off.

I laughed, and it felt surprisingly carefree. "I love him too, but I refuse to encourage you there."

"I need you to answer a question for me. Be brutally honest. Is this bad for you, what we do together? Am I like your father? We don't have to do any of the rough stuff, if it's too much for you. I don't want to be bad for you."

I traced his lips, choosing my words carefully. "I've been fascinated by the BDSM stuff since I can remember. It embarrassed me, and so I hid it well. Obviously, I had no experience with it, but I felt drawn to it, always. And the way you embrace it, with no shame, is liberating to me. My past has shaped me, that's true of anyone, but I don't think it's bad for me to confront it in this way. It's good for me to have someone like you, who can help me with this outlet. Someone who I think I could learn to trust. And you are *nothing* like my father."

I could see that my words reassured him. He leaned down to kiss my forehead softly.

"Thank you," he murmured against my skin.

"And we're getting off track. You owe me a painful revelation. A few of them, actually. Why do you hate alcohol so much?" I asked.

I knew there was something there. I just sensed it. His reaction to seeing me drunk, and his instinctive tensing every time he thought I might drink alcohol, was all just too personal.

He ran his hand up my torso, tracing my ribs.

I gave him a few minutes of silence while he watched me broodingly, and formed his answer.

"I told you about my first guardian when my parents died. He was an older cousin. His name was Spencer, and I despised him. Supposedly, he was a close friend of my fathers. I could see why, right at first. He seemed nice at the beginning, never giving me any rules or restrictions. I was barely fourteen and he would let me have wine with dinner. I thought he was the coolest guy in the world. Until I realized that he was drugging the wine."

A hand went to my throat at his words. I held my breath for him to continue, knowing with inexplicable certainty that the rest would be bad.

"It took me awhile. I would just have these blackouts. I

wouldn't remember anything after dinner.   But there were…
signs."

"I was sore in places that I shouldn't have been. I had marks
on my back, and wrists, and…other places.   And Spencer
changed.   At first it was just something knowing in his eyes.
After a time, he started to brush up against me in broad
daylight, and I just knew. I just knew that he had done things to
me, things that I hadn't consented to. Not that a fourteen year
old can consent to any damn thing."

Tears filled my eyes for the first time in many years, and my
hands stroked him reassuringly. It both broke me, and touched
me, that he would share such a thing with me.

He noted my tears, and brushed them from my cheeks almost
absently, continuing.   "It was just a guess on my part, but I
suspected the wine. So I pretended to drink it one night, and let
him lead me to his room.   He had me handcuffed before I
realized what he was doing. But by then, I was helpless. And
then I got to experience the whole disgusting thing without the
benefit of drugged wine."

I traced those tiny scars on his wrists, and he let me. He shut
his eyes tightly when I kissed them, but he didn't stop me.

"I think he knew that I wasn't as drugged out as usual almost
immediately, but I really don't think the bastard cared. He had
convinced himself that I was a willing participant, no matter
what I said or how I struggled."

"He didn't let me loose until morning.   That was the longest
night of my life. I was exhausted and sick down to my soul, but
I still had the gumption to beat the shit out of him the second I
was free."

"He steered clear of me after that. And not even a year later,
some angry lover choked him to death. He liked younger men
who could overpower him physically. I guess it finally backfired.
At least that lover wasn't underage.   It was a huge family
scandal.   All of my relatives were mortified. But I relished the

news." His eyes had glazed over as he told me the gory details, but they cleared as he finished, and seemed to focus back on me right away.

He leaned down and kissed me when he finished. I returned the kiss desperately. He pulled back, murmuring into my mouth.

"You're the first person, aside from my therapist, that I've ever told that to. I was so ashamed by it all. Does it change the way you see me?"

In answer, I kissed him with all of the emotion that I felt for this damaged soul that seemed, somehow, to match my own. And to complement it in just the way that I hadn't realized I'd needed so desperately.

We just kissed like that for long minutes. It was a soft and reverent kind of sharing. The type of intimacy that would have made my skin crawl at one time. But it didn't now. I relished the contact, something having changed inside of me.

He finally pulled back, but only to lift me. "I need you in my bed, Love. Say goodbye to the 4th floor, for now. But we'll be back, make no mistake."

He cradled me against his chest as he walked with seemingly no effort to the elevator, not setting me down or shifting me as he boarded the elevator and it rose slowly back to his room.

I nuzzled against his chest. He kissed the top of my head.

He laid me on his bed and made love to me. I imagined it was a lot like being made love to in a forest, the huge, wall-sized window flooding us with sunlight.

He was all tender lover, though even James's tender lover side had an edge. He pinned my legs down on the bed, parted wide, so that his every hard thrust rubbed my clitoris almost unbearably roughly. He made me come again and again before he allowed his own release.

"You're mine," he breathed into my ear afterward. We lay together, entwined. We were on our sides, and he was wrapped around me tightly from behind, a hand laced firmly with one of my own.

"Yes," I murmured back, and sank into a deep and peaceful sleep.

CHAPTER THIRTY-THREE

Mr. Beautiful

I awoke to darkness, disoriented at first, and uncertain of what had awoken me.

"Shh, love, go back to sleep," James murmured into my ear, rising and going immediately into the bathroom. I heard the shower turn on. I made myself get up.

I went into the closet, putting on my work clothes, since they were the only ones I had. I definitely needed a shower, but it could wait for my hotel room. I had a feeling that if I joined him in the shower now, he would talk me into staying at his place while he went out. I still wasn't willing to do that.

I dressed quickly, going to the bathroom door when I heard the shower turn off, speaking to James through it.

"I'm starving. Mind if I go try to find some food in your kitchen while you get ready?"

"Please. I'm sorry. I've been a negligent host. Help yourself. I'll need some time to get ready, but I'll join you in about twenty minutes."

I had seen the pristine tuxedo laid out in his closet, so I knew why he needed some time. He was obviously attending a black tie event. And one far fancier than anything I'd ever been to.

"Okay," I said.

I got a little lost navigating through his maze of an apartment, but it was a good thing that I did, since I found my suitcase. I had left it in the trunk of the car when Clark had driven away. I hadn't even given it a thought until the second I saw it again. I grabbed it gratefully, pulling it behind me as I attempted to place the kitchen, trying to retrace James's steps from the day before.

I found it more by sound than sight, inadvertently coming at it from a different angle. I could hear two female voices chatting, one warm and husky, the other friendly and tinkling with laughter.

I approached the open doorway cautiously. What I saw confused me, and I just stood there, blinking.

One woman was in her fifties and I recognized her friendly voice from overhearing her speaking to James when we had first arrived. She was the housekeeper. She was a plump hispanic lady and had the look of a kindly mom-type. Her words trailed off as she saw me. She took in my disheveled appearance wordlessly.

I wasn't surprised by her presence. It was the other woman whose presence I couldn't make sense of.

She was exceptionally beautiful, with coifed, curly black hair that shone brilliantly. Perhaps she was related to James, I told myself. She was beautiful enough to share his bloodline, if anyone could be as beautiful as James.

Her lovely gray eyes studied me with far less surprise than I studied her. She was decked out for a black tie affair in a silky, pale-gray gown that matched her eyes and belonged on the red carpet. It had a classic and simple strapless design that clung to her perfect body like a glove. She had a very tidy body, with the tiniest waist I'd ever seen in my life, but it still managed to be voluptuous, flaring out in the quintessential hourglass. She was the kind of woman that made every woman feel worse just by looking at her. She was several inches shorter than me, no taller than five foot six.

She made me feel instantly tall and awkward. Her tan skin was flawless, her lips lush and sultry, her nose pert and perfect.

"Another flight attendant?" the woman asked in a husky voice. She was speaking to the housekeeper. "Boys and their toys." Her voice was casual, and she rolled her eyes, but there was a certain tension around her mouth that spoke of cold anger.

"He'll be ready to settle down with you in a few years, my dear. Men are basically animals until they hit thirty. It's a well-known fact," the housekeeper said to the lovely creature, sounding kindly.

Her eyes weren't kindly as they sized me up, though.

I was starting to get a very sick feeling in the pit of my stomach. I looked at the lovely woman dumbly for a moment, then made myself ask. "Who are you?" My voice was small and pitiful. I really didn't want to hear the answer, but I had to ask.

The woman smiled, her expression warming in an instant, like magic. Either she was a consummate actress, or she had suddenly decided that she liked me. I was definitely betting on the former.

"I'm Jules Phillips."

"Are you related to James?" I asked. I was grasping at straws, I knew.

She laughed, and it was a warm, sensual sound.

I felt so sick that I thought I might lose the contents of my stomach right on her perfect red stilettos.

"No. If I were a relative, the things that James and I have done would certainly be illegal. I'm his date tonight. He's escorting me to a charity ball. It's for a charity our mothers founded together. Poor thing, did he not tell you about me? He can have a one-tracked mind. I've had to be very understanding of his peculiar…whims, over the years."

She fingered a necklace at her throat, eying up my own bared collar, where I had left the top few buttons undone. Hers was a diamond collar, not so very different from my own.

"Although he's always been generous enough to make it worthwhile," she continued, "as I'm sure you know."

That did it. I barely made it to the sink before I began to vomit.

Jules made a sympathetic noise, and I felt someone smoothing my hair back. The housekeeper made a disgusted noise.

"Too much to drink, dear?" Jules asked, stroking my hair. There was a bite to her question that she probably thought I wouldn't pick up.

She was a woman to be careful of. I knew it with grim certainty.

I brushed her off.

"Please, give me space," I said, feeling suffocated.

I straightened, wiping my mouth on my sleeve. I'd never felt so disgusting in my life. Never felt so dirty. He was a liar, I thought. I had fallen in love with a perfect lie. I had shared myself with a beautiful liar. I felt laid bare.

I have to get out of here.

I lurched out of the kitchen. I would rather be sick in the street than spend another second in *his* home. I made it to the elevator, punching the button.

I felt Jules hovering behind me, a heavy presence at my back.

"Do you live together?" I asked her, without turning.

The other woman didn't answer, and I assumed the worst.

There was a table by the elevator. I removed my necklace and watch with trembling hands. I laid them on the table carefully, but they still made a loud clanking sound.

I couldn't get into the elevator fast enough when it finally opened. It was only then that I turned.

On a landing above, I saw that James had just emerged from

his bedroom, immaculately dressed for his date. He was frozen in place, taking in the sight of the two of us below. He seemed to register something in my face.

"Bianca, wait," he said, panic in his voice, his eyes gone wild. He was running down the stairs in a frantic burst as the the elevator doors slid mercifully shut.

I spent the ride down taking deep breaths, trying not to be sick again. It would be too humiliating to leave his elevator stinking with my vomit. And I'd had enough humiliation for the night.

When I reached the street level, I nearly ran from the building. I stood at the edge of the sidewalk for a long moment, disoriented.

"Ms. Karlsson?" A voice called from my right, concern in the voice.

I turned and saw Clark approaching me cautiously, as though afraid I would bolt into the street.

"Let me give you a ride, Miss Karlsson. Please. You look upset." He spoke quietly, his voice kind and worried. "I'll call Mr. Cavendish, and he'll take care of whatever is troubling you."

At the mention of the name, I did bolt.

I ran across the crowded street without even looking, propelled by panic. I didn't want to see him. Horns honked, but I didn't care. A taxi had to careen to a halt mere inches from me.

I glanced inside. It was empty. I got in, dragging my suitcase topped with my flight bag in beside me. I directed the driver to my hotel.

He looked at me like I was crazy, but I reached into my flight bag, fished out my wallet, and thrust a twenty at him. I would normally never take a cab. It was an ungodly expensive way to get around. But at that moment, I would have paid just about anything just to get away. I wanted to get to my room and curl into a ball.

I knew Stephan would still be out. I debated calling him. I knew he would drop whatever he was doing and come back to comfort me. I wanted that. But I dismissed the idea almost immediately. It was a selfish instinct; to pull him away from a fun night and into my misery.

I got gracelessly out of the cab when it stopped. I felt around for my room key, relieved when I found the card still in a pocket. I didn't want to talk to anyone, not even the the friendly hotel staff.

I nodded at the girl manning the front desk when she called out a greeting. I didn't recognize her through my blurred haze of misery, even though she called me by name.

I moved quickly to the elevator.

I felt a wave of relief when I finally let myself into my room, bolting the door behind me. I'd had some crazy, paranoid idea that James was chasing me, trying to catch me before I could lock him out and never speak to him again.

I just leaned against the door for long minutes, trying not to lose it.

Of course, I'd known James had a long line of ex-lovers. Of course, I'd known he was a womanizer. Of course, I was a fool. When he'd told me he'd be exclusive, I had just believed him, as though a man like that wouldn't be a consummate liar.

I left my suitcase at the door, deliberately making myself go through the usual motions.

I pulled the top cover off of the bed, tossing it into a heap in the farthest corner of the room. I knew they never washed those things. I set the alarm by the bed, and then the one on my phone, plugging it in to charge.

I saw that I had eight missed calls. I just turned off the vibrator as well as the ringer, so that it wouldn't wake me with calls or messages. I'd set it up to only make noise as an alarm.

I unpacked the minimum. Just toiletries and my extra uniform.

I moved to the adjoining door. Even though I had been spending the day away, we had arranged to adjoin, as usual. I opened my side, relieved to see that Stephan had already done the same. I
heard movement in his bathroom, and jumped.

"Ste-Stephan?" I called, really hoping it was him.

He strode out of his bathroom at my call. He was shirtless, wearing only low-slung navy cargo shorts. "Hey, Buttercup. Some knucklehead got barf on my shirt, so I had to come back to change." He moved towards me as he spoke, drying his hair briskly with a towel.

He got a look at my face and froze. Scant moments later I was being enfolded into his arms. He held my face to his bare chest, stroking my hair.

"Oh, Bee, what is it?"

I had managed not to cry until then, but his sympathy undid me. I heard a broken sob escape from my throat, as though from a distance. I never cried, especially not like this. I wet his chest with my hopeless sobbing.

How had I let this happen? I asked myself, again and again. I had been so certain that I wouldn't let my heart get involved. But in the end, I'd had no control, even in that.

I felt a horrible crush of guilt as I realized that Stephan cried with me. He had always been like that. He couldn't watch me suffer and not suffer himself.

"Shh, it will be okay," he told me, his voice soft and soothing, despite his tears. "We will survive it, Bianca. Whatever it is, we'll survive it together."

CHAPTER THIRTY-FOUR

Mr. Duplicitous

Suddenly, there was a furious pounding at the door. It vibrated as heavy fists beat against it.

"Bianca, open the door. We need to talk. Don't lock me out. Open the door. Now." James's voice rang clearly into my room, since he was shouting to wake the dead. He pounded relentlessly. I had never heard his voice at any level even approaching a shout. It startled me, to say the least.

We tried to just ignore him in silence as he pounded at the door. It went on for a good five minutes.

Each blow to the door made me tense up, until I was just a quivering mess of nerves.

It brought me back to my childhood as almost nothing else could. The door pounding, my father breaking it down and beating us because we'd had the nerve to lock him out. Almost every violent episode in my childhood had begun with fists reverberating against a door. Just like this.

I was such an emotional wreck at that moment that I reverted back to a habit I thought I had weaned myself off of years ago.

Abruptly, I shot out of Stephan's arms. I found the safest looking hiding spot, on the far side of the bed. I curled in on myself, arms wrapped tightly around my legs. It was purely a child's defensive stance, but I couldn't seem to stop myself.

I heard the door swing open, then Stephan's voice, colder than I'd heard it since the last time he'd spoken to my father. That hadn't ended well. I was really hoping this scene wouldn't end up similarly.

"Don't do that. She doesn't want to see you. Just look at her! What have you done?"

His last few sentences were strained. I heard the sounds of a hard struggle, and I knew that James had rushed inside of the room, heedless of the huge blond man filling the entrance. Stephan had blocked him, from the sound of things.

The scuffling sounds paused for long moments. I knew that either James had stopped trying to get past him, or Stephan had James pinned in a good enough hold to restrain the other man.

The sounds of a struggle began again in earnest.

"Just let me see her. I just want to make it better. I'm not here to hurt her, Stephan," James said, and his voice sounded like it came through gritted teeth.

"You've already done that! Look at her! What did you do?" Stephan's words were a furious roar this time. "You need to leave!"

"I see her," he said, his raw tone making me cringe. "Bianca, just hear me out. That woman was just a friend."

I heard the sound of a fist meeting flesh, and a soft grunt of pain out of James. I thought it sounded like a blow to the stomach. That worried me. I knew that Stephan's gut punches could do some serious damage. Best-case scenario would be just a few days of coughing up blood.

"What woman?" Stephan asked, sounding angrier by the minute.

"Please, just let me go to her. I can't see her hurting like that. It's killing me."

"So leave. You made her like that, and you need to leave. If she wants to talk to you, she has your number."

"Bianca," James said again, a break in his voice.

The sound of a body slamming into the wall finally got me to turn my head around, just enough to see. Stephan had an arm at James's throat, but James was still struggling fiercely to get past him. He wasn't trying to fight, just move past the roadblock of Stephan.

Stephan, on the other hand, looked like he was on the verge of murder. I could see the hard muscles straining on his naked back furiously.

"Just say you'll hear me out, Bianca. If not now, then later. But promise me you won't just shut me out completely. Promise me, and I'll leave. If that's what you want," he gasped.

It wasn't my first inclination to agree, but seeing Stephan being pushed to just this side of murder went a good way towards convincing me.

My voice was a quavery mess, but I finally managed to speak. "I'll give you my word, just like you did, when you said we were exclusive."

That seemed to send Stephan over the edge.

"Fucker," he roared, punching James hard in the stomach again.

I cursed myself. I had only made things worse.

"We were. We are. I never lied to you. I tell you the truth about everything, even when it hurts, because I want you to trust me," he told me, his voice labored and harsh from the blows.

His words made me so furious that I forgot that I was trying to defuse the situation. "You said you didn't date. That was a lie, since I met your date for tonight."

Stephan slammed James against the wall, cursing. "You Bastard. You swore to me that you wouldn't hurt her. But I haven't seen her this hurt since the last time her dad got his hands on her."

That seemed to take all of the steam out of James. He stopped struggling even as Stephan tried to push him through the wall.

"Bianca, please, you can't just leave me. Just agree to talk to me again, when you feel up to it. I'll let you pick the time and place, but I can't just let you go without a fight."

"Fine, if you'll answer one question for me first."

"Anything."

"First, agree not to come near me, so Stephan can let you go."

His eyes held a desolation that I could see even from across the room. "If that's what you want."

Stephan let go of him abruptly, pacing across the room, his hands in his hair. He hated when he lost it, more than anything, and tonight he'd been pretty damn close. I felt a crushing guilt at the knowledge that it was all my fault. I vowed never to become involved with another man.

"You can come to my house Monday afternoon, at five. We can speak then."

It was hard not to feel anything when I looked into his seemingly sincere, pleading eyes.

"Sooner, please. Waiting until Monday will be pure torture."

I shook my head, holding my ground firmly. "No. Monday. Now answer my question."

He nodded. He shoved his hands in his pockets, looking absolutely devastating in his black tux with its crisp white shirt. His hair was messed up from the struggle but still somehow managed to just look artfully disheveled.

"Have you fucked Jules?" I asked.

He tensed up, and I knew the answer before he spoke.

"Yes. But it's been a long time."

I didn't want the question to leave my mouth, but it did anyways. "When?"

"A year, at least. I'm not sure exactly how long."

And he's known her for years, I thought.

"Was it just the one time?" I asked.

He closed his eyes. "No. But it never meant anything, I swear."

"So you've been sleeping with her for years, and you were going on a date with her after I left tonight, and it didn't mean anything?"

"I know it sounds bad, but it's not like that. I've known her since high school, and our families have ties that go far back. Her brother Parker is a close friend of mine. And she is only a friend to me. I swear it."

"But you obviously fuck your friends." My voice sounded dead, and I wished I could just shut up.

His eyes pleaded with me. "Not anymore. Anything I had with her means nothing. It never did."

"And you've only known me for a week. What does that say about us?"

His jaw clenched. "Please don't do that. It's different. *We're* different."

I turned away from him, finally done with talking. I just wanted him to leave.

"Please go. I'll talk to you on Monday. And please don't be on any of my flights. If you are, I'll go work in coach to get away from you." My voice was getting steadier by the moment. I sincerely hoped that meant that all of my hysterics were finished.

He didn't leave for a long time, but he didn't speak either. I heard the door open and close, then the latch being secured.

Stephan picked me up, carrying me to the bed. He held me and cried.

I knew he was hurting, and all because of me. His violent outburst would trouble him, as well as thinking he'd vetted James well, only to learn that I'd wound up hurt. And my hurt would hurt him too.

We hugged each other, and I found that my crying was far from done.

           Stephan and I were both surprisingly functional the next morning, which was odd, considering how little actual sleep we got. Odd, but good.

We couldn't miss work from a layover unless we were close to death's door. Missing the return flight home from a trip had cost many a flight attendant their job. So we trudged down to the hotel lobby five minutes early, quiet, but in working mode.

Everyone had to ask Stephan why he'd never made it back to the bar the night before. He had forgotten to even text anyone, which was unusual behavior for him. He was normally considerate to a fault.

He made the excuse that he'd passed out on his bed, drunk and exhausted. The excuse served, and the chat shifted away from the issue.

I wasn't in the mood to talk, so I stayed silent and remote for all of the crew chatter, only coming to life when it was time to work. The familiar routine helped, and I was grateful for a very busy morning, free of James.

I noticed the Agents were on the flight, one in first class, one in coach, as usual.

We had a full house. Every seat on the plane was occupied. So it was three hours into the flight before I asked the agent, James Cook, quietly, "Do you work for James Cavendish?"

He looked a little startled, but put his poker face back on almost instantly. "I'm not at liberty to say, Ms. Karlsson."

I just nodded. I thought I had my answer.

Captain Damien surprised me by being oddly sensitive to my mood. He dropped his usual flirtatiously friendly routine, and took the time to step into my galley briefly, touching my arm, his eyes serious and sad.

"I won't ask what's made you so sad, but I just want you to know that I'm your friend. If you ever need anything, even if it's just a sympathetic ear, please don't hesitate to call me. I actually do sympathetic very well, if you can believe it." He smiled gently as he finished speaking. He was so earnest, and seemed so sincere, that I found myself oddly touched.

I smiled back. "I can believe that, actually. I'll keep that in mind, Damien. Thank you."

My small contact with Melissa as she made a trip to the cockpit was the polar opposite of that. She eyed my bare wrist with a catty smile.

"Trouble in paradise?" she asked. She continued without waiting for an answer. I never would have given her one, so it was just as well. "You still have to wear a watch, you know. You can get written up for going without."

Stephan spoke, surprising us both. He had approached without a sound.

"I doubt that would be as serious of a writeup as you ditching the other flight attendants in coach to go into the flight deck to sexually harass the pilots. Again," he finished blandly.

She gave him a look that was positively murderous, but didn't say a word. She stormed back to the main cabin.

Aside from his words to Melissa, Stephan was both quiet and affectionate that morning. I got reassuring pats and hugs that actually did reassure me.

I might be stupid when it came to romantic relationships, but maybe it was fair, since I had Stephan.

Who needed more than that? Who deserved more? Not me.

We never got much downtime during full morning flights. It was hours before we got a spare moment to relax and scarf down some food in the galley. We ate our usual rejected greek yogurt, leaning against the beverage carts as we took quick bites, our shoulders touching.

"I'm going to research James online. I should have from the start. I guess I just wanted to get to know him as a person, and not his image. But now I see that what I don't know could hurt me," I told Stephan quietly, after I had finished eating.

I had an old computer, and I used it when I needed to, but I wasn't the type to spend much time online. I didn't really care about the news. When I had spare time, I almost always preferred to paint or spend time with Stephan and our other friends. I avoided Facebook and anything similar like the plague. I was sure James probably had a Facebook page, though I'd never thought of it before.

I wondered dejectedly what his relationship status would say. I shook the thought off. A simple name search would probably tell me plenty.

Stephan nodded, sliding his finished food tray into the trash cart. He held a hand out for mine, discarding it as well.

"That sounds like a good idea, considering. I should have researched him better, but I didn't. I just trusted him. I saw the way he looked at you, and I knew that he cared. I thought it was enough. And I didn't want to interfere with the one guy you've ever been interested in. Want me to be with you when you look?"

I shook my head. "No, I'll be fine."

He straightened, moving close to rub my shoulders comfortingly. "I'm sorry I got so violent last night. I almost lost it."

I patted his hand. "Don't, Stephan. It was my fault, for bringing my mess to your doorstop. You were just being protective."

"James keeps texting me. I had eight texts when I checked my phone before the flight. He's asking to speak to me. Should I? Or would you prefer that I not?"

I shrugged. "It's up to you. Deal with him however you need to."

"I do believe that he has strong feelings for you. There's no doubt in my mind that he cares about you."

I held up a hand. "I don't want to talk about that. It doesn't matter to me what he *feels* if I can't live with what he *does*."

"He never threw a punch last night, never even tried, but *he's* apologizing to *me*."

I turned to meet his eyes, letting him see my resolve. "Drop it."

He leaned into me, kissing the top of my head. "Of course, Buttercup. I'll drop it."

CHAPTER THIRTY-FIVE

Mr. Celebrity

It seemed like it took an eternity to make it to my house. And when I did, I passed out for an unprecedented six hour stretch.

I had turned my phone off first thing that morning, and I left it off. I had told James that I would speak to him on Monday, but that hadn't kept him from calling and texting me, over and over again.

Just thinking about reading those texts made my stomach churn, so my phone had stayed off.

When I awoke, I ate some eggs and sat down at my computer with no small amount of dread.

My computer was an old, refurbished piece of junk, but it served its purpose. I typed the name James Cavendish into the search engine with trembling fingers.

What came up was overwhelming, and filled with even more unpleasant surprises than I was prepared for. I had been aware that he was a young but well-known billionaire. I had expected some attention from the media in his direction, just from his looks and money alone. But I couldn't have anticipated what I found.

I was out of touch with current events, to say the least. I didn't watch the news, and you couldn't pay me to watch some of the celebrity entertainment shows that were on television, and I certainly wasn't interested in print tabloids. I'd never understood the appeal of things like that. I had just never been able to relate to anything about them. They usually centered around spoiled rich people, and I just didn't get the appeal. That could perhaps excuse the fact that I was utterly clueless about the man I'd had a brief affair with.

I clicked on the images portion first. It was mostly shots on red carpets. He seemed to have endless pictures posing with countless women, though Jules was in a sickening majority of them.

He wore tux after tux, some fashion forward, some classic. She wore gowns in every color, always looking beyond stunning. The two of them together made a dauntingly beautiful pair. He wore suits in other pictures, to what I assumed were less formal red carpet events. I was shocked to see that I even recognized some of the other women he had dated.

I recognized a very famous actress. I hadn't realized she was so tiny until I saw her standing beside James's tall figure. She barely came to his chest. I had liked a few of her films, but I felt an unreasonable rush of dislike for her when I saw that she had attended at least three events with him.

I recognized yet another woman, a voluptuous, dead behind the eyes reality star. She was dark-haired and dark complexioned. Her curves very nearly ran to fat, I decided cattily. She was so short that they looked ridiculous side by side.

I felt sick when I saw him next to one woman who had the caption 'fetish porn star' right under the picture.

He always looked spectacularly handsome, regardless of who he had on his arm, but I was getting a bigger and drastically different view of him now. And I didn't like what I was seeing.

Farther down on the image page I saw a picture of him and Jules dressed down in jeans. It was a rare sight, so I clicked on it. I got a larger view, with a small gossip article. They were holding hands in the picture. The article said that she was rumored to be his longtime on-again off-again girlfriend.

I turned on my phone just long enough to send James the image.

Bianca: You Liar. I'll speak to you on Monday because I said I would, but I've begun to do my research, and I'm quickly seeing that I don't know anything about you.

I didn't bother to read the dozen unread messages above the one I had sent him, but I got a response almost immediately, and I did read that.

James: Please don't believe that tabloid garbage. I'll admit I never discouraged the rumors about Jules being my girlfriend, but they were only rumors. She has never been my girlfriend. She's my best buddy's sister. I promise I will never escort her to another event for the rest of my life, but last night was not a date with her. It was a long standing social obligation. If I had tried to put myself in your shoes, I would have seen how hurtful it could look to you. I apologize for that. I would give anything if I could do it differently. But please, just try to give me the benefit of the doubt, and stop looking at tabloids. I'm still in New York working, since you won't see me, but it's killing me that I hurt you and that I can't make it right. I could be on a flight within the hour. Just say the word, love.

I turned my phone off after that. His one message almost had me softening towards him, and I just wasn't going to let that happen. *Fool me once...*

I went back to my own personal torture of sifting through gossip about James Archibald Basil Cavendish, The Third. I hadn't even known his middle names, or that he had two of them. A random gossip site had had to tell me. Of course, he didn't know mine, either.

I found articles about his parents, and even a few pictures. They were a stunning couple. His mother was a dark-haired, dark-eyed, ravishing beauty with James's golden skin and pretty mouth. His father was devastatingly handsome and blond, with beautiful turquoise eyes that made my gut clench with recognition. I could see how such a combination of people could create a masterpiece like James.

An article I found about them wrote about how they had died in a car accident. Their tragedy, and a beautiful young James, a billionaire before he was even fourteen, had quickly been propelled into the spotlight and romanticized.

I caught little snippets and even a picture of his infamous deceased guardian, and the full details of that scandal. The man was in his early thirties in the first picture. He was handsome, with light brownish-blond hair, like James, but a paler complexion. And he was slender to the point of frail, with creepy, pale green eyes. Spencer Charles Douglas Cavendish had been a predator in the skin of a lamb. I felt a hate for him that made bile rise in my throat.

I read the article about his death. Spencer Cavendish had been killed by an enraged lover. One Lowell Blankenship had been drugged and handcuffed by the frail Spencer. Lowell had commented that he had consented to have sex with Spencer, but that he hadn't agreed to any of the other 'sick shit' the man had forced upon him. Spencer had been strangled to death when he had unlocked the handcuffs of the much larger Lowell. I personally thought he deserved a far more painful death.

There were countless other articles about James's numerous business ventures. I just skimmed over these. I did learn that he was into much more than just the hotel industry, and I wasn't surprised.

I read through a three page article about his two month affair with a platinum hit singer. She was barely nineteen, and it had been less than six months since their split.

Dammit, I have some of her songs on my mp3 player, I thought in disgust. He had his hand on her nape in one of the pictures. I wanted to throw something.

There were a few articles that hinted briefly about him being a kinky sex partner, but that was all that I found that was even close to touching on his BDSM lifestyle. I wondered how he'd kept it so well under wraps.

I turned off my computer, striding into my bedroom and tearing the painting of him from the wall. I tried to make myself tear it up, but I just couldn't do it. Instead, I put it into my chest of old watercolors.

I turned my phone on again. I ignored all of the new missed calls and texts from James. I texted Stephan, asking if I could come over. He answered instantly with a yes.

I went over, and we watched TV and ate too much ice cream. It helped, but as soon as we stopped watching, I started thinking again. That's how we ended up catching up on my TV until nearly two a.m on a work night. We had an early morning, but Stephan didn't complain.

"I spoke at length to James today," Stephan told me after we'd been watching TV for hours.

I just nodded.

"Want me to tell you about it?"

I shook my head.

"Okay. Let me know if you do."

"I need some time. I read up on him online. I'm feeling less inclined than ever to even speak to him again."

Stephan took a deep breath. "That's something I wanted to talk about, actually, if you're willing to hear what I think about the whole thing right now."

I just studied him for a minute. He looked nervous, which meant I wouldn't like what he was going to say. "Not right now," I said.

"I think I can at least understand now why he wanted to keep his relationship with you private."

I held a hand up. "No more. It sounds a lot like you're taking his side right now. I just can't handle that at the moment." Unwilling tears welled up as I spoke.

He pulled me against his chest, kissing the top of my head. "Never, Buttercup. I'm always on your side. *Always*. We'll talk about it when you're ready."

CHAPTER THIRTY-SIX

Mr. Cavendish

I was grateful for busy flights at work the following day. We had full planes going both ways on our turn. I barely had time to eat, and I was avoiding thinking at all costs. I didn't even have my phone. It was still at home, by my bed, and turned off.

The Agents were present, and I felt a moment of unreasonable anger at them when I first spotted the one in my cabin. I squelched the emotion, just serving them as they alternated cabins on the return flight. I made myself brush off the implication that James still had a reason to keep an eye on me. I would set him straight on Monday, and then this nonsense would be over for good.

I was, thankfully, exhausted by the time I got back home that night. I only performed the minimum bedtime preparations before practically falling into bed.

I slept in late the next morning. Even after I woke up, I moved slowly. It took me nearly an hour to prepare and feed myself breakfast.

I felt like a zombie, too numb to even cry. I thought it was an improvement.

Stephan and I had a monthly lunch date with several of the other members of our flight attendant class at eleven. I was skipping out. It was a boisterous, funny, close-knit group. The lunches were always a great time. There were twelve of us in total that went, and we usually caught up with each other over lunch. We often caught a movie afterward or even headed to Stephan's house, on occasion. I wasn't up for any of it. Stephan had promised to make my excuses. He had offered to skip out with me, but I wouldn't hear of it. I knew he was a social creature, and the lunches were always a highlight for him.

I tried to paint. One look at my canvas of a nude James changed my mind . I put the painting in my spare room with trembling hands. I just didn't have it in me to deal with it at that moment.

Finally, I went the masochistic route, turning on my computer again. I set out to do more painful research on my famous ex-lover.

If I had been shocked by what my search had turned up the first time, I was utterly floored by what I found then. What a difference a few days had made.

Now, typing James Cavendish into the search engine brought up an entirely new batch of photos that the first search hadn't. Pictures of *me*. I had never thought of myself as a beauty. My features were even and symmetrical and my coloring was a soft natural blond, but I had always just considered myself attractive, if I was in a kind mood. I usually photographed well. I even had a picture-ready smile. If it wasn't all that sincere, it was at least polished and convincing enough at a distance. These weren't those kinds of pictures.

They had obviously been snapped as I was stumbling out of James's building. I looked disheveled, and, well, horrible. I was ghostly pale, my eyes red and bloodshot. There was mascara running down my face in dark lines. It made me look at least forty years old, instead of twenty-three.

My uniform was in shambles, the buttons of my blouse misaligned by at least three. I hadn't even noticed at the time. My shirt was untucked, and the top was hanging low, showing an almost obscene amount of cleavage. My hair was a tangled mess.

I looked like I was drunk and about to throw up in the street. I was teetering on the edge of the sidewalk. Apparently, I had looked as awful as I had felt that night. And the pictures were everywhere. One gossip site after another had scented the story of trouble in paradise. Though they all seemed to have a slightly different slant on it.

One site named me a 'Vegas floozy' who had come between Jules and James, though the site claimed that their love would endure the scandal. I saw that they were commonly referred to on the gossip sites as J&J. It made me want to throw up.

One site called me a 'Low Class Inflight', who had broken the heart of a distraught Jules. That one hurt, with side by side pictures of the two of us. The picture of Jules showed her in the pale gray gown she'd been wearing that night, giving a stiff smile at the camera. She looked strained, but at least she'd known she was being photographed. I saw farther down on the same article that they had indeed still attended the charity event together, in spite of the obvious strain yet another of James's affairs had caused on the beautiful couple. The article concluded that their love would prevail over James's weakness for cheap women.

I wouldn't have been surprised if Jules had written the article herself, it was so biased towards her. It made her out to be a long-suffering Saint. I'd met the woman, if only briefly. She was no Saint.

One site called me a 'Blond Sky Slut,' and claimed that I was trying to trap James with a baby. I couldn't believe all of the lies that could be concocted from a few short minutes worth of unsolicited photos, and all of a woman no one had ever heard of. It was shocking, and infuriating, and sickening.

One site resorted to drawing giant penises all over my face, saying that I 'gave the best head', and that was the only reason James would risk his long-time lover's wrath. Supposedly several of the site's sources knew it first-hand. The lies made me feel ill.

One site claimed I was part of a high-priced flight attendant prostitution ring, and that James obviously needed to ask for his money back.

I was almost flattered for a moment as I read the headline of one article. It claimed I was a 'Swedish Bikini Model'. That sounded complimentary. Until I scrolled to the bottom of the article, which had a link it claimed went to a porno, starring me. I didn't bother to click on it. I knew for a fact that it wasn't me, and I didn't want to see what it *actually* was.

Another said I was a cocktail waitress, and yet another said that I was a stripper with the stage name 'Glory Hole'. The slurs went on and on, and I felt humiliated, angry, and heartsick.

This was the price I had to pay for one week of pleasure? I thought in disgust. I was going celibate for the rest of my life.

And I hated myself, for being just as upset that James and Jules had still gone out together that night as I was by all of the horrible lies being spread about me...

I got my phone out of my bedroom, finally turning it on after days in the off position. I went straight to Stephan's name in my texts, completely ignoring all of the other messages and calls that I had missed. I'd missed one from Stephan as well. It had been sent twenty minutes ago.

Stephan: Buttercup, I'll be home soon. Finishing up lunch now. We need to talk. Please don't look at anything online until I get there.

I snorted. He should have known better. If I hadn't already

looked, his odd message would have sent me straight to my computer.

I heard the doorbell ring.

That was quick, I thought, as I strode directly to the door.

I wondered why he didn't just let himself in. He was rarely so formal. He even had my alarm code.

A cold shiver ran through me. I couldn't place why. Cautiously, I checked the peephole. It was covered.

By a hand, I thought. It made me angry.

I swung the door open, ready to chew Stephan a new one. "You know better than to mess with me like that, Stephan. It's a mean prank-"

I couldn't finish as a huge hand seized my throat, shoving me back into the house. I couldn't even scream as the hand tightened. I blinked, trying to focus on the coldly furious face in front of me. The familiar pale-blue, bloodshot eyes. I could do nothing as the huge blond man picked me up by the throat, and shoved me across the room, my back hitting the wall with a jarring thud.

I clawed at the giant hand that held me suspended like a rag doll. It had no effect. My throat burned, and the impact with the wall had knocked the wind out of me, but the pain was secondary to the terror that gripped me.

A question consumed my thoughts. It was an old familiar pattern for me, when this madman, who exercised so little control over his rage, held me in his grasp. The question circled my brain like a persistent cancer. *Would he kill me this time?* He always threatened to. Ever since I had stood, not more than four feet away, and watched in horror as he pushed the gun my mother held into her mouth, and pulled the trigger. I had watched in helpless horror as his finger covered hers on that trigger, and pulled so slowly.

Blood had splattered all three of us, but he hadn't seemed to notice.

At the moment, his words were a confusing tangle of Swedish and English, and I couldn't for the life of me understand it. I had never been fluent in Swedish, but I'd had to understand it as a child, since my father stubbornly insisted on using it at home. But, either from terror or disuse, any ability to understand it was failing me. I tried to speak, to tell him that, but his hand was still at my throat, cutting off my ability to speak.

His hand relaxed on my throat just enough for me to take a breath. I gasped, then grunted and whimpered as his fist made hard contact with my ribs. I sobbed in another breath, still desperate for air.

He spoke again. This time it was a heavily accented but understandable string of English. "Don't get the idea that a rich boyfriend will keep you safe from me. If you even think about speaking to the police, I will still kill you. Do you understand?"

I couldn't speak, but I tried. God, did I try. Finally, I just nodded, but it wasn't enough. One of those massive fists made contact with my stomach once, and then again. I started to crumble, but he pushed my shoulder into the wall hard enough to keep me upright.

"Look at me," my father's cold voice ordered.

I did, getting a good look at him for the first time since he'd charged, like a madman, through my door. It had been six years since I'd seen him, but he'd aged twenty. He was even heavier now, his face dissipated with the signs of a life lived in excess. He was a drunk, a smoker, a chronic gambler, a murderer, and God only knew what else. It had all taken its toll on his once handsome face.

I called myself a thousand kinds of fool. I'd known he would never leave Vegas. He had gambled to stay afloat since his parents had disowned him at least twenty-four years before. I had prayed that his destructive lifestyle would take care of him on its own, but it had been too much to hope for.

Thinking it was Stephan at my door was no excuse. I was an

idiot for letting my guard down for even a second. But he had somehow known when to strike. I was so depressed and despondent that my brain wasn't working properly. The thought of a real threat had been so far from my mind...

"People have been asking about me, people I don't know. What did you tell your rich boyfriend about me? Did you tell him about your mother's death?"

"No," I sobbed. "I don't know what people you're talking about. I didn't tell him anything. I swear it."

My words were useless. They always were. My father was a man of action. He grabbed my arm with one hand, punching me in the side with the other. He always spread his punches out. He caught a spot at my back and my spine bowed in pain.

He swept my legs out from under me. I went down easily. He kicked me once, hard, in the back. He walked around me, bringing a booted heel to my neck. "It would be easier than taking a simple step for me to kill you. You understand this? My weight alone will crush your windpipe. Is this how you want to die? Because if you tell anyone what I did to your mother, there is no reason why I shouldn't kill you. I would not hesitate. Do you understand, sotnos?"

"Yes," I croaked out. It was a struggle to get that one word out with that huge boot on my neck.

He picked me up, effortlessly propping me back on my feet. "And your man needs to quit poking around in my business." He raised an enormous fist above me, bringing it down on the back of my head. My world went black.

CHAPTER THIRTY-SEVEN

Epilogue

I awoke to the biggest, baddest headache of my life. It was a doozy. I wanted to sink back into unconsciousness immediately. It was my first conscious thought.

I opened my eyes the tiniest crack. It made the pain even worse, so I shut them again.

I'm in a hospital, was my second conscious thought. Everything, from the way I was propped up, to the smell, to all of the little beeps, clued me in. My third thought was that my head wasn't the only thing wrong with me. Almost every part of my body throbbed, head to toe.

My hands seemed to be unharmed. My right hand was clutched in a warm, hard hand. I knew that it must be Stephan at my side, and I felt better just from the knowledge of his steady presence. I was in bad shape, but I was alive. And I had Stephan.

I made a second attempt to open my eyes. It was marginally more successful than the first try, but agonizing pain still shot through my temples. I glanced toward the man sitting at my right. I was more than a little unsettled to see that it wasn't

Stephan.

Golden-brown hair trailed into an achingly beautiful face as James leaned over my hand, his face stark and desolate, his eyes red, his pretty mouth pursed as though he were in pain. He had the posture of someone who had been sitting slumped over that way for hours, if not days. He looked so tragic that way, and so heart-achingly handsome, that I felt an instant softening towards him. I wasn't thinking very clearly, but I tried to reach out briefly to comfort him.

My arm didn't move much, but I was able to grip his hand with a tiny, reassuring squeeze.

His head shot up, his eyes searching. Those vibrant blue eyes looked on the verge of tears. It was surreal to see him like that. He swallowed hard.

"How are you feeling?" he asked. He reached over and pushed a button just to my right, but behind me. And then both of his hands gripped mine, stroking it softly.

My voice was raspy and weak, but I answered him. "Alive."

He blinked, and a tear slipped down the planes of that perfect golden cheek.

I blinked at him, wondering if I was dreaming. This was such a strange James that sat in front of me, nearly a stranger. But then again, he had always been a stranger. *Hadn't he?*

"Where's Stephan?" I asked him. It hurt to talk, so I vowed to keep my talking to a minimum.

"He went to get coffee. He's been glued to your side." He nodded at a spot on the other side of me. There was another chair placed right at my side. "He's even been sleeping there."

I processed his words, then almost immediately broke my vow of silence. "How long have I been out?"

He lowered his head, touching his forehead to my hand. "Three days. Forever."

I sighed, feeling a little relieved. It could have been worse. "How long have you been here?" I asked him.

His face looked impossibly tired as he gazed down at our joined hands. "I showed up at your house as the ambulance was taking you away. We followed it to the hospital. Stephan and I were both just minutes too late..."

"You came to my house early," I said, a small thread of accusation in my voice.

He just nodded. "Yes. But not early enough," he said, and I could tell that he was blaming himself for what had happened, for showing up too late to stop it, which was crazy, of course.

I supposed, in a disconnected kind of way, that someone who needed so badly to be in control, must also feel the need to take a disproportionate amount of responsibility for things, even things that were completely *out* of his control. I squeezed his hand.

"How long have you been at the hospital?" I asked again.

He just blinked at me. "Since then, Love. Do you think I could leave you like this?"

My brow furrowed. "Don't you have work to do?"

He laughed, and it was a rusty sound. "I'm taking some time off."

I noticed for the first time that the private room we were in was filled to bursting with flowers. They ranged from exotic bouquets, to decadent roses, to simple carnations. It seemed that every flower was represented in the many vases around the room.

"You did this," I said, as I took it all in.

He kissed my hand. "Not just me," he said. "The white lilies are from Stephan. And those sunflowers are from Damien and Murphy. The mixed wildflowers are from your airline. And that mixed bouquet is from a group of flight attendants from your class. I got the rest."

"They're beautiful. Thank you."

"My pleasure," he murmured, watching me like a hawk.

Stephan came in then, and rushed to my other side. Tears

ran down his face as he grabbed my other hand.

"How do you feel?" he asked, sitting in what was obviously his chair at my other side..

I grimaced. "Alive."

"I should go get the nurse," Stephan said, starting to stand.

"I buzzed her. She's usually prompt, so she'll be here any time now," James told him.

Stephan sat again. He stroked my hand comfortingly. "I was just speaking to the police. They want to talk to you when you feel up to it. I told them that I thought it was your father, but I didn't see him, so they won't take my word for it. It *was* your father, right?"

I just nodded, wincing. "Later. I'm definitely not feeling up to it right now. What day is it?"

"Thursday," Stephan told me.

My eyes widened, my mind automatically going to work. "We fly out tonight?" I asked him.

He patted my hand. "I talked to the director of inflight. He had no problem letting us switch our vacation time, with you being hospitalized. He was actually really great about it, knowing we couldn't take that much time off unpaid, and that I couldn't work with you hurt like this. We've got two weeks off, so don't worry about work."

I shut my eyes in relief. "Thanks, Stephan. You're the best."

James's hand tightened on mine. "That's not enough time. And if you're that worried about money-"

"Don't," I told him, my eyes still closed.

His mention of money opened the floodgate, and I suddenly remembered, quite vividly, why he had no reason to be by my side. I started to withdraw my hand.

He clutched it, and my eyes snapped open, glaring at him. The look in his eyes stopped my hand, and I just didn't have the heart to glare at someone who looked so...desperate.

"Okay, I won't. I'm sorry. I just wanted to help," he reassured me in a way that seemed foreign to him. No one could say he wasn't trying...

The nurse arrived, checking on me. She asked me about the pain, and I saw her pushing the painkiller button several times. I drifted off.

Both men were seemingly unmoved when I roused again. I could see from the slightly opened shades that it was dark outside. Both of my hands were still warmly enveloped.

"How long was I out that time?" I asked.

Stephan seemed to be dozing, but James had his eyes open. He looked like he was praying over my hand.

"Fourteen hours," James said, and kissed my hand. "I think you've taken ten years off my life this week." He reached to punch a button, and I knew he was calling for the nurse again.

It was a different nurse this time, I absently noted, as she left after checking and medding me. They had both been pleasant and quick. I wondered if the hospital always had such good service, or if this was the James Cavendish effect.

"You don't have to stay here," I told him, as I began to drift off again. He sent me such a hurt look that I tried to take it back even as I sank into a drugged sleep.

Days went by like that, floating in and out of consciousness while my body healed. It was five days before I was up and about. And even then it was a limited amount of activity.

I had a severe concussion, some internal bleeding, and some badly bruised ribs. From the way they felt, I found it hard to believe they weren't broken. I hated to imagine what they would feel like if they were actually broken, if this was what bruised felt like.

I found out from the doctor that I would be in the hospital for several more days, under observation. All of my injuries were painful, but survivable. I was lucky, I knew. It could have been so much worse.

I had several visitors. The rest of our crew even visited once, pilots included. They wished me well, and chatted pleasantly about nothing important. Neither of the men at my side even offered their spots to the other visitors. I wasn't surprised.

James's hand tightened on mine once, when Damien reached down to pat my leg. I knew Damien was just being friendly. He would have patted my hand, probably, if they weren't both already taken.

James and Stephan never wandered far from their seats at my side, day or night. Occasionally, they took turns sleeping on a tiny bed that folded out from the wall in the far corner of the room. I couldn't imagine either man was getting much sleep on the uncomfortably hard looking bed. It was both heartwarming and baffling to me, these two amazing men that insisted on watching over me, completely unconcerned for their own comforts.

A neat, business-like blond woman kept coming in and out of the room, silently handing James his phone, or his laptop, or even the occasional stack of papers. I supposed that was how he was able to spend so much time at my side.

"You don't have to stay here," I told him. "I understand that you have work to do."

He just gave me a dismissive glance, working on his laptop.

I was nearly recovered enough to be discharged before Stephan brought up the attack again. "Why did he come after you again, after all these years?" he asked in a hushed voice. James was dozing in his bedside chair.

"He mentioned something about people asking questions about him, people that he didn't know. He saw me in the tabloids, I suppose, and blamed me. He also seemed to think that dating a rich man would make me more likely to get brave and go to the police about him."

"This was my fault," James spoke, making me start in surprise. His face was ashen. "I'm so sorry."

I arched a brow at him. "That's a bit of a stretch. And,

anyways, my father wasn't wrong. I *am* feeling brave now."

James tried to get me to explain what I meant, but I wasn't sharing anymore. And there was nothing to share with Stephan. He already knew everything.

I caught the tail end of a hushed conversation as I woke up one morning, days later.

"I think that will do more harm than good," Stephan was saying to James. "She won't like it. Just give her time, James. I know it's hard, but you'll have to be patient."

"What're ya talkin' bout?" I mumbled, as my brain crawled out of sleep.

Both men looked a little guilty at being caught discussing me, but neither answered.

"Spill it, Stephan."

He sighed. "James would like to take you to a quiet place to heal. He was suggesting a place on the beach, maybe. And we were trying to figure out how to handle the media circus that seems to follow James around."

I went from groggy to alert as he spoke.

James gave me a very solemn look. "I can't tell you how much I didn't want you to get caught in the crossfire of my media circus of a life. That is the entire reason that I wanted to keep our relationship quiet, at first. I was suggesting that I release a statement about our relationship so it's clear that you and I are together and exclusive. And that Jules is and only ever has been a friend of mine. I hate the implication that you are usurping on her territory. Nothing could be further from the truth."

I pulled my hand away from James, then raised it when he tried to protest.

"Stephan, give us a moment, please," I said solemnly.

He left without a word, beating a rather hasty retreat.

James's jaw had clenched, and he looked angry and pleading all at once. "Please don't shut me out, Bianca," he said quietly.

I took a deep breath. My chest hurt. It wasn't just from the fists that had marked it. It was a deeper pain. "James, this has all happened too quickly. I need to take a step back."

He looked down, hiding his pain-filled eyes, that lovely mouth twisting in a heart-wrenching way. "Please." His voice was quiet. "I can't stand the thought of losing you. What can I do?"

I swallowed past a very thick lump in my throat. "Just give me time, please. Things between us happened too fast, and everything that's happened since has just made me realize that. I can't think when we're together. You just sweep me up and I seem to lose all semblance of sane thought. I don't know that I can be a part of your life, or that I can even accept whatever little piece of it you would carve out for me." I could tell he wanted to argue, but I quieted him with a look.

"Just give me some time," I finally repeated. "That's all I ask. We can discuss this thing we have in a few weeks, maybe a month, if you still want to. Frankly, I half-expect you to just move on in that time."

He looked very angry now, but he studied me, and I could see that he tried to tamp it down.

"Please have more faith in me than that," he said quietly. "Will you at least allow me to call you? Or even text you?"

I closed my eyes, wanting to go back to sleep, wanting to cry like a baby. "I'll contact you," was all I said.

He clutched my hand. "It feels like you've already written me off. I wish I knew the words to say to help you understand how serious I am about you."

There were tears in his voice, and it broke my heart. But he didn't really try to find any of the words. He never spoke of love, or even how much he cared. It made it easier for me to do what needed to be done. It helped me to tell myself, *We barely know each other. This could all mean nothing to him in a month.* If he had said he loved me, I might not have been able to manage it.

"I haven't written you off. I just need time, and space. As you've seen and heard, I'm going to be fine. I'll be released from the hospital anytime now. Today, probably. Stephan will take care of me after that."

I kept my eyes closed. It was so much easier to say the words when I wasn't looking at him.

"Goodbye, James," I told him, my voice oddly thick. It was a dismissal.

He kissed my forehead. I felt him watching me for long minutes. Finally, after a suspenseful wait, he departed.

I felt tears slip down my cheeks, but only after he'd gone.

Stephan re-entered some time later. I suspected he had walked James out. He came right to my side, seeming to know, without a word from me, what had transpired. "Are you okay, Bee?"

I nodded. "I want to get out of here. And I'm ready to talk to the police, Stephan. I'm going to tell them everything."

JAMES AND BIANCA'S STORY CONTINUES IN,

MILE HIGH
BY R.K. LILLEY

AND COMING FEBRUARY 12, 2013, THE EXPLOSIVE CONCLUSION TO THE UP IN THE AIR SERIES,

GROUNDED
BY R.K. LILLEY

CPSIA information can be obtained at www.ICGtesting.com
Printed in the USA
LVOW01s1458271013

358781LV00012B/315/P